DEATH
of the
CITY MARSHAL

ANNE LOUISE BANNON

Healcroft House, Publishers

Altadena, California

Healcroft House, Publishers, a subsidiary of
Robin Goodfellow Enterprises,
Altadena, California
United States of America

ISBN: 978-1-948616-06-5

Library of Congress Control Number:
2018914706

DEDICATION

To my niece Justeen Pierce, who is doing the toughest work of all: raising three wonderful, smart young women.

AMDG

ACKNOWLEDGEMENTS

In addition to Mr. Scott Zesch's excellent book, The Chinatown War, there were a number of terrific references that I used, most importantly, Michael Holland, archivist for the City of Los Angeles, who also happens to be my beloved husband.

I must also recognize the wonderful librarians of the Los Angeles Public Library's history and science departments. They are paragons of patience and determination, no matter how obscure a question I ask.

Then there are the fabulous people who support me in my craft and in my life. My dear friend Carol Louise Wilde, an amazing line editor and even better friend. Ginko Ching Lee, whose cover for Death of the Zanjero was the model for this cover, and whose friendship has been a revelation. The above-mentioned Michael Holland, who is always ready with the thirty-minute answer, never mind that I only wanted the thirty-second one. Often what I want is not what I need. Thank you, darling.

DRAMATIS PERSONAE

Some of the characters in this story have the real names of people who were living in Los Angeles in 1870. However, since this is a work of fiction, they are technically fictional characters who may, in varying degrees, bear some resemblance to the real people they are named after. Those with real names I have noted. As for anyone else, the reader may assume that he or she is fully the product of my fevered imagination.

RANCHO DE LAS FLORES
Maddie Wilcox, owner, winemaker, physician

Sebastiano Ortiz, winery manager, husband of Olivia, brother to Enrique

Olivia Ortiz, cook, and wife of Sebastiano

Enrique Ortiz, vineyard manager, husband of Magdalena, brother to Sebastiano

Magdalena Ortiz, housekeeper, and wife of Enrique

Armando Ortiz, son to Magdalena and Enrique

Hernan Mendoza, field hand, husband of Maria, cousin to Emilio and Pascual

Maria Mendoza, maid, wife of Hernan

Rodolfo Sanchez, field hand, husband of Anita

Anita Sanchez, nanny, wife of Rodolfo

Emilio Mendoza, field hand, brother to Pascual, cousin to Hernan

Pascual Mendoza, field hand, brother to Emilio, cousin to Hernan

Wang Fu, field hand, physician

Wei Li, field hand, brother to Wei Chin
Wei Chin, field hand, brother to Wei Li
Juanita Alvarez, personal maid to Maddie

MADDIE'S FRIENDS
Angelina Sutton, undertaker's wife who prepares the bodies for burial

Walter Lomax, a deputy on the city police force

Regina Medina, madam, sister to Thomas Mahoney

Thomas Mahoney, saloon owner, brother to Regina Medina

Ernesto Navarro, a deputy on the city police force

James Rivers, mill owner

LADIES OF LOS ANGELES SOCIETY (and their husbands)
Mrs. Carson, she and her husband Mr. Carson are presumed to have existed. Mr. Carson owns a stationery store

Mrs. Glassell, she is presumed to have existed, as her husband, Andrew Glassell, was a prominent attorney in town at the time, he also founded the Glassell Park neighborhood and helped found the City of Orange, California

Mrs. Judson and her husband, the banker Mr. Judson

Mrs. Hewitt and her husband Mr. Hewitt may have existed. They own and run the buggy manufactory

Mrs. Elmwood, and her husband, Reverend Elmwood, pastor of the Congregationalist church

OTHER ANGELENOS
William Warren, City Marshal and recognized as Los Angeles' first police chief, husband of Juana Lopes Warren. As in he was a real person

Juana Lopez Warren, wife of William Warren and landowner. She, too, is real

Joseph Dye, deputy, former friend of Warren, real

Robert Brooks, constable

Jose Redona, deputy and real

Mrs. Redona is presumed to have existed

Lon Yu, prostitute, sister to Lon Cao

Lon Cao, grocer, brother to Lon Yu

Doctor Skillen, a local medical man

Reverend Jeptha Bennett, an itinerant preacher

Leander Wills, notary

Mrs. Lawrence, sister to Robert Brooks

Frank Hill, an employee at the Hewitt manufactory

Señora Mendoza, grandmother to Hernan, Pascal, Emilio, mother to Emanuel

Emanuel Mendoza, shoemaker, uncle to Hernan, Pascual, Emilio, mother to Mrs. Mendoza

Father Jimenez, pastor of the Catholic Church

Councilman Wilson, insurance agent and on the city council

Jorge Villega, a worker at the Rivers' mill

Sam Bonner, ranch hand

Lavina Gaines, daughter to Robert Gaines, sister to Timothy Gaines

Robert Gaines, land agent, father to Lavina and Timothy

Timothy Gaines, land agent, son to Robert, brother to Lavina

Mr. Sedonez, saloon keeper

Biddie Mason, landowner and real, one of the wealthiest people in Los Angeles at the time

CHAPTER ONE

When the shooting stopped and the smoke cleared, there were five people bearing wounds from the bullets that had flown so fast and furiously. I had made a point of diving for cover the moment I'd seen City Marshal William Warren pull his derringer from behind his back. Most of the other women in front of the Clocktower Courthouse that fateful afternoon of October 31, the Year of Our Lord 1870, had quickly left the street for some safe indoor place the moment they'd heard Deputy Joe Dye screaming at Marshal Warren. The men and I had stayed to see the show.

My father often said that I didn't have the sense that God gave a goose. However, in my defense, I must point out that the closest indoor cover was a saloon, from which those of my fair sex were barred, and that any effort to seek cover across the street in the market on the first floor of the courthouse would have been impeded by the crowd that was gathering. I was looking for some other safe haven when I saw the marshal's derringer and decided that down on the board walkway was safer than anywhere I could reach.

As I rose, I was not surprised to see the marshal and a Chinaman on the ground and bleeding. What did surprise me was that Mr. Dye was bleeding from his forehead and his leg, but so enraged was he that he had pounced upon Marshal Warren and was biting his ear. Two men, I did not see who, grabbed Mr. Dye by the throat, and pulled him off the Marshal. Deputy

Jose Redona was easing onto the ground, a bullet hole in his upper right arm. Deputy Constable Robert Brooks was bent over his bleeding right hand. The young Chinawoman Marshal Warren and Mr. Dye had been fighting over sat huddled near Mr. Brooks, too frightened to move.

I went first to the Chinaman and saw that the bullet had struck his jaw. I grabbed some bandages from the huge bag I always wore and began to gently bind his head, but another Chinaman eased me away and took over. So I went over to Marshal Warren.

"I'm killed," he groaned.

"Not if I have anything to say about it," I told him.

I began to bandage the nether region above his limbs in spite of his embarrassment. I did not like doing so in public, but he was bleeding and the bandage was necessary.

Perhaps I should explain, even though this is the second volume of my memoirs. My name is Madeline Franklin Wilcox, called Maddie by my intimate friends, and I am a trained medical doctor. Nowadays, in our supposedly enlightened Twentieth Century, sadly, a woman medical doctor is almost unheard of. But when I finished my training in 1859, it was not all that unusual, though still fairly rare. My father had been so ashamed of me he forced me to marry Albert Wilcox, who promptly dragged me here to Los Angeles, then still a tiny pueblo of five thousand people. Mr. Wilcox bought a vineyard and promptly died, leaving me to make my way as a winemaker who happened to have a talent for the healing arts. I'd been forced to finally reveal myself as a doctor the previous spring. Not everyone, including Marshal Warren, was entirely comfortable with my true vocation.

Marshal Warren was an average-sized man with dark hair and eyes and an overgrown and unruly mustache and beard of the sort that was favored by men of that time. We'd never gotten on well. However, we had developed a grudging respect for each other, and if he did not appear happy that it was me that had come to his aid, at least he wasn't fighting me.

Four men took the marshal on ahead to his house. I told them that I would be there as soon as I checked on Mr. Redona and Mr. Brooks. Mr. Brooks' wound was superficial and barely needed bandaging. Doc MacKenzie was tending to Mr. Redona. Mr. Redona called out to me. He, apparently, had as little confidence in Doc MacKenzie as I did.

It wasn't entirely fair. Doc MacKenzie had many years of experience, even if he had no formal training. And he would give me the benefit of the doubt, which was more than most of the other doctors in town would. Fortunately, that day, we were both in agreement that the bullet had passed through Mr. Redona's arm without harming the bone and little more needed to be done beyond stitching the holes shut. I told Mr. Redona to keep the wound clean (which also served to remind Doc MacKenzie that sanitation was of the utmost importance). Then I hurried off to the marshal's house to tend to him.

Mrs. Warren was waiting for me as I ran up. Doctor Skillen came running up and glared at me. He generally approved of me when I tended to the women and children in town. However, he firmly believed that I had no business treating men. But Mrs. Warren told him in no uncertain terms that she wanted me tending to her husband and sent him off.

"How is he?" I asked Mrs. Warren as she led me upstairs.

"Complaining like a little girl," she said, then frowned. "That's good, isn't it?"

"Usually, yes," I said, not wanting to say more.

The case could go either way, based on what I'd seen on the street. He'd been hit in the pelvis. Had the bullet pierced his belly, we would have been facing a long night that would end in a slow, painful death.

As it was, I was able to dose him with some morphine and ether, then opened up the wound. The bullet had landed next to his bladder. I got it out, then stitched the wound up, then cleaned and stitched his ear. You'll note, I did not sterilize anything. We didn't yet know. Mr. Lister's and Mr. Pasteur's work had yet to reach our benighted little corner of the world. All I knew was that keeping things clean made it less likely that wounds would fester. I was considered somewhat radical because I used ether and morphine to dull the pain of surgery.

It was a good two hours before I was done. My work apron was a mess, but it couldn't be helped. Fortunately, Juanita, my maid and confidant, worked miracles with blood stains. I was equally happy that I had on my third best riding habit that day, a somewhat faded cotton and wool suit festooned with ruffles around the skirt. I finished washing my hands to find that Mrs. Warren had brought a guest into the room.

He was a tall man, his dark hair neatly combed as it curled slightly around his ears. His eyes were bright blue and rather striking, actually. He wore the usual dark suit which looked fairly new, although there was some dust from the street on it.

"Reverend Jeptha Bennett, Ma'am," he said, nodding at me. His voice was deep and he had a Yankee accent even thicker than my own. "I helped carry the marshal home and have stayed to help bear up Mrs. Warren and the marshal in prayer and spiritual comfort."

"That's kind of you, Reverend," I said, glancing at Mrs. Warren.

She was small and dainty, with a narrow face that often reminded me of a cat. Her hair was coal black, as were her eyes. She was a Mexican, and as such, a Catholic. I'd heard the marshal was, too. Which meant that the Reverend's offer was more kindly meant than practical.

I'd been hearing about Reverend Bennett through the previous months, although I hadn't yet met him. He supposedly espoused the fire and brimstone kind of religion that I do not hold with at all. A traveling preacher, he'd arrived in the pueblo in the middle of the summer and his revival meetings had become so popular, he'd decided to stay indefinitely.

"Father Jimenez is on his way," Mrs. Warren told me, eyeing the reverend with mild annoyance.

"It's a pleasure to finally meet you, Reverend Bennett," I said, returning to cleaning my surgical tools for a couple minutes and hoping he'd recognize this as the dismissal it was. He did not, so I turned to him. "Reverend, I would like to speak to Mrs. Warren privately, if I may?"

"Of course." The reverend bowed his head slightly and left the room.

"How bad is it?" Mrs. Warren asked the second he was gone.

"The good news is that the surgery went well," I said. "We'll have to see if he takes sick from it. We should know in a few hours. I'll wait here with you."

"Thank you, Mrs. Wilcox," she said, going over and stroking her husband's face. "Oh, Mr. Ortiz came by. He thought you might be here and said to tell you that he will tell Mrs. Ortiz not to expect you for dinner."

I couldn't help smiling. I didn't know whether Mr. Ortiz meant Sebastiano or Enrique. They were the brothers who helped me manage my property, with Sebastiano overseeing the winery and Enrique the vineyards. They had started as my workers, but we had become fast friends and I'd recently made them my partners. Their wives managed my household, with Enrique's wife Magdalena as the housekeeper and Sebastiano's wife Olivia as the cook. It didn't matter which of the two brothers had delivered the message to Mrs. Warren, it was clear they knew me well.

"That was a kindness," I said and went back to cleaning tools. "Are your daughters at home?"

Mrs. Warren's three girls were still fairly young.

"Their grandmother is here but can take them to her house at any time."

I glanced over at the marshal, who stirred. "I'm hopeful, but best keep them close."

Mrs. Warren nodded, her eyes filling with tears. She knew as well as I did what peril the marshal was in, and that it would be best for the girls to be able to say goodbye to their father if need be. Still, he was breathing evenly and his color was good for his condition.

I grew more hopeful as the afternoon wore on. Father Jimenez arrived and sat next to the window, muttering over his beads. Marshal Warren mostly slept. He awoke once just before sunset, chided me briefly, then went back to sleep again. Outside the house, several of the marshal's friends ambled back and forth, waiting.

Mr. Leander Wills, a notary of the local court, came by after dusk to get the marshal's testimony for the court's examination of Deputy Dye, which would be the next day. Mr. Wills was so insistent, I could hear him all the way upstairs. I told Mrs. Warren to wait with her husband and went to the front door.

Mr. Wills was a small man with a rounded belly and pince-nez glasses. He was meticulously clean-shaven and his suits were hand-tailored of the best wool, and his vests usually a shade of blue or yellow. He was wearing one the color of marigolds that evening.

"I am here as an officer of the court," he announced. "I must get the marshal's testimony."

"I'm afraid you're not going to get it," I told him. "The marshal is asleep and neither I, nor anyone else, is going to wake him."

Mr. Wills' eyes narrowed. Standing behind him was Mr. King, one of the two men who ran The Daily News. Mr. King did most of the reporting for the newspaper. Mr. Wills harrumphed a couple times. I continued to glare at him. Mr. Wills harrumphed one more time then turned away from the door. As I shut it, I saw him shrug at the reporter.

Half an hour later, Constable Brooks came by to

visit and was able to speak briefly with the marshal, as did Deputy Redona.

"You should be in bed," I told the deputy. "You could still take sick from that hole in your arm."

Deputy Redona laughed loudly and the smell of whiskey washed over me. It was patently obvious how Doc MacKenzie had chosen to dull Mr. Redona's pain.

"It'll take more than this little hole to knock me down," Deputy Redona said, his body listing slightly to the right.

Deputy Redona did leave shortly after, promising to return, and left Constable Brooks in the front parlor to watch. Reverend Bennett stayed with them. Father Jimenez had stayed until dinner time. In fairness, it didn't look like the marshal was going to need last rites. When the family's eight-day clock struck ten that night, I checked the marshal for fever, found he didn't have one, then motioned Mrs. Warren outside the room.

"I can't say for sure that he's out of danger," I told her. "You know as well as I do, wounds can look perfectly all right, then all of a sudden start festering. But I do think it's unlikely at this point. If you want me to stay, I'll be happy to. However, I see little point in it."

"I don't either," she said, looking through the door at her husband. "He just needs rest."

"As do I," I said. "If anything changes, don't wait to send for me. But I'll be back by dawn. Would it be all right if I didn't knock? I don't want to wake anyone unnecessarily."

"Oh, please, just come straight in."

I returned to the room to gather my bag and other things. I almost always carried a large leather bag, not unlike a saddle bag, with me wherever I went. The long strap crossed over my chest and wore my dresses terribly. However, I had my surgical tools and my most useful drugs with me at all times. The gunplay that we'd seen earlier that day was all too common, along with knife fights and other forms of violence. Even if it weren't, malaria, assorted poxes, and scarlet fever lurked everywhere, not to mention typhoid and cholera. Then there were the accidents from runaway horses or cattle or in the mills or on the farms and vineyards surrounding our tiny pueblo. I never knew when I'd be called to the side of an ailing ranch hand or child or young mother struggling to give birth. It was best to keep my most-used remedies and tools with me.

I had folded the work apron into the bag and looked, at least, mostly presentable as I left the Warren house. The crowd outside had lessened to around five or six men. Armando Ortiz, Enrique's eldest son and a strapping youth who had just turned sixteen, was lounging on the porch. He bounced to his feet the second he saw me.

"Tío had me bring the buggy for you," he said softly in Spanish.

"That's a mercy," I replied in the same language. I had already seen the conveyance, hitched to my roan mare, Daisy, and tied up outside the house.

"Tía Olivia says that she will have soup ready for you when we get home." Armando helped me onto the trap's seat, then pulled himself up and took the reins.

Daisy ambled her way along the street toward my vineyard, winery and home, Rancho de las Flores. The wheel on the buggy squeaked exceptionally loudly and I made a mental note to ask Enrique about it when I saw him.

"I hope she will not be too put out if I'm not hungry," I said. "Señora Lopez made sure that there was plenty of food and insisted that I have some."

Señora Lopez was Mrs. Warren's mother. The Lopez family was one of our more distinguished. They had vast holdings in the area and raised cattle for beef, tallow, and hides. I can't remember if Mrs. Warren was from the third or fourth generation since the family had settled here, but they'd been here almost from the founding of the pueblo in 1781.

Armando shrugged. We both knew that Olivia considered my care and feeding her personal domain, and it was impossible to say how she would react to my having eaten. Sometimes, she would regard someone else feeding me as interference and become quite resentful. Other times, she'd be grateful that someone had actually taken care of it. Heaven knows, she did not trust me to see to feeding myself, alas, with some justice on her part.

Olivia was waiting on the outside porch as Armando and I drove in through the gate of the ranch. The adobe where I and the Ortiz families lived was not far from the gate and across the yard was the huge barn which was our winery. There was a livestock barn just beyond that, which housed Daisy, a pair of mules, a family of goats, and the three ranch dogs. The chickens had a good-sized coop closer to the barracks house, where most of our ranch hands and their families lived.

Armando helped me down off the trap's seat, then went to lock the ranch gate. I tried to read Olivia's mood. It was not an easy task. However sweet and even merry her heart was, Olivia's face was permanently set in a scowl. Her black hair was sprinkled with gray and her dark eyes were the one clue to whether there would be a tongue lashing in store for me or not.

That night, the soup she had prepared had actually been made in advance of the morning's breakfast, as the weather was turning cold and we'd even had some solid rain the week before.

"I knew Señora Lopez would feed you," Olivia said as she ushered me inside the adobe. "She's a good woman."

Olivia sniffed as if to add that however good a woman Señora Lopez was, her food couldn't possibly match Olivia's.

"It wasn't as good as I'd have gotten here," I said, dutifully.

Sebastiano, who ran our winery, was waiting for me in the front parlor, which opened directly onto the yard. He was about average size, with broad shoulders and a drooping black mustache. I can't remember if it had started to go gray by that time or if that happened later. His dark eyes usually flashed with good humor, but that night, he was not happy.

"We found two more barrels," he told me.

I bit back the foul words that sprang to my mind. "Two? How many more could there be?"

Sebastiano shrugged. Just over a week before, yet another group of young men had broken into the winery and tainted several barrels of the brandy we'd distilled the year before to make our angelica. It was the local sherry that was made all over the area, although ours was considered among the best. With the harvest done and that year's grapes mostly done fermenting, we needed the brandy to add to the new wine to fortify it so that it kept better.

We were, sadly, quite frequently the target of such vandalism. Sometimes it was from competitors. But mostly it came from men who believed a woman had no place owning a business, never mind that I had no other means of support. Even though I was getting some money for my doctoring services by then, it was hardly enough to keep me in bandages, let alone support my sizable household.

"We have enough good barrels for this year's wine," Sebastiano said. "But just enough."

"I'm assuming you made sure that they are soundly locked up?"

"Naturamente."

I thought for a moment. "Are the chickens locked in their coop?"

"Sí. You want to let the dogs loose in the yard?"

"It can't hurt."

Sebastian smiled. "I was about to suggest it."

"I'm afraid I've got to get to bed," I said, trying to stifle a yawn. "I told Mrs. Warren I'd get back to the marshal by first light."

"So he's likely to live a while longer?" Sebastiano

said, his face rather neutral. He did not like the marshal, with good reason, alas, but he was too kind a man to wish anyone ill.

"It looks that way but we both know how fast that could turn."

I went on to bed. As I had planned, I was up well before the sun. Sebastiano had risen, also, and gotten Daisy, saddled for me. I thanked him, mounted, and trotted off. The first rays were lightening the sky as I approached the door of the marshal's house. The household was still asleep. Deputy Redona snored softly from the sofa in the front parlor. I slipped upstairs quietly. Mrs. Warren was asleep in her daughters' room. Señora Lopez had, apparently, gone home.

I knew the second I entered the marshal's bedroom that something was amiss. The covers around him were completely rumpled as if he'd been struggling. A pillow lay at his feet. The marshal's eyes were wide open and he was dead.

CHAPTER TWO

I have to give Mrs. Warren credit. She was devastated by the death of her husband, but she took the news without hysterics. She wept, of course, and stroked his cold face, shaking her head.

"So the wound went bad after all?" she asked.

"I don't know," I said. I had, at first, felt considerable shock when I first saw Marshal Warren's body. But then I began to feel extremely cross, as I became confident that his wound had not caused his death. "If I may examine him?"

She nodded and I pulled back the blankets and sheet. As I had expected, the wound was perfectly clean, with no sign of festering. I checked his eyes and saw the tiny hemorrhages in the whites, then looked into his mouth. Sure enough, there were white strands of cotton caught in his teeth and a small, white, downy feather near the back of his throat.

"Why are you checking his mouth?" Mrs. Warren asked.

"Because your husband was murdered and not by means of a gunshot wound," I said, pulling the feather free.

"What?"

"Somebody came in here last night and smothered him." I straightened and showed her the feather. "See? I found this in his mouth. The blankets were rumpled as if he'd been struggling and this pillow was at the head of the bed when I left him."

Her eyes grew big. "Could Mr. Dye have come in

and finished him?"

"I doubt it, but perhaps one of Mr. Dye's friends did. I'll have to ask around."

"No!" Her vehemence startled me. "No. You can't."

"But don't you want justice for your husband?"

"Yes, but..." She sank onto a chair, crying full out now. "I don't want anyone to know how he died. He would be humiliated."

Being dead, I thought he was past humiliation, but I saw Mrs. Warren's point. The marshal may have been best known for being quick to shoot, but he was still strong enough to engage in a fist fight and leave his opponent the worse for the wear. I still remember treating a particularly large and obstreperous teamster who'd had the living daylights pounded out of him by the marshal. And I could well understand why Mrs. Warren wanted his reputation left as intact as possible. She clearly cared deeply for the man.

"You have to promise me you won't tell anyone," Mrs. Warren cried. "That Joe Dye, he caused this as much as anybody. He might as well be hung for it. Please. Promise."

I swallowed. I could not let an innocent man go to the gallows, although I seriously doubted that Deputy Dye would be hung for killing Marshal Warren. The marshal had clearly drawn first, which meant Dye had shot in self-defense. I also did not want to add to the sorrow of a newly bereaved woman.

"Mrs. Warren, I will only say something if I must," I said, finally. "But I know from my own horrible experience that whoever did this terrible deed must be caught before he kills again. Not seeking him out could put you and your daughters in the gravest danger."

Mrs. Warren shuddered, then nodded. "Then do what you must, but please be careful of his reputation."

"That I can promise."

With her permission, I saw to sending for the undertaker, Mr. Sutton, whose wife, Angelina, was my dear friend. Leading Daisy by the reins, I followed the men bearing the marshal's body to the Sutton's funeral parlor.

I think Angelina and Mrs. Warren were cousins. They were similar in stature, although Angelina's figure was somewhat fuller and she had a rounder face. Her hair and her eyes were dark and shining and she smiled a great deal. But she was as strong as an ox.

Angelina was waiting when we arrived at the back room where she prepared the bodies for their coffins. The men put the body on the table and left quickly.

"So what's going on?" Angelina asked. "You don't normally walk the bodies in here."

"You were bound to spot it, so I thought I'd better tell you right away," I said. "The marshal was murdered."

"I know," Angelina said. "Deputy Dye and him are all anyone is talking about."

"It may yet have been one of Dye's cronies. But Marshal Warren did not die of a gunshot wound." I held open one of the eyelids, which had been closed, but were already starting to stiffen.

Angelina looked over my arm. "Oh, my. What happened?"

"I found a pillow at the foot of the bed and cotton threads in his teeth. I also found a feather near the back of his throat."

"He was suffocated?" Angelina immediately opened the mouth and looked. "Who could have done this?"

"One of Dye's cronies, I would imagine. It was beginning to look like the marshal was going to survive."

"Yes, but it's in the paper this morning that he was not expected to live."

"It was?" I frowned, then remembered Mr. Wills shrugging at Mr. King. "I think I know what happened. Mr. Wills was trying to get the marshal's testimony for Deputy Dye's examination today. I told him the marshal was asleep and that neither I nor anyone else was going to wake him up. Mr. King, from the newspaper, was standing right there. I was wondering why Mr. Wills had given up so easily when he had been so determined before. He must have thought the marshal wasn't going to live."

"And that's what was in the paper." Angelina looked over the corpse. "So does this mean we have another killer to find?"

My heart sank. "We do, but it's going to be difficult. Mrs. Warren begged me not to tell anyone how the marshal died."

Angelina looked at me. "I don't doubt it. Can you imagine the scandal if it got out that he was smothered in his sleep? Poor thing."

"Which is the essential problem. His girls deserve better than that, as does Mrs. Warren, herself." I sighed deeply. "But we must find the true killer. The family also deserves justice. And if there's another killer operating in secret to hide his crimes, he needs to be caught and kept from more mayhem."

The previous spring I had uncovered just another sort of hidden killer. I could have left well enough alone, and had I done so, perhaps the killer's second victim might have lived. But the killer had been bent on killing again, and I shudder to think what additional havoc might have been wrought if I hadn't intervened.

Angelina smiled. "We don't have to tell anyone how the marshal was really killed. It could be the test. Who knows more than he should?"

"That is an effective test," I conceded. "But it will still not be easy asking questions when we have no apparent reason to."

"Then we will find a reason." Angelina came around the table and laid her hand on my arm. "You're a very smart woman, Maddie. And so am I. I think between the two of us, we'll find a way to catch this killer. And catch him, we must. It would be too dangerous to let him get away with this."

I suddenly frowned. "Do we want to ask Deputy

Lomax to help? After all, several of those of whom we must be suspicious are his comrades in arms."

Our police force, at the time, was quite small, no more than ten men, including the marshal. The Common Council seemed to consider that number quite adequate, whilst the more settled of our population felt that the reverse was true. I'd been told that requests for more police officers was among the most common petitions placed before the council. To the best of my knowledge, most of the officers were friendly with each other, but little more.

"This is true." Angelina thought. "On the other hand, Deputy Lomax is going to know who is the more honest of the policemen in the pueblo. But I agree. Let's wait to tell him anything. We've been proven good witnesses before."

"But the court still required the voice of a man to confirm what we told them." I bristled at the memory. "We'd best send for the deputy and show him what we've found."

It didn't take long, in spite of the early hour, for Angelina's houseboy to find Deputy Walter Lomax. News of the marshal's death had spread even faster than the newspapers could be sold and all manner of folk were coming into town for more news or to pay their respects. Some simply wanted a good seat at the courthouse for the examination. In any case, the good deputy appeared far more quickly than I would have expected.

He was of average stature, with brown hair and eyes, broad shoulders and a square jaw, and was reserved as much by nature as by needing to protect his family's secret. He carried his brown hat in his hands and looked somewhat wary of being called to Angelina's preparation room. Laconic, as always, he didn't say much as I explained and showed him what I'd found on the marshal's body.

"One of Dye's pals?" he asked me when I'd finished.

I shrugged "It seems likely, but I can't say with

any certainty."

"And we absolutely cannot tell anybody," Angelina said. "The scandal would be too terrible for the family. Besides, we need to know who knows too much."

"Then how are you going to find out who really killed him?" Mr. Lomax asked. He knew without us telling him that we would be on the hunt for the killer.

"I haven't thought that far," I admitted. "I suppose we could begin with the people who were at the house yesterday. I saw quite a crowd on the street in front."

Angelina picked up the corpse's hand. "It doesn't look to me like he's been dead all that long. If he died in the middle of the night, he'd probably be a lot stiffer."

"There were still people waiting when I left at ten o'clock last night," I said. "Unless he was killed by someone inside the house, someone would probably have seen the killer go in or out unless the killer came by before first light."

Mr. Lomax shrugged. "Sounds right. That's when there would be the fewest people on the streets."

I thought about it for a moment. "Deputy Redona was asleep on the front parlor sofa when I went into the house this morning to check on the marshal. I assume he was there to guard the marshal, but I slipped past quite easily."

"Didn't their housemaid wake him when she went to the door?" Angelina asked.

"I didn't knock. I wanted to be there by first light, just in case the marshal developed a fever overnight. So I asked Mrs. Warren if she'd mind if I came straight in, which I did."

"Mr. Redona is a good man," Mr. Lomax said. "He wouldn't have been sleeping if he thought the marshal was in danger."

"He'll be at the examination, won't he?" Angelina asked.

"I think I'd rather talk to him sooner rather than later," I said. "Where does he live?"

Mr. Lomax gave me the address, which was on

the north side of town on the Calle de Eternidad. It was a small house but kept immaculately clean by Mrs. Redona, a heavy woman with dark, flashing eyes, and black hair that kept escaping from her pins. She invited me into the front parlor and stayed when her husband came in.

He was the worse for the wear, in a rumpled shirt and with stubble on his chin, although I thought that his head was causing him more pain than his arm.

We spoke in Spanish.

"How are you feeling today?" I asked.

"How do you think?" Mr. Redona grumbled.

"It's your own fault," his wife snapped. "You should have waited for la bruja."

She meant me. Many of the Mexicans in town referred to me as la bruja from when I went about as a woman skilled in healing rather than a medical doctor. The word means witch, but in their case, it means a healing woman, rather than one who has sold her soul to the Devil.

Mr. Redona grunted.

"May I check your wound?" I asked.

He grunted again. I undid the bandage and checked the stitches. Doc MacKenzie had done a competent enough job, and the wound looked mostly clean. It was oozing a bit, but it didn't have the fiery red of contagion that could spell disaster. I cleaned it again, applied a poultice for gunshots, and put on a fresh bandage. He winced but held his peace.

"You're going to want to change that bandage a few times a day," I told him. "How's your head?"

He groaned. I looked up at Mrs. Redona.

"Do you have any willow bark for tea?" I asked her. "It will help his head. If not, I have some here."

"I've got it," she grumbled. "Why he let that idiot near him..."

"That was my fault, I'm afraid," I said. "The marshal was in much greater peril, and there was some hope. It was pretty clear your husband only needed stitches and Doc MacKenzie can do that reasonably well, as long as someone reminds him to keep things clean."

"But he got poor Jose drunk!" Mrs. Redona did not approve of spirits, which was why Deputy Redona remained among the more sober of our policemen.

"I should have given him some morphine." I sighed. "My only excuse was my concern for the marshal."

Mrs. Redona snorted but refrained from arguing whether my concern was warranted. And she did have some justice on her side. Given the location of the marshal's wound, it was more likely than not that it would have killed him, and given that likelihood, I probably should have made more of an effort to make sure Deputy Redona did not take sick from his injury rather than focus on an almost certain lost cause. That the marshal did not, in fact, succumb to his wound did not entirely lend justice to my decision to care for him first.

I turned to the deputy. "You were at the Warren home when we found the marshal was dead."

"I went to relieve Constable Brooks," Mr. Redona said. He sighed deeply. "I was supposed to be there by two in the morning but didn't wake up in time. I think the clock struck half-past four right after I got there. Pobre Bobby. He'd fallen asleep."

"Did you go upstairs to see the marshal?"

Mr. Redona began to shake his head, then winced. "No. I didn't want to wake him. Bobby said he'd talked to him sometime after midnight and that he was in a foul temper."

I could well imagine that. "Were you able to stay awake long?"

"I wasn't asleep!" Mr. Redona said.

"You must have just been closing your eyes when I came in."

"You fool!" Mrs. Redona snapped. "I told you to stay home. Send someone else, I said. Ask Mr. Lomax, I said. Did you? No. You had to go out and fall asleep on Mrs. Warren's sofa."

"Basta!" Mr. Redona snarled. "Woman, you'll make me an old man before my time!" He glanced up at me. "All right. I was asleep. I thought you'd come in through the back. I never heard you."

"It's hardly your fault, Deputy," I said. "You were wounded, and stronger men than you couldn't have stayed awake after all the whiskey Doc MacKenzie gave you." I looked over at Mrs. Redona. "Doc does tend to be over-generous in that regard. I suspect it accounts for his popularity."

"I don't need to be excused. I failed in my duty," Mr. Redona sighed.

"It was no duty of yours," I insisted. "You had no business being there, wounded as you are. Now, I expect you to stay in bed today. Change that bandage several times and keep that wound clean. If you don't, you could lose your arm. Do you want to sacrifice your arm to your pride?"

Mr. Redona lifted his chin defiantly but then ducked it as his wife folded her arms and glared at him. I felt sorry for the poor deputy. He really shouldn't have been trying to be on watch. I did not want to burden him with the fact that the marshal might still be alive if someone else had assumed this duty.

Which, as I mounted Daisy and left the house, made me wonder why someone would have felt the need to ensure the marshal's demise. After all, if the newspaper report that morning was reflecting what was generally thought, then there was no need to smother the marshal. He was supposedly as good as dead. Unless the ill-intentioned visitor either knew that the marshal had been faring surprisingly well, or had come to gloat over his impending doom only to find that he was not nearly as close to that final trumpet call as had been rumored.

I also realized that I did not know the particulars of the dispute between Deputy Dye and Marshal Warren. Having witnessed the argument, I knew that Mr. Dye felt that the marshal had cheated him out of something, and I didn't doubt that the young Chinawoman was at the center of it. I had assumed there was a bounty involved but didn't know whether that was certain or just the usual assumption one made. And it was a direction that I could pursue without saying why I needed to know. I might not even have to ask about it.

I would have to speak with Deputy Lomax. There were strong feelings on both sides of the dispute. Marshal Warren had a great many friends and supporters in the pueblo, as did Deputy Dye. I also decided to go to the examination. At least, that was my intent. As I rode up to the Clocktower Courthouse, I saw that the tie ups on the street were filled with horses and buggies. I managed to squeeze Daisy in at a tie up across the street, then headed toward the courthouse. But the courtroom was far too crowded for me to even approach the hallway. So, I chose to linger in the market downstairs.

I was not the only woman there. The moment they saw me, Mrs. Carson and Mrs. Glassell bustled over. They were two of a kind, even though, to my knowledge, they had no familial relationship. Both were of medium height and rather round, with gray hair. Mrs. Carson was somewhat rounder, and her hair had dark strands through the gray. She wore her favorite blue walking suit, trimmed with black lace that gathered in the back of her hoop skirt. Mrs. Glassell's suit was obviously brand new, in a brown wool serge with matching silk ruching all over the newly in fashion narrower skirt with a back peplum. Her matching feathered hat was piled on top of hair that had once been a lighter brown. They were both the worst gossips in the pueblo, and, as such, the best source of news.

"It's utterly dreadful," Mrs. Carson gasped. "We couldn't get into the examination."

"At least, Mr. Glassell is there," said Mrs. Glassell.

"Is he representing Mr. Dye?" I asked.

"Oh, heavens, no!" gasped Mrs. Glassell. "I wish

he was."

I didn't doubt it. Mr. Glassell was quite a prominent attorney in the pueblo. He also owned several farms and huge swaths of land in the Anaheim colony to the southeast. He was an excellent source of news since he was inclined to rant about whatever was going on in the pueblo in front of his wife, who was quite happy to pass the news along.

"Everyone is saying it was clearly self-defense," Mrs. Carson said.

"The marshal did shoot first," I said.

"Hmph!" Mrs. Glassell snorted. "Mr. Glassell thinks a case could be made that the marshal shot first in self-defense, given the way Mr. Dye was coming after him with a cane, no less."

I thought back and vaguely remembered Dye carrying a cane as if he were carrying a cudgel. I still did not think much of Mr. Glassell's supposition, though I would have never dreamed of saying so. And, as it turned out, it was a good thing I didn't. Even before Mrs. Carson or Mrs. Glassell could continue the conversation, there was an uproar from the courtroom upstairs, one that quickly filtered down to the marketplace.

The word that was passed from mouth to mouth was that Deputy Dye had been ordered to stand trial and bail was set at $2,000, at the time, a huge sum, to be sure. One could have bought several acres of prime farmland for that amount. But then, there was an even greater rumble and uproar And we presently learned that someone, it was not clear who, had paid the bail right then and there. It was so astonishing that even Mrs. Carson and Mrs. Glassell were lost for words.

Soon the crowd shuffled, quieted, and eventually parted as Deputy Dye and several of his friends made their way downstairs and out to the street. I knew the deputy could not have killed the marshal, as he had spent the night in the jail. I believe Dr. Skillen had tended to the deputy's wounds, and from the way Mr.

Dye limped, it looked like the leg wound was causing him no little pain. Fortunately, he did not appear feverish, and so I surmised that he wouldn't take sick from his injuries. I was not entirely surprised. Dr. Skillen and I may have had our differences, but he also advocated for better sanitation during surgery and the like. If I was occasionally more popular, it was mostly that there were more Mexicans in the pueblo than Americans, and the Mexicans seemed to trust me more.

There seemed to be little I could do there. Mrs. Carson and Mrs. Glassell had moved off, chattering about Mrs. Glassell's beautiful new buggy. As I watched the crowd sift through the market, I realized that I hadn't seen Constable Brooks among them. I decided to seek him out and speak to him. He lived with his sister and her husband on a small vineyard on the western edge of the pueblo. Mr. Lawrence, Mr. Brooks brother-in-law, was one of the two schoolmasters we had. He and Mrs. Lawrence had been missionaries to China before coming to Los Angeles and eventually produced fourteen children, not counting the ones who didn't live to their first birthdays. At least twelve of them would live to adulthood. At that time, however, they had only seven children in the house and Mrs. Lawrence was expecting another.

The three oldest were at school that morning when I rode up to the Lawrence home. Of the four that remained, three were playing in the yard out front not far from a buggy and horse that I knew did not belong to the family. Indeed, Dr. Skillen was leaving the house as I dismounted.

He was a portly man with white hair surrounding a balding pate and full white whiskers. His blue eyes were often rheumy, thanks to the hay fever from which he suffered dreadfully.

"Good day, Mrs. Wilcox," he said, looking at me a little suspiciously. "What brings you here?"

"Mrs. Lawrence," I said. I was lying. But I knew Dr. Skillen would not appreciate me looking in on Mr.

Brooks, never mind that I was there to ask questions rather than offer treatment. Fortunately, Mrs. Lawrence's condition allowed me an excuse.

"Ah. Yes." Dr. Skillen pulled a handkerchief from his pocket and dabbed at his nose. He frowned. "She didn't say you were coming."

"I hadn't planned to," I said. "However, I was taking a ride and found myself in the neighborhood."

"Excellent idea." Dr. Skillen nodded. "You must be feeling quite desolated after this morning's events."

His concern was kindly meant. After all, one of the louder arguments against women practicing medicine, even now, is that our more delicate constitutions are not up to the mental and emotional rigors. So naturally, Dr. Skillen was sure that I was devastated by the loss of my patient. I was saddened by the loss, of course, as one always is, but hardly devastated. I was almost tired enough to give the doctor a piece of my mind about the supposed delicacy of the female constitution, which would only have confirmed his belief. Fortunately, I composed myself and tried to focus on the kindness behind his concern.

"It's good of you to think of me," I replied. "But I was hardened to the loss."

"So I tried to remind a couple of our colleagues in town." Dr. Skillen shook his head. "There are more than a few folks about who seem to think that had I seen to the marshal, he might be still alive. I do not, of course, hold that view, as you well know."

"I do, indeed, Doctor." I briefly considered explaining what had really happened but realized it would only make me sound as though I were telling a tale to cover my perceived incompetence.

"And I did make every effort to correct their ill-conceived perception," Dr. Skillen continued.

"Which I appreciate."

The doctor paused. "Still, I suppose I should caution you, Mrs. Wilcox, that there are those in town who are made quite happy by even the least of your failures."

I tried not to roll my eyes but did anyway. "Dr. Skillen, I am well aware of their attitudes. It is pure jealousy. I have at least as many successes as does any other doctor in town."

In fact, I had more than all of them except Dr. Skillen, and even there, we were closely matched. And that was in so far as we could call what we did successes. We had so little knowledge then. We didn't even know about germs, let alone sterile surgery. It was a wonder any of my patients survived.

"I am well aware of your skill," Dr. Skillen said, stuffing his handkerchief in his pocket. "In fact, if it weren't for the impropriety, I would recommend you to our men over the rest of those charlatans in town. I have already commended you to many of our women."

This was high praise, indeed.

"Why, thank you, Doctor," I said stepping back a little.

"Nonetheless, there is, as you have pointed out, much jealousy, and I have heard from some people who claim they would do almost anything to ruin you."

I sighed. "I am afraid, Doctor, that while I do very much appreciate your concern, this is nothing new to me. I am well aware that I am not approved of in many quarters of the pueblo, whether as a physician or as a winemaker."

"Perhaps if you married," he suggested.

"And can you think of any man in this pueblo who'd want to be saddled with me, even with my acreage?" I asked, knowing full well that he would not be able to think of any.

"Yes. I dare say you have a point." He smiled congenially as if to soften his statement.

He, of course, thought that I would find it insulting for him to acknowledge my statement. I knew, actually, that there were a couple men who did want to take me on. But I was not willing to take them on, not that Dr. Skillen would understand that. Thank Heavens, I am finally old enough now that it is no longer presumed that I am on the desperate hunt for a husband. Back then, however, I was still young enough, and I like to think pretty enough, that it was generally believed that I wanted and needed nothing more than a husband. Indeed, many of the women in the pueblo worried that I was out to turn their husbands' heads, which was patently ridiculous. The number of women in the pueblo was growing, but there were still significantly more men, many of them fine catches. That I didn't want any of them never occurred to anyone, and so it was much easier to complain that they didn't want me when marriage was suggested. I suppose I should have taken it more to heart when others accepted my complaint without questioning it but it never bothered me that they did. At least I didn't have to explain why I had no interest in marrying.

Dr. Skillen shifted. "Well, I'll leave you to your patient, Mrs. Wilcox. Good day."

"Good day, Dr. Skillen." I smiled at him as he got into his buggy, pondering his unexpected kindness and worrying about his warning.

CHAPTER THREE

Admittedly, to call the Lawrence home a house would be something of an exaggeration. It was mostly a sprawling shack that Mr. Lawrence had cobbled together in between teaching children and caring for the almost seventy acres of grapes and beans that he grew on his land. Constable Brooks also helped out. But from the state of the house, it was clear neither of them was a carpenter. The front part of the house was a long adobe, of the style favored by the Mexicans. But as his family grew, Mr. Lawrence had added rooms higgledy-piggledy, creating the most curious twistings and turnings among the rough boards and unglazed windows.

Fortunately, that morning, I did not have to wend my way around cots and bedrolls. Constable Brooks was ensconced on an aging sofa in the front room. Oddly enough, in spite of the dirt floors and cracks in between wall boards, the house was kept quite neatly, an amazing feat when you consider Mrs. Lawrence had no maid. Her children helped, of course, but at this point, most of them were too young to do more than roll up their bedclothes and herd the current youngest child around.

Mr. Brooks and his sister were much alike in appearance, with nut-brown hair, fair complexions, and slender figures. She was the elder of the two by several years, and while quite youthful in appearance, still had a maternal calm about her. She sat by the fireplace, sewing, as she was constantly doing. In addition to keeping her own brood clothed, she also took in bits and pieces from the other women in the pueblo to help get enough money to keep her family.

I smiled at Mrs. Lawrence since ostensibly she was the reason for my visit. But I couldn't help looking at Mr. Brooks, whose face was slightly flushed. The front room was in the adobe part of the house and the walls were not only whitewashed, there were two good windows letting in light, so it was a bright, comfortable little room, indeed.

"And how are you, Constable?" I asked kindly. I couldn't help approaching him and lifted my hand in query.

"Feeling okay," he sighed and nodded.

I felt his forehead. "You've a bit of a fever."

"It was worse earlier," Mrs. Lawrence said. "His wound was starting to fester. That's why I called Dr. Skillen. I gathered you were busy with Mrs. Warren."

"I was." I caught the faint odor of herbs and wine. "I take it the good doctor applied his famous poultice?"

"He did," Mr. Brooks said, grinning and lifting his bandaged hand.

"The wound had gotten all red and Bobby was quite feverish when he came home this morning," Mrs. Lawrence said. "That's when I sent for the doctor. He'd just come back to check on Bobby when you arrived."

"It's a good thing you called him," I said.

I was not surprised to see Mr. Brooks getting better. Dr. Skillen's gunshot poultice was remarkably effective. It was his special secret but he had been kind enough to share the recipe with me even back before he knew me as a medical doctor with a degree. The poultice contained laurel and a couple other herbs, along with a bit of gunpowder, all steeped in wine. Of course, we know now that it was probably the alcohol in the wine that served as a disinfectant. But even if we didn't know why it worked, both Dr. Skillen and I were profoundly grateful that it often did.

"What happened to the marshal?" Mr. Brooks

asked, a little petulantly. "You said it looked like he was going to make it."

"You're right," I said. "It certainly looked like he would. But I never said he would and I have reason to believe it was not his wound that actually killed him."

What with Dr. Skillen's warning in my ears, I debated briefly whether I should say that the marshal had actually been murdered in his bed. After all, Constable Brooks complaint was just. Fortunately, Mrs. Lawrence saved me.

"So it could have been an apoplexy or a stroke?" she asked.

"Those are some of the things that can happen," I replied, skirting around the issue. "Nor is there anything that can be done if they do."

"See, Bobby?" Mrs. Lawrence said, soothingly. "Mrs. Wilcox wouldn't have left him if she thought she would be needed."

"And I came back by first light to be sure," I said. "The wound could have gone bad, too. Sadly, there will be no autopsy."

"That's just as well," said Mrs. Lawrence. "It seems a terrible desecration to cut into somebody's body like that and it's not going to change anything for the family."

That and we already knew what had killed the marshal, but I couldn't say that.

I looked at the young constable. "Deputy Redona has told me you spoke with the marshal sometime after midnight. How did he seem?"

Mr. Brooks sighed. "Cussed, as always."

He flushed even more deeply as he recalled the conversation.

"What were you talking about?" I asked

Mr. Brooks winced. "Nothing much. He was always riding hard on me."

"Was Mrs. Warren there?"

"No. She went to bed right after you left."

I nodded. "So why did you go upstairs to talk to

him?"

"I didn't." Brooks shifted uncomfortably. "I was just walking around, trying to stay awake. He must have heard me and called out. So I went in to see if I could get him something."

"And did he want anything?"

"Some water. There was also some of that laudanum you left. He seemed like he was in a lot of pain, so I got him a dose of that, too." Brooks blinked and shivered in fear. "I hope I didn't do anything wrong."

"How much of the laudanum did you give him?" I asked.

"Just a couple droppers full. I put it in some of that angelica, and he drank almost all of it."

"Only two droppers? Are you sure?" I waited as the constable nodded. "I can't imagine that would have hurt him."

Mr. Brooks seemed relieved.

"Did anyone else come into the house?" I asked.

"No." Mr. Brooks hesitated again.

"I understand from Deputy Redona that you were asleep when he arrived."

"It was only for a few minutes!" Brooks looked as though he were about to burst into tears. "I swear, Mrs. Wilcox!"

"Easy now," I said. "If you were in as bad a shape as your sister says, it was probably the contagion taking hold. Why, in Heaven's name, were you over there in the first place? Shouldn't you have been here resting?"

Mr. Brooks got even more riled up. "It was my duty as a constable, and I am not going to let any man or woman say that I do not do my duty!"

"That's enough, Mr. Brooks," I snapped. "No one is calling you a malingerer. My only concern is that it might have better served the marshal if you had not put your hand and your very life at risk by not taking care of yourself."

Mr. Brooks snorted. Obviously, as a woman, I

would have no idea what would best serve the marshal. I could have remonstrated, however, it would have had little effect, so I chose not to.

"Nonetheless, I also fail to see why you thought a guard was necessary," I said more calmly. "Would you be so good as to explain?"

"Maybe it wasn't. But Joe was so dadblamed angry..." Brooks glanced up at me and flushed again as his sister gasped at his coarse language. "Begging your pardon, ma'am. He's a nice enough fellow, but when he gets riled, well, you saw what happened. We weren't sure but that he might put one of his friends up to finishing the job. Jorge Villega and Sam Bonner, they were almost as mad as Dye. Or we were afraid Dye would find a way out of jail and do it himself."

"I hardly think that would have been possible," I said. "Still, the marshal was not universally loved."

Brooks snorted again. "There were lots of folks who hated him. You know that Mr. Wills, he's the notary? Marshal shot his little brother, Pericles Wills, about a year back. It was my first night as a constable. Wills, Pericles, I mean, was a land agent's clerk and had gotten drunk, then drew on the marshal and got shot."

"Did he die?"

"Yep. Right there on the street. Marshal caught him right in the eye. Mr. Wills, the notary, blamed Marshal Warren for killing his brother, even if his brother had drawn first. Heck, even Jose Redona was getting pretty riled at the marshal."

"Whyever for?" I asked.

Brooks shifted. "I probably shouldn't say this. You know we get part of the fines and bounties that we collect. Well, the marshal usually oversaw who got what commissions and Jose was thinking that maybe the marshal wasn't giving him his due. Also, the marshal always managed to keep the best bounties for himself."

"Is that why Deputy Dye was mad at him?"

"That wasn't all of it. See, the girl they were fighting over, Lon Yu, she'd been kidnapped last summer. They said she'd stolen all sorts of cash and jewelry. But that was just her boss man Sing Lee swearing out a complaint to get a warrant for her arrest and get the lawmen interested in finding her. But she'd been kidnapped. Both Marshal Warren and Joe Dye had found out from different folks that this fellow Juan Espinosa had her. Only Marshal Warren got to Espinosa first and got the bounty. Then three weeks ago, Lon Yu escaped. Sing Lee swore out another complaint that she'd stolen from him and the judge issued the warrant again and Sing Lee offered a hundred-dollar bounty on her. Well, Jose and Marshal Warren finally found out that she was in San Buenaventura. So had Joe Dye and he'd even telegraphed the marshal there to hold Lon Yu. But Jose and Marshal Warren got there first and got her, and so Marshal Warren got the bounty again. Well, Joe thought he deserved it because he'd sent the telegraph and after Warren beating him out last summer, he was pretty riled."

"He was, indeed," I said, remembering the yelling. "I wonder who else felt cheated by the marshal? Or was angry with him?"

"I would imagine there were quite a few people," said Mrs. Lawrence. "He's shot so many, and not every time was he justified."

"I am well aware of that," I said. I was about to ask another question when I noticed Mr. Brooks eyeing me curiously. "In any case, I am here to see you, Mrs. Lawrence. How are you feeling?"

I was able to get her alone to do a thorough examination. She was well along, but we both agreed she probably wouldn't deliver for another couple weeks or so.

"I'm getting so good at this, I could probably deliver myself," she said, laughing gaily.

I chuckled. "Probably, but let's not take that chance."

She immediately sobered. Granted, we do not lose as many mothers in childbirth these days as we did then. But I know of no woman who, when she feels the first twinges of labor, doesn't wonder if she'll survive the birth.

I left soon after and realized that I had missed the midday meal. Olivia would have something saved for me and would probably be quite annoyed if I didn't get home in time to eat it. Since I'd also missed dinner the previous evening, I knew it would be more politic to go home and eat.

Sure enough, there were chicken stew and warm tortillas waiting. Olivia had obviously heard about the marshal but was kind enough to offer her condolences on the loss of my patient and let me alone. I ate quickly, then, there being considerable work to be done at the rancho regardless of the need to find the marshal's killer, changed to my work dress, got an apron and went to find Sebastiano.

I found Enrique, instead, out in the yard, helping a young man fit a new wheel onto the buggy. Enrique looked much like his older brother, Sebastiano, although Enrique was taller, did not wear a mustache and had skin tanned quite dark, thanks to spending his days in the harsh Los Angeles sun. The young man was a sturdy fellow, broad-shouldered, with brown hair and mustache. His plaid shirt and canvas pants were stained with red, brown and green paint. I thought he looked familiar, but couldn't quite place him.

Even though our pueblo was still rather small, the population had swelled to over five thousand people. It would be impossible to put a name to every person, and that's without allowing for the transience of much of that population. Teamsters, cowhands, miners, land agents, manufacturers' agents and all manner of drifters wandered in and out of our fair pueblo, some staying, many moving on when there was work to be found elsewhere. It was one of the reasons the pueblo was such a violent place, which perhaps necessitated a man like Marshal Warren, who shot first and then asked questions. Mr. Lomax had told me once that was probably why the marshal had lived as long as he had.

"This is Mr. Frank Hill," Enrique told me when he saw my puzzled look. "He's from the carriage manufactory."

"Oh. I have met you before, Mr. Hill," I said, smiling.

The carriage manufactory was owned by Mr. and Mrs. Hewitt. I was on friendly terms with Mrs. Hewitt, though we never became close. It was not well-known in the pueblo for, sadly, rather obvious reasons, but Mrs. Hewitt ran the manufactory rather than her husband, who was generally too drunk to be of much use to anyone. He was sufficiently able to keep the appearance of sobriety that few in pueblo society realized this. Better yet, Mrs. Hewitt had the complete loyalty of her foremen and almost all of her employees. She sometimes complained to me how much that loyalty cost her in the excellent wages she paid her workers. As for those employees who bristled at being under the management of a mere woman, the foremen insured that they held their tongues. I never wished to question how.

Mr. Hill, the employee in my yard, nodded politely. "Yes, ma'am."

I looked over at Enrique. "I see you're replacing the wheel. The old one couldn't be repaired?"

Enrique looked at Mr. Hill. The young man kept his eyes fixed on the ground as he answered.

"The rim was split, ma'am. That's the outer wooden edge that we bind with steel."

I waved him silent. "Yes, I understand the parts of a wheel. But thank you for explaining, nonetheless." I looked at him again. "You're rather new to the manufactory, are you not?"

"Yes, ma'am. About five months."

"Hm. You sound as if you're from up north somewhere."

"Yes, ma'am. I was born and raised in Washington Territory. Came down to California about three years ago, and here to Los Angeles last summer."

I smiled. "Not our best time of year, I'm afraid. You'll like the winters, though."

"Yes, ma'am."

"Well, thank you for your efforts and I'll leave you to your work."

"Yes, ma'am."

I smiled again and nodded, then turned for the small cabin on the other side of the winery. The afternoon sun flashed against my eyes and I quickly adjusted my bonnet.

I couldn't help checking my hands, as well. Over the ten years I had been in Los Angeles, I had done the best I could to keep my face and hands as milky white as the rest of my skin. I was very vain about my appearance, and my complexion was my greatest vanity of all. Even though I was thirty-one at the time, my skin was still smooth and blemish-free. Even now that I am old enough to recognize my wrinkles as part of the grace of living a long life, I blush to disclose that on those few occasions I consult a mirror, I am happy to see that there aren't as many wrinkles as could be and that my skin is still quite white and mostly smooth.

My late and much-lamented mother had often encouraged me to put aside my vanities in favor of greater Christian charity. It was, and even now still is, a constant struggle. And that afternoon, as I turned back to my other work, I resolved once again not to let my fear of turning brown keep me from my proper duties. But I did hide my hands under my work apron as I walked to the still cabin.

Sebastiano was already there, scrubbing out the main tub of the still. After pushing my bonnet back off my head and letting it hang by the ties, I picked up a scrub brush and the funneled cap to the tub and began scrubbing, as well.

"I saw Enrique in the yard," I said, attacking the

cap with perhaps more fervor than was absolutely necessary. "Where are the others?"

"Wang Fu and Emilio are in the garden," Sebastiano said.

Wang Fu and Emilio generally were in the garden or in the several fields or the vineyards. Wang Fu, in particular, took great delight in growing an impressive variety of herbs for various medicinal purposes, as he had been trained as a doctor in his native China. He had been teaching me some of his favorite cures and I have to say they were as successful as many of ours at the time, which is to say, not very. I also found his emphasis on Qi, or lifeforce, rather queer, but it was hardly more queer than the belief that the human body was governed by humors, a belief that was only just giving way to solid science at the time.

"The Wei brothers and Hernan are cleaning the press," Sebastian continued. "Rodolfo and Pascual are getting ready to pour the cabernet wine off the must." He stopped scrubbing a moment and looked at me. "You are not happy about the death of the marshal."

We had been speaking in English, but aware of Mr. Hill in the yard, I switched to Spanish.

"Sí. So you've heard."

"Maria came back from the market with the news of the death and of the examination." Sebastiano nodded back at the house.

Maria was Hernan's wife and helped Magdalena, Enrique's wife, who was the housekeeper. That was one of the great joys of my rancho. Even though I was the mistress of it all, my servants were as much dear friends as they were people who depended on me for their livelihoods. Everyone except Mr. Wang and the Wei brothers all lived on the property. Many of them, in fact, were relatives. Pascual and Emilio were not only brothers, they were Hernan's cousins.

And that's not counting the children on the rancho. Sebastiano and Olivia had five who were alive at that time, and they managed to survive to adulthood. In fact, the oldest two were pretty much adults already. Enrique's and Magdalena's six were somewhat younger, and they all survived, although Juan died when he was twenty-seven. Hernan and Maria had two little ones, Ignacio, who was six at the time, and Adriana, who was three. Maria's third was due to arrive in another month.

I was of the opinion that she should have been resting more at the time, but Maria loved going to the marketplace and running other errands for Olivia or Magdalena, and as such, cheerfully ignored me. I must concede she had the better of me on that one, for as Olivia pointed out, Maria would have been devastated had she not been able to get and bring back news of the pueblo.

"She must be all atwitter," I remarked, glaring at the brush in my hand before I dipped it in the water bucket.

This was not said to disparage Maria. One could hardly expect anything else from the goings on in the pueblo. Alas, I was feeling quite unsettled. I have always tried to master my passions and because I am a woman working as a doctor, have made every effort not to let them rule me lest some man or woman claim that I am unfit for my vocation. But that does not mean that I do not feel things, and the death of Marshal Warren had raised all manner of unseemly feelings in my bosom.

"According to her, the whole pueblo is." Sebastiano went back to scrubbing. "I'm sorry about the marshal, especially since you had such good hopes for him."

I slammed my brush onto the floor. "He was murdered, Sebastiano. Foully, cruelly murdered in his own bed. An act of utter cowardice, to smother a man at his weakest, lying wounded in bed. What vile worm does such a terrible thing? And how dare he do that to one of my patients?" I suddenly sniffed. "And the worst of it, Sebastiano, is I can't help being afraid that someone thought I should look the worse for it."

"Ay, Maddie, people die all the time. Nobody's going to think you didn't do your best for him."

"I should know that. And I am ashamed to be so worried about what people will think of me when I should be worrying about Mrs. Warren and her three daughters. Who's to say that the killer might not want to harm them, as well?"

Sebastiano gently tipped the huge metal tub over onto its side. "A man doesn't usually kill someone just to kill. He usually has a reason."

"And yet, we both know that someone committing such a heinous crime is not likely to stop killing."

"Unless it was Mrs. Warren who did the killing." Sebastiano may have been concentrating on getting water out of the tub, but I knew he was watching me for my reaction.

I frowned and picked up my brush. "She does appear to have been the best able to do it. But it doesn't make sense. She seems to have been genuinely fond of him and from what I have heard, he was quite full of tender regard for her."

"That's what I've heard." Sebastiano shrugged. "But that doesn't mean it's true."

"As we know all too well." I attacked the funnel cap again. "And we know that appearances are not necessarily to be trusted. But almost always, when you look at things more closely there are little hints and signs that don't generally mean much unless something terrible happens, and then you realize they did mean a great deal. But I can't remember seeing anything that would hint that Marshal and Mrs. Warren were anything but companionable toward each other."

"Have you talked to Mrs. Sutton?"

"And Deputy Lomax. I had to. Mrs. Sutton would have seen the same traces of smothering that I did and we needed a man to stand as witness." My lip curled at the thought, though I did hold Deputy Lomax in considerable esteem. "Worse yet, I know of at least four men who might have had cause enough to have wanted to kill Marshal Warren, in addition to Deputy Dye. And one other who could have done it quite easily, although I don't think he had reason to."

Sebastiano snorted. "There are many who had cause to want Marshal Warren dead. Even Hernan and his family."

"Hernan?"

"And Pascual and Emilio. The whole Mendoza clan. They hated the marshal because he killed Elias Mendoza."

"I don't remember the fellow, I'm afraid."

"There were five brothers, I think," Sebastiano said. "You should ask Hernan. He can tell you better."

I looked over the funnel cap to the still. It was clean. "I think I will. I need to inspect the press anyway."

I set the brush on the shelf next to the wall of the small cabin, and got my bonnet back on. As I went through the yard to the winery, I saw that Mr. Hill was just finishing up. Enrique gave me a pained looked and as I passed by, I heard what was causing it.

"These are the end times, you mark my words, Mr. Ortiz," Mr. Hill was saying. "All this lawlessness, it's just the first sign. You gotta have your soul right before God."

I hurried past without saying anything. Alas, I'd had truck with fellows of Mr. Hill's ilk before and knew very well that anything I said would not merely fall on deaf ears, it would provoke yet another sermon about the evils of allowing women to rule over their husbands, never mind that I had none. I looked quickly at Enrique and was reassured that he was not seeking rescue but offering me a warning. Alas, Mr. Hill's beliefs were not unique in the pueblo, and as I recalled, we'd been hearing more and more about the End of Time and the Return of Jesus ever since Mr. Bennett had become part of our fair community.

In the winery, the Wei brothers, Li and Chin, were helping Rodolfo and Pascual with the cabernet wine. The grapes had been harvested about two weeks before. I believe it was a slightly early harvest that year, but the weather had cooled down and slowed the fermentation down, as well. Like the other red wines, we'd run the grapes through the masher, and then let it ferment fruit and juice together. The next step was considerably more difficult in that the vats, which held well over a hundred gallons, had to be emptied of that juice which had separated from the fruit, without taking the remnants of the fruit with it. That juice, or wine, would go into the aging barrels. The must, or remaining fermented fruit, would then be pressed and the resulting wine would go to the still cabin and be distilled into brandy, which would then be aged and used to fortify the next year's angelica. The wooden vats had drains at the bottom, but the fruit would frequently block the drain, or pass through the wire mesh.

Hernan was in the final stages of preparing the press for the coming must. He was a small man, with jet black hair and eyes, and strong, but slim shoulders. He did not seem to ask much of life other than good, purposeful work, a good wife and children, and was a generally pleasant soul. He smiled when he saw me approach.

"We're clean and ready for the next pressing," he told me in Spanish.

"Yes, I can see that," I said. "Gracías. But Hernan, may I have a word with you privately?"

He shrugged, then glanced over to the vats where Pascual was muttering something probably profane as he tried to unblock a drain.

Hernan and I moved over to the other side of the winery, behind some of the taller aging casks.

"Hernan," I began slowly. "Sebastiano was telling me that your family has cause to be angry at Marshal Warren."

Hernan's face became still and blank. "We do not speak his name."

"I understand the marshal killed one of your own."

"Mi tío."

"Pascual and Emilio's father?"

"No. Tío to all of us. It happened years ago. We do not talk about it."

"I see."

Hernan nodded at the front of the winery. "It is time to start pressing."

He pushed past me back to the vats where Rodolfo, Pascual, and the Wei brothers were pulling the juice. He barked at Pascual, then Wei Li, but shortly settled down and became his usual placid self.

Bewildered by his strange reaction, I left him and the men to their work, and entered the house. Maria was busy with her feather duster in the front parlor. She was not unlike her husband in stature, although she was more rounded. And she was more jolly than placid. She hummed to herself as she dusted, one hand resting on her swollen belly.

"You've had a bit of excitement today," I said, untying my bonnet.

"You mean the news about the marshal." She smiled then nodded somberly. "I am so sorry that he didn't make it after all."

"That's as it may be," I said. "I was talking to Hernan. Apparently, the marshal killed his uncle?"

"He told you that much?" Maria's eyes opened wide in surprise. "The men in that family, they never talk about it. They're ashamed they could not get justice in the courts and that no one went after the marshal."

"So do you know what happened?"

"Of course. Tío Elias Mendoza was in San Buenaventura, I think. It could have been San Gabriel. Anyway, the marshal's horse had died, so the marshal told Tío Elias to give him a ride back here. At least, that's what the man at the stable said. Tío Elias was a good man and was happy to give the marshal a ride. Except somewhere between here and there, the marshal got scared or something. Anyway, he said Tío Elias had drawn on him, so he shot in self-defense. Anyone who knew Tío Elias knew that was a complete lie, but the judge believed Marshal Warren. It all happened about five or six years ago. No longer ago than that. I don't think Ignacio was born yet."

"Do you think somebody in the family would have tried to hurt the marshal?"

"They were going to, but Abuela Mendoza made them promise not to. She could see that it would have been suicide. If they survived drawing against the marshal, they would have been hung and had the trial afterwards."

I could well see that eventuality. I was impressed that Grandmother Mendoza had such a firm hold on the behavior of her offspring, but it didn't surprise me. I knew many such a matriarch among the Mexican families and a couple among the American ones. That the courts were that corrupt was appalling but all too common, especially toward anyone not an American.

Unfortunately, this left me with little to do at the moment. I went to my study to write up my journal for that day and the day before. It was a task I generally left for the hour or so between dinner and hearing the children's lessons, and going to bed, myself. However, on those rare occasions that I had an idle moment or two, I would go ahead and write, often transcribing notes I'd made the night before while waiting at the bedside of a patient.

As I looked over the notes I'd made the night before, I felt the ire rising again within me. I am generally well in control of all my passions and not given to fits of temper. My beloved mother taught me well to keep my anger in check and not let it rule me, even when my wrath was completely justified. Still, it was infuriating to have worked as hard as I had to beat back Death only to have the marshal murdered in a most cowardly sneak attack.

And, if I am to be completely honest, I was also afraid. Dr. Skillen's warnings rang all too loudly in my ears, despite the truth of Sebastiano's reassurances.

It had been a most awkward time the previous spring when it became known that I was a medical doctor. But as many of the Americans started seeking me out and paying me, I began to flirt with the idea of working as a doctor all the time and selling the winery and rancho to the Hermanos Ortiz. That, actually, had been part of my intent when I made them full partners in the venture that summer. I hadn't said so, although I doubt they were fooled. I enjoyed winemaking, but clearly, my passions were centered on the healing arts. But if Dr. Skillen had accurately described the current rumors, then it would be that much harder to make my living as a doctor. Doctors were paid so poorly then, it was hard enough as it was.

I was not left long to wallow in my fears. I had barely begun to transcribe my notes when I received a most peculiar note from Mrs. Warren. She had arranged to have the viewing and prayers for her husband that night at the Catholic church instead of at home because of the tremendous interest in the event. I was invited, naturally, but her note asked that I stop by the house before the viewing so that she could talk to me about a matter that concerned her greatly. The language was formal, but I could sense that she was afraid.

CHAPTER FOUR

I arrived in good time at the Warren home that evening wearing my brown bombazine visiting dress. It was a rather sedate gown, but still smart with a little ruffle in the back and silk ribbon trim. Mrs. Warren met me alone in the front parlor. She was wearing a well-made black wool dress and her widow's weeds, which were thrown back from her face. Her eyes were red from much weeping, but she was more frightened than grieved at that moment. Her face flushed with relief when she saw me.

"Oh, Mrs. Wilcox, I don't know what to do!" she sighed softly, glancing back at the rest of the house. "My brother says I am being foolish and a nervous hen. But he doesn't know about, about..."

I frowned. "What's happened?"

"Someone has been creeping around the house, listening at the windows. I can hear him, and I've seen him at least twice. But every time my brother went out to look, he didn't see anything."

"That is most disturbing," I said.

"Mrs. Wilcox, you were right." Mrs. Warren shuddered and began weeping again. "You must find out who killed my husband. But how are you going to do that without telling everyone how he really died?"

"An excellent question." I went over and put my hand on her shoulder. "However, there is a bit of good news. I have already asked some questions merely as a matter of course. I should be able to continue asking without revealing why I want to know. It may even help. Now, when did you first think someone was listening at the windows?"

Mrs. Warren shook her head. "This morning, I think. I don't really know. People have been coming in and out all day. I saw a shadow during lunch and then again, this afternoon."

"Well," I pressed my lips together, trying to think. "Who has come to visit?"

"Mostly my family." Mrs. Warren blinked, then dabbed at her eyes and nose with a black trimmed handkerchief. "And, of course, Father Jimenez. He was able to stay all day. And that Reverend Bennett. He said he helped Mr. Warren home after he was shot and feels as though it's his duty to offer aid and comfort."

"It might be if it were wanted, and it appears it is not."

"We're Catholics. What do we care about a revivalist? I let him stay for a while. He was no bother. But that Councilman Wilson." Here, Mrs. Warren glared as she twisted her handkerchief. "He kept coming to the door and I kept turning him away. He has paid me attentions before. Can you imagine being so foolish?"

Indeed, there were those, myself among them, who would have considered it bordering on suicide to pay attentions upon the wife of the hot-tempered marshal.

"And my husband not even in his grave yet," Mrs. Warren went on, growing more and more angry. "What impropriety! It's as if he thought I had no regard for my husband, no constancy. As if I had no tender feelings for him when I have nothing but!" She began weeping again. "He was a kind and loving husband and a gentle caring father to our daughters. I know he was a hard man in his work, but at home, he was kindness, itself."

If I was nonplussed at that moment, one could have hardly expected otherwise. It was not her tears, however, that left me floundering. One expects tears from a newly-made widow, and if I could not help but wonder if she was grieving over much, it was only because she had the easiest opportunity to harm her husband. Her tears seemed quite genuine, however, and there seemed to be no appropriate way to ask her if she had done the deed. If anything, it seemed quite unlikely she had done so.

Fortunately, Mrs. Warren recovered herself quite quickly. Her eyes were still watery, but she squeezed my arm in thanks, sniffed and made use of her handkerchief. A minute later, her brother came in and announced that the buggy was ready to take her and the family to church. Armando Ortiz was outside waiting in my buggy to drive me there, as well. I took my leave and only waited for the buggy bearing Mrs. Warren to leave before asking Armando to follow along to the Catholic church in the pueblo.

It was a long service and all in Latin, with the Catholics all fingering their beads and muttering along with the priest in intervals and the rest of us trying not to show how utterly bored we were by the abundantly repeated Ave Marias, with Pater Nosters sprinkled in. One of the younger priests led the service, but Father Jimenez was close by. It was a sign of Marshal Warren's standing in the community that Father Jimenez, who as the pastor of the church oversaw the five other priests there, had taken it upon himself to attend to Mrs. Warren the previous day, and then attended the viewing and service that night.

I was considerably surprised when, after the service, Father Jimenez approached me. He was small of stature, but so uncommonly handsome, with graying temples, and beautifully shaped cheekbones and jaw, that I would have thought his appearance would be a hindrance to his vocation. Nonetheless, I'd heard nothing but good of the priest, and on the few occasions when our paths had crossed at the bedside of the sick or injured, he'd always seemed appropriately compassionate, as well as reasonably courteous to me. That being said, however, ours was the most passing of acquaintances, usually when I had done all I could and needed to place the patient's healing and care into the hands of our most merciful Lord.

I've had more cause than most to rue the clay feet of our men of God. However, I must say that I have seldom run across one who cannot offer succor to a sick or injured person. There was one old codger under Father Jimenez who I dreaded seeing, and another younger fellow who came along after the pueblo got big enough to support a dedicated Episcopalian congregation, rather than the combined Episcopalian Methodist one we had at the time. But most flowed with the milk of human kindness when suffering and even fear of immediate death hovered. Even Reverend Elmwood, the pastor of the congregation to which I belonged, and with whom I had locked horns on multiple occasions over his tendency to condemn sinners rather than encourage and aid their reform, even he could be counted upon to be kind and compassionate at the bedside of one who needed his prayers and comfort.

When Father Jimenez spoke, it was almost too softly for me to hear.

"Mrs. Warren has told me you alerted her to the true cause of her husband's death," he said.

"Yes, I did. I'd only just discovered it, myself, when she came into the room," I replied.

"Then I must ask you to not to let anyone know," Father Jimenez continued with a quick look over his shoulder. "It would not be kind to sully his memory and might even be dangerous for Mrs. Warren and her daughters."

"I understand that full well, Father. I will only reveal what I must to prevent an injustice. Or to hopefully prevent further harm. Has she told you about the man lurking under her windows?"

Father Jimenez sighed. "Yes, she has. It is a most difficult situation."

"Then, since you are fully apprised of what happened, perhaps you can help me. I've been able to ask a few questions here and there as a matter of course. But I can ask you directly. Who did you see at the house last night?"

"Nobody you couldn't expect. Many of Mrs. Warren's relatives, her mother and sisters, and her brother. No. He came later the next day."

"Was there any ill feeling among her family toward the marshal?"

Father Jimenez shook his head. "None that I ever saw. Believe me, Mrs. Wilcox, I see and hear a great deal, as you can imagine. Marshal Warren and his wife, theirs was an exceptionally companionable marriage, and he was very friendly to his wife's family, and they to him."

"Anyone else there? I saw Mr. Redona and Mr. Brooks both there, neither of whom should have been, given their wounds. Oh, and that Reverend Bennett."

"I saw him, too." Father Jimenez suddenly perked up. "And Councilman Wilson. He was there a large part of the afternoon and again today. He said he was there as an official representative of the city. But Mrs. Warren did not seem happy to see him."

"She told me he's been paying her inappropriate attentions."

"I'm not surprised." He looked over his shoulder again and then smiled and acknowledged some other member of his congregation. He smiled at me once more, then left to speak with someone else.

I looked around but was not terribly surprised to see that both Mr. Redona and Mr. Brooks were not present. Mrs. Redona was and kindly assured me that while Mr. Redona had a slight fever, his wound looked clean. I made a mental note to visit the next day, after the funeral. I also didn't see Reverend Bennett, but as a preacher of another religion, one could hardly expect him to be there.

Reverend Bennett did make an appearance at the funeral mass the following day. Indeed, even Reverend Elmwood did, and he had little use for Catholics. Later, I stumbled into Reverend Elmwood as we jostled our way into the graveyard. He righted himself with a small sniff and moved on. I debated asking after his catarrh, for I had smelled oil of turpentine on him, and that was commonly used in chest plasters for such maladies. However, it was far too crowded. The streets had been jammed with buggies and traps, and people were packed quite closely to the gravesite as Father Jimenez began chanting something in Latin.

I, like most educated people, learned Latin as a young woman, but quickly forgot most of it. What I have retained is directly related to the practice of medicine. I had, at that point in my life, attended many a Catholic graveside service. It would have been hard not to, given my ties to the Mexicans in the Pueblo. But I had somehow escaped learning the Latin used in their services.

I saw Reverend Bennett standing next to me, but because we were on a slope, I was actually almost level with him, his much greater height notwithstanding. He muttered something.

"Excuse me, Reverend?" I adjusted my bonnet so that he could see me.

"Mrs. Wilcox," he replied.

"Did you say something?"

"Oh. No. I was merely contemplating our fate before God, praying that I should be among those of the elect."

"A worthy meditation, indeed," I said, softly, looking at the coffin with its array of roses and other late blooms. That was one of the gifts of Los Angeles. We were able to get many flowers well into December, and even January in the case of roses, without resorting to hothouses. "You spent quite a bit of time at the marshal's house that night."

"I felt responsible," the reverend said. "I helped him home."

"That's right. You did. Did you see anyone else there?"

He looked at me sharply. "Why do you ask?"

I swallowed quickly. "Mrs. Warren told me last night that she feared someone had been listening at her windows. She didn't see anything, but was worried."

"Shouldn't she be talking to one of the other policemen?"

I couldn't help letting out what I hoped was a lady-like snort. "Only to have him see her as a nervous, flighty woman and ignore her? No, she came to me because she thought I might have seen something that night. And I, like you, felt responsible. After all, I know what it's like to be left alone as a widow."

Reverend Bennett shrugged. "I left the house before you did, Mrs. Wilcox, and retired promptly to my room and stayed there."

"I'm sure you did, Reverend," I replied softly. "But did you see anyone skulking around the house that night as you left?"

"No. I did not." He shifted away from me as some of the others in the crowd began glancing our way.

I turned my focus back to the coffin, hoping my bonnet hid the blush on my face. Graveside was most definitely an inappropriate place to ask questions. Questions I had to be careful about asking, I suddenly realized, lest the killer decide I was learning too much and set his sights on me. It was only good fortune that I'd thought of a legitimate reason to be asking about the night the marshal was killed or at least a reason that the Reverend accepted. I could not guarantee the same would continue. I had to find a more circumspect way to find out who had been at or around the house that fateful night.

After the marshal was laid in his grave, I made my way home. I was intent on getting there as soon as possible, but the crowds, with all their buggies, and even more people on foot, made hurrying impossible. I was glad I had decided to walk, and even more glad that the current fashion decreed smaller hoops. As much as I appreciated, and still do appreciate, fashion, I have to concede that the hoop skirt was a singularly ill-considered style. For all its elegance in a grand ballroom, it made movement in small or crowded spaces almost impossible, which may have been the point, now that I think about it. In any case, it took far longer than it should have for me to wedge my way around the buggy wheels and whalebone hoops to where I could stride with some comfort, my mannish gait being yet another trial to my Grandmother Franklin, who despaired of making me a lady to her dying day.

Once I returned to the rancho, I found a note that left me rather perplexed. But I agreed to the arrangement and sent a return note with one of the younger Ortiz children. That left little for me to do but change into my work dress. Mrs. Redona had reassured me at the funeral that her husband was doing much better and did not require a second visit. So I went to see to the distilling and to check that the aging barrels were well-secured. I was surprised to see that the three dogs we had on the place were, for a change, lounging contentedly around the huge aging barrels.

As a rule, I am very fond of dogs, including some of the more ridiculous lap dogs, and I had been all but devastated the previous winter when we'd had to destroy the two we'd had on the rancho, who had become rabid. I had been quite happy and utterly relieved when Negrito, a large black dog with short hair, and Beauty, a yellow short hair, had found their way onto our rancho. Negrito was some sort of hound, based on his baying, and had been a year or so old when one of the children found him late the previous spring. Beauty we'd gotten as a puppy in the middle of April. Both were filled with the energy of young dogs.

But neither of them could keep up with ChiChi. He was a small Mexican dog, not even twelve inches tall at the shoulder. He had been the companion of someone's abuelita, or grandmother, when she had passed away last summer. I was offered the dog and agreed to take it. Little did I know. ChiChi yapped constantly, bit all of us until he realized we were his new family, but then commenced to biting anyone else who did not belong on the rancho. He ran everywhere and could leap almost as high as my waist. We'd seen him jump clear over Negrito in one of his mad dashes across the yard. The children and Olivia doted on him. The rest of us tolerated him, especially Juanita, who'd had to mend all our skirts and pants when he'd still been biting us. The only person on the rancho who could control the beast was Wang Fu, whose own personal calm somehow calmed ChiChi.

As I entered the winery, ChiChi bounded up to me, his high-pitched barking once again piercing my ears. Sebastiano appeared from behind one of the large barrels, the tops of which were almost twice Sebastiano's height.

"Basta!" he snarled at ChiChi, who continued yapping.

"Why are the dogs in the winery?" I asked, feeling somewhat nettled.

They were not allowed in the winery because however delightful they may be, dogs are not sanitary, and I kept my winery scrupulously clean.

"It was Pascual's idea," Sebastiano said. "It will make it harder for anyone to tamper with the wine. And now that it's sealed in the barrels, it will be clean enough."

I pursed my lips. "I must concede the sense in that. We'll have to make sure we clean extra carefully when it's time to rack again."

"Of course."

Together, we checked the barrels, and satisfied that all was as it should be, we returned to the distilling hut. All was in good order there, so I returned to my study and began writing my journal notes, dealt with a couple of letters I had received, then wrote one letter each to my younger sisters, Carrie and Abby. And finally, out of duty, wrote two more, one to my father and the other to my brother, Merriam, or rather to Merriam's wife, Gertrude.

After that, it was time for supper, then listening to the children's lessons, as we preferred to teach them ourselves, given that Mexican children often got short shrift in the two city schools that we had at the time. By close to eight o'clock, the children had been put to bed and the rest of my household was probably chatting amongst themselves in the barracks' sitting room, it being much larger than the front parlor in the adobe.

I first heard ChiChi yapping from the barracks. There was, of course, a good, stout rail fence surrounding the rancho. Unfortunately, ChiChi could work his way through the rails and did at every opportunity. Hence, he had to be kept in the barracks at night. Negrito and Beauty, who were always better behaved, ran loose in the yard. After ChiChi began his noise-making, Negrito began baying and Beauty added her fierce bark.

A minute later, I could hear a horse and buggy rolling into the yard and I went to the front parlor door. I'd told Magdalena, Enrique's wife and my housekeeper, that I would see to my guests, myself. However, she did make sure that there were plenty of pan dulces, or sweet bread cakes, and a full decanter of angelica set out on the credenza in the front parlor.

Angelina Sutton was already at the front door when I opened it, and I could see my second guest daintily getting down from the buggy, never mind her tall stature, hoops, and layers of petticoats. She was one of the few women in the pueblo who could drive herself without causing comment. But then, given Regina Medina's decidedly odious profession, if a woman driving herself could be considered a sin, it was certainly the least of hers.

Regina tied her horse at the post near my front door, then stooped as she entered the front parlor. Already overly tall for a woman, she wore her luxurious dark hair piled on top of her head, then adorned that with a tall hat. The hat and the lace jabot she wore at her neck were her trademarks. That and her incredible wardrobe, which was the bane of every lady in the pueblo's society. No one knew how she did it, but Regina managed to get fashion plates before anyone else and many a lady would purchase a gown or suit of the very latest style, only to be humiliated when someone realized that Regina had been modeling that same style for a month or more. It was embarrassing enough to find your latest style wasn't the latest. It was made worse because Regina owned and ran one of the most popular houses of ill-repute in the pueblo.

It is a constant source of surprise to me that I had formed a close friendship with Regina. I most certainly did not approve of her profession. Indeed, I was repulsed by it, as any right-thinking woman would be. However, Regina was excellent company and had opened my eyes to the plight of the young women in her care, who fell into their vile trade thanks to having little alternative. It did not surprise me that once they were introduced, Angelina and Regina would form an attachment. Angelina had a decidedly wicked sense of humor and neither of them had much use for the conventional mores of society. If Angelina paid more heed to the expectations, it was simply because her husband's business depended on it. Although, if I am to be completely honest (as I hope I always am), Angelina did almost all of the work in that business, and as such, one could quite rightly call it hers.

In any case, the three of us were soon settled, Regina and Angelina on the red velvet sofa, and I in my chair, pan dulces served and angelica poured. Angelina called us to order almost before we'd taken our first sips.

"Maddie, I hope you will forgive me for including Regina," Angelina said, rushing through her words. "But if we are to find Marshal Warren's true killer, then we need her help."

"I do know things, dearest," Regina said her soft throaty voice that held a hint of an Irish brogue. "And the marshal and the deputy were fighting over a prostitute. I don't have much entrée into the Chinese

Companies but I have a better chance than you."

All of this was quite true, however I hesitated. Angelina frowned.

"Please, Maddie, I know you want to keep this in the strictest confidence," she began.

I held up my hand. "Actually, I'm quite grateful you brought her." I looked at Regina. "I am merely puzzled by your interest in the matter. There's no love lost between you and the marshal."

"And if I had been the victim, I would expect you to look at him first," Regina said with a smug smile. "But in spite of my over-hasty incarceration last spring, I bore Marshal Warren no ill will. If he had any complaint against me it was that I deprived him of a source of income by paying my girls well, treating them fairly, and letting them go when they run off."

"Nor is that much of a reason to kill someone," I said.

Angelina sniggered. "As if anyone around here needs a reason."

Alas, violence in the pueblo was quite a common thing, and Angelina, as an undertaker, saw the results of it more than even I did.

"Certainly they don't when they are drunk and angry." Regina finished the last of her small glass and lifted an eyebrow at me.

I handed her the decanter. Regina refilled her glass and passed the decanter to Angelina. As I mused on the death of Marshal Warren, Dr. Skillen's warnings echoed again in my ears.

I frowned. "But there was stealth involved in this killing. It may have been an act of rage, but it was accomplished in secrecy, unlike most killings in the pueblo. Worse yet, Dr. Skillen told me yesterday that there are those who are hinting that the marshal might have survived had he been left in the care of a man."

Regina scoffed. "Dearest, they're saying it outright."

"Oh, no!" I blinked back the tears that had

suddenly rushed to my eyes.

"They say it all the time." Regina reached over and patted my hand with her own overly large one. "It's nothing new. But when someone is in grave danger, who's the first person they call? You. And that was even before they knew you were a medical doctor."

"But what if someone killed the marshal to taint my reputation?" The anxiety filled me and I could not hold back my deepest fears.

"Why kill someone to do that?" Angelina asked. "Maddie, you're the best doctor in the pueblo, but even you can't fix everything. If somebody wants to taint your reputation, all he has to do is wait. Why risk going into a house full of people who would probably be up and about watching?"

I accepted the decanter from her and poured myself another glassful of angelica. "It does sound rather ridiculous when you put it that way."

"And everybody thought the marshal was going to die, anyway," Regina held out her glass. "In fact, the mood at my house was fairly celebratory the day of the shooting. You'd have thought he was dead already."

"But I thought your men liked him," Angelina's brows knit together in puzzlement.

She didn't say so outright, partly because neither Angelina nor I knew it for certain and partly because Regina prided herself, and deservedly so, on her discretion. However, we were both under the impression that most of her customers were members of the City Council and prominent businessmen in the pueblo. It was one of those widely accepted rumors and I'd heard just enough from the back rooms, those times I was there delivering a baby or otherwise helping one of the girls, to believe it.

"The funeral was huge," Angelina continued. "How many buggies did you count, Maddie?"

"I didn't, but there were more than I've ever seen."

In fact, the newspaper the next day would report that there had been one hundred conveyances and even more people on foot. They had, as usual, exaggerated the number, but not by that much.

Regina laughed. "They probably wanted to be sure the marshal was really dead. I won't say he didn't have his supporters, but they were not as numerous as you might think. I know many a prominent man in this pueblo who supported him to his face, but did not care for him a whit in private."

"Why was that?" I asked. "I thought they appreciated the way he kept peace in the pueblo."

"Oh, they did," said Regina. "But they couldn't trust him not to blow their heads off if they were in the wrong place at the wrong time. The man had quite the temper. They would probably never admit it, but they were all terrified of him."

I thought that over. "That might account for the stealth attack on him. After all, if you were afraid to draw on the man, and what rational person wouldn't be, smothering him while asleep would be the safest way to murder him."

Angelina pulled a sheaf of blank paper from the small wooden lap desk she'd brought with her. She loved to make lists. She was also prone to scribbling all sorts of odd notes to herself, as well as drawing whatever struck her fancy. In fact, she was quite an accomplished artist, although she often demurred on that point.

"It's time to make a list of everyone we think had reason to kill the marshal," Angelina announced, opening her ink pot.

"How late do you want to stay tonight?" Regina asked with a laugh.

"It certainly feels that way," I sighed. "But I think we can limit our list to those men, or their families, who have suffered a serious personal injury at the hands of the marshal. And I have to include Hernan Mendoza and his cousins, Pascual and Emilio. Indeed, their whole family was grievously injured when their uncle was killed by the marshal."

Angelina's eyes widened. "I know them! It was terrible. But which of them would do such a thing? Mrs. Mendoza was very firm that they were not to go after him."

"Sadly," I said. "Hernan and his cousins would have been among the few who would have known that I expected the marshal to live. They might have seen his being wounded and weakened as an opportunity to get their revenge."

"It's possible," said Regina. "But wouldn't someone else here on the rancho have noted that they were not at home that night?"

"It would have made it more difficult for them to leave and commit the murder, to be sure," I said. "But it would hardly have been impossible, especially if they chose to collude amongst themselves."

"But would they have felt safe going into the house?" Angelina fidgeted with the edge of her paper.

"It's hard to say." I glared at my sherry glass. "If they assumed that because I had left, there would not be anyone watching or that they could use my name to acquire access, they might have attempted it."

Regina sipped again. "Unfortunately, that does bring to mind the one person who would not have had a problem acquiring access. Indeed, she would have been expected to have been there."

"You mean Mrs. Warren." Angelina frowned. "It's possible, I suppose."

I shook my head. "It would be extremely unlikely. She seems genuinely grieved. In addition, I've been privy to some information that certainly suggests that she did not do it."

I suppose I could have mentioned what Father Jimenez had confided in me regarding Marshal and Mrs. Warren. Certainly, Regina's and Angelina's discretion was not to be questioned. Still, it felt uncomfortable to divulge what may have been meant for only my ears.

"I'm surprised that given the depth of Mr. Dye's ire, someone did not find a way to guard the house,"

Regina said, reaching again for the decanter.

"They did," I finished off my glass. "But the worse luck is that the two deputies who decided to stand guard were the two that were wounded in the affray between the marshal and Mr. Dye. That is, Mr. Brooks and Mr. Redona."

"Why, in Heaven's name, would they have done so when they probably should have been at home in bed?" Regina asked.

"They did not think they were that seriously hurt," I said.

"Men never do," sighed Angelina. "And to think I heard that Mr. Brooks took sick from his wound."

"He was improving as of yesterday," I said. "Mrs. Redona told me today that Mr. Redona was doing quite well and did not require me to come by. And she most certainly would have asked me to come if she thought he needed it. In any case, neither of them saw anything because each had managed to spend part or most of his watch asleep."

"That may be," said Regina. "But it also means that both of them had the opportunity to kill the marshal."

I frowned. "And Mr. Brooks said that Mr. Redona was becoming quite irate with the marshal over getting more than his share of the bounties and fines. Of course, Mr. Brooks also said that he was there standing guard because of fears that Jorge Villega or Sam Bonner might try to finish what Mr. Dye had started, as they are friends of Mr. Dye and were almost as angry at the marshal as he was."

Regina lifted an eyebrow. "Now, there would be an avenue to explore. But again, we face the question of whether either of these men would be likely to risk going into a house where one could surmise that people would be awake and watching. We have to remember most people thought that the marshal was about to die."

"Which means they would also have less reason to assure his death," said Angelina.

I sat up suddenly. "Wait. Mrs. Warren told me yesterday that someone had been listening at her windows. What if that same person or another accomplice had been listening the day before, as well? What if that person went unnoticed in the concern over the marshal?"

"The weather seems rather cold for the windows to be open," Angelina said. "Or for anyone to be standing outside trying to listen in."

"Oh, you poor native child," Regina replied archly. "Where most of us are from this is hardly cold at all."

This was an exchange that could lead to nothing good, so I spoke quickly.

"That is neither here nor there. Windows do not have to be open to be heard through. And because some of us are more habituated to cooler weather than others doesn't mean that it is so cold that one would freeze to death while standing outside. And if someone had been listening at the Warrens' windows, then that man would know that there was little fear for the marshal's life and would also have been able to ascertain before entering whether there was someone awake and on guard at the moment he needed to enter. Ergo, we can likely dispense with those particular concerns. Now, is there anyone else we should be considering?"

Regina sighed and put down her glass. "Possibly, but more for what he may have seen. Mr. Mahoney came to visit me that night."

Angelina and I looked at each other then at Regina as we tried not to gape. It was well known in the pueblo that saloon owner Thomas Mahoney kept his distance from Regina Medina. Indeed, the two barely acknowledged the existence of the other. However, only Angelina and I knew that it was not out of enmity that the two avoided each other, but because Mr. Mahoney was Regina's brother.

"May we ask why?" I finally said. "I pray it was not some dire news?"

"It was nothing dire in the least," Regina said,

pouring herself another glass of angelica. I had lost count of how many she'd had, but I was not concerned. She could hold her liquor amazingly well. "Thomas merely came by to visit. He does that now and again to see how I'm getting on. We talked over the affray and the reactions to it, and the men in his saloon had largely the same reaction mine did."

I looked at Regina. "Does he have a reason to want to harm Marshal Warren?"

Regina shook her head. "None that I know of. But, having come after he'd closed the saloon, it was quite late when he arrived and even later when he left. Which means he would have been abroad at an hour that makes it possible he saw the person who helped the marshal to his appearance in the heavenly court."

"Could Mr. Mahoney have done it, himself?" I frowned. "He is such a mild soul that I cannot imagine him striking out that way, and yet, I suppose it is possible."

"The fact that I'm still alive speaks a great deal to his mildness," Regina said with an almost sour laugh. "In addition, he bore the marshal no ill will. I would very seriously doubt that he did it. It's far more likely that he could have seen something and did not remark upon it."

"Now, all we have to do is find a way to ask him about it," said Angelina.

"That will have to be my job," I said. "I'm the one with the most reason to speak to him."

And, indeed, I did speak with Mr. Mahoney on a quite frequent basis as he was one of the more regular buyers of my wines.

"Then I will try to find out more from the Mendoza family," Angelina said. "That way, Maddie won't have to risk ruining her relationship with her servants."

"For which, I thank you," I said.

"And I will continue to collect observations and see if I can gain access to the Chinese Companies," Regina said, polishing off her glass.

Thus arranged, she and Angelina left soon after. It had been a good meeting and it was somehow comforting to know that I had help in my mission. I had yet to learn that I would soon have a good reason to ask all the questions I wanted, which would have been a happy coincidence had it not been due to something so terrifying.

CHAPTER FIVE

The next morning, I must confess, I was not at my best. I arose at my normal time, however, but was not happy to find that I already had a messenger waiting for me before I'd even had a chance to break my nightly fast. Olivia did see to it that there was a cup of strong coffee and would not let me leave until I had eaten something.

I had Armando drive me to the Warren home in the buggy to get there as quickly as possible. What I saw as we drove up was utterly appalling. The house was made of clapboard and painted white, with two stories and gable windows to the attic. A medium-sized porch sat on the front corner of the house with a small turret above it. To the left of the porch as you looked at the house was a generous picture window that had cunning wooden cutouts at the bottom and top. Several shrubs grew underneath it.

Someone had splashed red paint all over the front window and porch. Not caring to get paint on my blue wool and linen riding habit or my boots, which I'd newly bought, I went around to the back of the house. As it turned out, Mrs. Warren was waiting there for me, anyway.

"It must have happened last night," she told me as we made our way to the front parlor.

There was a lamp lit near the sofa, as she'd pulled the heavy green curtains closed to hide the window.

"And it wasn't just the paint," she said, picking up a large sheet of paper from an end table. "We found this nailed to the porch pillar."

"This was the home of a sinner!" was written across the top of the sheet in uneven, but clear block letters made in red paint. The rest had been penned in smaller block letters adorned by the occasional blot of ink. "These are his sins, to wit: Murder, A lover of whores, In the pay of The Devil."

"Oh, dear," I said.

Mrs. Warren tried to blink back more tears. "I am so afraid for my darling girls. Who could be doing this to us? Why? I know Mr. Warren was no saint and there were people who were angry with him. But why hurt his family?"

"I have no idea," I said. "But the first thing to do would be to get that mess cleaned up. I'll send over some of my men."

I mentally debated sending Hernan and his cousins, but it did occur to me that they may have, in fact, been the perpetrators of the vandalism. While it would have been just, in that case, to have them clean it up, I did fear that they could use it as an opportunity for more mischief. I'd have to ask whether Enrique and Rodolfo might be spared, and perhaps Ramon, Sebastiano's eldest, assuming he was not needed at his job at the Pico House.

"Who is doing this?" Mrs. Warren asked again, as she began pacing the room. "He probably killed my husband, don't you think?"

"That would seem to be the logical conclusion," I said. "And the fortunate part of this miserable episode is that we probably won't have to reveal how your husband died to find the miscreant."

"That's a relief." Mrs. Warren blinked back more tears. "It's hard enough to have lost my darling husband. It would be worse having to protect his memory from cowards who would only attack him in secret."

"I agree." I looked over the sheet of paper again. "I'd like to keep this. I don't know how it might help, but it could."

"I don't want it," Mrs. Warren said.

I left through the back and sent Armando back to the rancho to fetch the help. I, however, went straight to the Sutton home. Angelina was happy to receive me and took me back to her little parlor. She, too, was appalled by the vandalism and read the paper with great interest while I paced the floor.

"It's somebody educated enough to write and spell correctly," she noted, then shrugged. "Poor Mrs. Warren. Although, she should be glad the marshal wasn't accused of adultery."

"I fear I had the same thought, myself." I paced some more. "It seems a very odd turn of events. Could it be a coincidence?"

Angelina shrugged. "It's possible, I suppose. After all, why do this after killing your enemy? Unless someone wants the manner of the marshal's death exposed."

"That makes sense," I said. "And coincidence or not, it does give us an excuse to ask after those who hated the marshal."

"Which I've got to do today," Angelina said. "I'm going to have tea with Mrs. Mendoza this afternoon. That should help."

"Thank you. I hope it does." I sighed. "I hate suspecting my dear friends of such an atrocity."

Angelina put her hand on my arm. "I know." She suddenly yawned.

"Forgive me for coming by so early," I said. "But I thought you'd want to see this as soon as possible."

"I did," said Angelina with a smile. "It's just that meetings with Regina make it very hard to get up the next morning. Penance for our sins, right?"

"I suppose. I'll leave you to your work."

Angelina's eyes twinkled merrily. "I'll send you to yours."

However, what my next step would be did leave me momentarily somewhat flummoxed. There was Mr. Mahoney to speak to, but given that he worked late into the night at his saloon, he would hardly have been awake at that hour. I was pondering who else I could speak to when I saw a banner hanging from a wagon that made me smile.

One wonders at how our Gracious Lord works, at times. It seemed as though He was favoring my work with proper cover to protect Mrs. Warren in spite of the questions I needed to ask, and had just pointed me to where I could go next. The Races. It was opening day at our new horse racing track, with the meets to start at one o'clock. I know that there are those who find a horse race a less than salubrious place for a lady, given the low sorts engaging in gambling and even pickpocketing that one finds there. However, in a small pueblo that was somewhat starved for entertainment, opening day at the race track was quite the event. All of the pueblo's society attended, and it would give me a rare chance to speak to a wide variety of men.

I did have several chores at home to complete first, but by noon, I was dressed in my green bombazine walking suit and waiting in the buggy with Olivia for Sebastiano to finish hitching the mule to the carreta so the rest of the household could come, as well. I did so love that particular walking suit, with its swept-back skirt, matching silk ribbons and silk ribbon ruching on the bodice. I'd even had a parasol and hat made to match it. With my new boots, a new beaded purse, and new black kid gloves, I thought I made rather a smart and striking appearance that day. I suppose that was vanity, but it was a useful one at that moment. I wasn't feeling at all confident that I should be able to find, let alone talk to some of the fellows I was hoping to.

It was a good thing we had thought to leave at noon, a full hour before the first race was to start. Even as we drove up, the trotting park was surrounded by all manner of buggies and sulkies and even wagons. The park grounds and stands had been meticulously built up over the summer and were looking quite fine. The ladies were all wearing their best walking suits, adding large swaths of different colors among the dark suits of the men. Even the cowhands, teamsters and laborers had made an effort to clean up. The betting was quite lively and I had to hold back Armando from placing a wager or two. He was barely sixteen at the time. Ramon, Sebastiano's eldest, managed to place several wagers and even secured bets for each of the younger children. That was when he wasn't flirting with every young girl there.

It did seem like the entire pueblo was there, although they couldn't all have fit in the park. Even Regina was on hand, circulating among several of the factory foremen. She caught my eye shortly after the first race had ended and nodded. Fortunately, she had situated herself close to a stand selling tea, punch, and water. I made my way over to get a drink for myself, then managed to stand so that Regina's back was to me, but I could hear a great deal of what the fellow she was talking to was saying.

"It's knowing the horses, Mrs. Medina," the man told her in his moderately heavy Spanish accent.

I managed to gaze about me at the crowd and turned just enough to see him. He was of average height and wore a dark suit with a stained shirt. His mustache was quite dark and full and his small hat identified him as a worker of some sort or other.

"It was quite a generous bet, nonetheless, Mr. Villega." Regina's voice was just barely audible.

"But I won. You can't be afraid to put real money down. That's how you win big."

I couldn't hear Regina's response, but the two moved off toward one of several fellows offering varying odds on the second race. I could no longer hear them but could see Mr. Villega pull out several bills and even a gold coin. I was shocked. That coin was twenty dollars, probably a week's wages for the fellow and it looked as though he had even more in his pocket. He must have made quite a generous wager on the first race, indeed.

As the afternoon wore on, Regina also pointed out

to me a man who appeared to be a ranch hand, more likely a foreman, based on the way he carried himself. His mustache and beard were blonde and full and his hair hung in greasy strings from under his well-worn hat. His dark suit was surprisingly well-cut, new and dust-free. However, I could not tell who he was and assumed Regina would explain later. I made my way back to the stands where my household had established itself. Looking at some of the lines for those stands offering refreshments, I fully appreciated Olivia's insistence on packing a small feast for us.

There were three races total, which made for quite a full afternoon. The crowd was well-pleased with the entertainment. My party waited until much of the crowd had left, although I couldn't help noticing the park begin to empty before the third race had even begun. As the crowds filed out, I watched to see if there was anyone else I could talk to. I saw Councilman Wilson with a lovely young woman on his arm. Indeed, she was almost young enough to be the middle-aged councilman's daughter, although it seemed fairly clear from the way he was paying her attention that she was not.

They passed by quite close and as they did, the councilman doffed his top hat. He was a tall man, with dark hair and mustache, both shot through with gray and neatly trimmed, and pince-nez glasses. His clothes were very well tailored and that morning, he wore a dark frock coat and blue satin vest.

"How do you do, Mrs. Wilcox?" he said with a pleasant smile, completely ignoring the rest of my party. Apparently, he'd forgotten that the men were all citizens and could vote.

"How do you do, Mr. Wilson," I replied, nonetheless.

"May I present Miss Lavina Gaines, Mrs. Wilcox?" he said, indicating the young woman at his side.

She had a pretty, round face with a small, perfect nose. Her brown hair was in ringlets that bobbed charmingly as she nodded in greeting. The only thing that marred her appearance was her obvious discomfort at being on Mr. Wilson's arm.

"How do you do, Mrs. Wilcox," she replied, very politely.

"Did you enjoy the races, Miss Gaines?" I asked.

"Very much, thank you. Mr. Wilson has been most kind about explaining them to me." There was just enough of an edge in her voice to make me suspect that she had not needed the explanation.

"Are you two related?" I asked. "Mr. Wilson, I wasn't aware that you had any relatives in the pueblo."

He had been a widower for some time, and to the best of my knowledge, had only lived in Los Angeles for four years. As the owner of a very successful business selling insurance, in addition to owning quite a few houses, he had quickly established himself among the more respected of our citizenry.

Miss Gaines blushed and Mr. Wilson sputtered.

"No, no. Miss Gaines is the daughter of a dear friend of mine," Mr. Wilson said, then patted her hand as she winced. "He very kindly allowed me to squire her this afternoon."

Or pushed Miss Gaines into going with the old goat, I thought, but could not say. I decided to further my acquaintance with Miss Gaines when I could, if only to find out more about Councilman Wilson. There was something else about Miss Gaines that I was trying to remember, but could not.

At last, the park was empty enough that we could make our way home without being hampered by traffic. Hernan and Maria's two young children were completely exhausted by all the excitement and slept in the carreta. Their parents were in excellent spirits. Maria had picked the three winning horses, although Hernan had made the actual bets, and they were quite happy with their winnings.

I do not usually hold with gambling. Heaven knows, we saw the problems it could cause all too often in our little pueblo, between inciting fights and causing all manner of impecunity. But there was little harm in indulging the spending of a few dollars once a year at the trotting park.

Once we returned home, I stopped Maria before she went to the barracks.

"Are you feeling quite well?" I asked.

"Perfectly well," Maria asked with a twinkle in her eye. "Why?"

"All the excitement today. It can be dangerous for your condition."

Maria laughed. "Dear, dear, Maddie. I am very well and a little excitement is not going to hurt me."

"Hmm. That's as may be. However, if you feel the least bit of cramping, or there's even the tiniest bit of bleeding, you are to call me immediately."

"I will. Don't worry."

We were all very merry that night. The children ran about, imitating the horses and sulkies they'd seen. Armando even went so far as to fashion a racing sulky out of an old barrow and played trotter for the younger ones, to their great delight. If I hadn't been so worried about Mrs. Warren, it would have been an entirely satisfactory day.

Which made the visitors who arrived the next morning all the more irritating. They were three prominent men of the pueblo: Councilman Wilson, Attorney Andrew Glassell, and Councilman James Judson, who owned the biggest bank in the pueblo. Mr. Glassell was the opposite of his rather round wife in shape and was generally more jovial. However, that morning, he had on his most serious face, thoughtfully stroking his gray mustache and beard to presumably hide his nerves. Mr. Judson's figure was well-padded and his mustache also gray, but his chin was clean-shaven.

It was Olivia who brought the tea and pan dulces, to spare the men the sight of a pregnant woman. I sat in my chair in the parlor and bade them make themselves comfortable, with Mr. Wilson sitting in the other chair and Mr. Judson and Mr. Glassell on the sofa. Once all were served and settled, Mr. Judson cleared his throat.

"Mrs. Wilcox," he said, shifting uncomfortably. "We have been told that the Marshal did not, in fact, die of his wounds from the affray with Deputy Dye."

"Yet he was murdered," I said. "I, Mrs. Sutton, and Deputy Lomax can all stand as witnesses to that."

Mr. Judson shifted again. "Well, you may have been mistaken."

"I can assure you, I was not."

The men all looked at each other.

"Mrs. Wilcox," said Mr. Glassell, fidgeting with his teacup. "We want you to understand that we hold you in the highest esteem and believe that you are sincere in your belief. But we must encourage you to consider otherwise, for the good of the town."

Mr. Wilson smiled with all the warmth of a rattlesnake. "You see, Mrs. Wilcox, we wouldn't expect you to understand the intricacies of the dilemma we are faced with."

"Of course you wouldn't," I said. "That does not mean I am incapable of understanding said intricacies. So what are you three so anxious about that you came in such a number to my home, rather than send a letter or find some other way to talk to me?"

The men all looked at each other again.

"The problem, Mrs. Wilcox," said Mr. Glassell. "Is that it is imperative that Deputy Dye is tried, and hopefully convicted, of the murder of Marshal Warren."

"Even if he merely wounded the marshal," Mr. Judson jumped in. "He should still be tried for that, wouldn't you agree?"

"Yes, probably. But why come to me about that?" I asked.

Mr. Judson cleared his throat again. "We would appreciate it if you allowed the popular conception of the marshal's death to stand so that Deputy Dye can be tried and convicted."

"As in, you would like to get rid of the deputy

without it looking like you're trying to get rid of him," I said.

The men all sat back, utterly shocked.

"As a matter of fact, yes," said Mr. Wilson, smiling his snake-like smile again. "Alas, it would not be politically expedient to dismiss him without good cause and given that the marshal had sorely tried the man's patience, there is considerable sympathy for the deputy."

"That and you're all terrified he'll lose his temper and blow your heads off," I said.

Mr. Glassell puffed himself up and Mr. Wilson casually swept his suit coat back so that I could see the gun at his side. Mr. Judson merely shook his head and set his teacup down on the table next to him.

"We're not terrified," he said. "However, one does not have to be terrified to know that the wiser course would be to avoid direct confrontation with Deputy Dye."

"Indeed, Mr. Judson," I replied. "I've patched up enough of his victims to know full well what a menace he is to our community."

"Then you will appreciate our desire to see to it that he is tried and convicted," Mr. Judson said.

"That I do, but I cannot leave it at that. I will do everything in my power to find the marshal's true killer."

The men sputtered, with Mr. Wilson collecting himself first.

"I'm afraid you do not understand how crucial this is," he said, looking as though he were about to pat me on the head.

I glared back at him. "I do understand perfectly well. What you do not understand is that there's a killer in the community trying to hide his crimes, one who can wreak just as much havoc on the largely innocent. You are aware, are you not, about what happened to the Warren home yesterday morning? That family is living in fear of their very lives. And I might point out,

Mr. Wilson, that you have been paying quite a bit of attention to Mrs. Warren, even before her husband died."

"You can't be accusing me!" He leaped from his chair, again swishing his coat back from his gun.

"Not at the moment, no," I said, far more calmly than I felt. I hoped and prayed neither he nor the others could hear how hard my heart was beating. "However, it would be helpful to know why you were spending so much time at the Warren home that evening and the next day, especially when Mrs. Warren did not encourage your advances."

"I made no such advances," Mr. Wilson insisted, plopping back into the chair. "I might in the future, as I have no reason to believe they would be unwelcome."

I sighed. Mr. Wilson clearly believed he truly hadn't paid any attentions to Mrs. Warren. And from the way he smirked at me, he also clearly believed that not only would Mrs. Warren be delighted should he do so, but that I would be similarly delighted should he pay his attentions to me. I feared disabusing him of this notion would be impossible and did not care to attempt such in front of his fellows, which may have been kinder than he deserved. However, if one is to subscribe to Christian charity, then one must offer kindness even to those who do not deserve it, although I knew that in the spirit of that same charity, I would have to let Mr. Wilson know that he was not nearly as desirable as he thought, if only to spare Mrs. Warren.

"In any case, you spent a great deal of time at the Warren home," I continued.

"I am a member of the city council. It was my duty to be on hand, as a city employee was gravely injured."

"Had the others asked you to do so, or did you decide to take up this service on your own?" I asked. "I know Mr. Judson is on the council and he did not appear."

Mr. Wilson shifted as Mr. Judson cleared his throat.

"I was, em, glad that Mr. Wilson took this on," said Mr. Judson, who was possibly the most honest and upright person in the pueblo. "But I am not aware of him being asked by any of us to do so. I certainly did not ask him to."

"That's neither here nor there," said Mr. Glassell abruptly. "There is no reason to believe that Mr. Wilson had anything to do with the marshal's death and I would expect that a woman in your position, Mrs. Wilcox, would not want to bandy about someone's good name."

"I have no intention of doing so. However, Mr. Glassell, you know as well as I do that having a good name in this community does not mean that one has no ill intent." I set my cup down and stood. The men bounced up with me. "Now, thank you for your visit. If you will be so kind as to excuse me, I do have a great deal of work to be done today, including safeguarding the interests and lives of a bereaved woman and her daughters."

CHAPTER SIX

Fortunately, I was already wearing my best blue riding habit when the men had arrived. I did not, however, get the opportunity to ride right away. As I went to the barn to collect Daisy, Rodolfo, who had seen to getting her saddled, held me back.

"I need to talk to you," he said softly in English.

Rodolfo was a very large man, with a bent over back and drooping mustache. He had come to California from Mexico as a young man. Even though he had been in Los Angeles for many years, he still found speaking English rather difficult. So, I was surprised that he'd chosen to address me in that language. He knew I spoke Spanish as well as he did, perhaps even better, as I could read in that language, as well.

Rodolfo looked around to be sure we were alone, and I realized that he was speaking English for the sake of privacy.

"You must know. Hernan, Pascual, Emilio, they did not kill the marshal," he said quietly.

"I had no reason to conclude that they had," I stammered, feeling somewhat taken aback that my hands were concerned that I would doubt them.

"Yes, but you thought so."

I began to protest, but Rodolfo waved me to silence.

"I thought so, too," he continued softly.

"Rodolfo, por favor, en Espanol."

He sighed but answered in Spanish. "We all worried you would think los hermanos Mendoza, that they would have done such a thing. But I know they did not. They did not leave the rancho all week. I know. I was watching."

"You were afraid they would?"

"No." Rodolfo sighed. "It was my turn to keep watch the night the marshal died. Against those who make mischief, you know? But then, when you asked Hernan about the marshal, Emilio got worried that you thought that they had done it. And they did not want me to say anything to you because they did not want to embarrass you. They are very proud."

"Yes. I know."

"So I watched the rest of the week so that if anything else happened, you could be sure that it was not them. They do not want you to be worried about them."

I could not help but be touched by their tender concern, never mind how much easier it would have made things if they had simply spoken to me about their fears.

"Rodolfo, I thank you for your concern," I said gently. "Please tell the Mendozas that my first priority was to make sure that they were innocent. The last thing I wanted to think was that they were guilty." I then took Daisy's reins. "I'm afraid I must be leaving. Thank you again."

Rodolfo helped me into the side saddle and I gently nudged Daisy into a trot, heading into town and the Sutton home.

Angelina was happy to see me and upon settling ourselves in her tiny sitting room, I told her about the deputation I had received that morning. We both fulminated for several minutes on the vanity of men, then we brushed that aside and I told Angelina about what Rodolfo had told me.

"That is in agreement with what Mrs. Mendoza told me," she said, sitting up and pulling her little writing table around to her chair.

"Ah, yes. Am I to assume your meeting with her went well?"

Angelina sighed. "It went well enough for your sake. Still, I have a very strong feeling that I know where we should look for Marshal Warren's killer."

"How do you mean?"

"Mrs. Mendoza was very certain that her grandsons had nothing to do with the murder, although that was because she was far more worried about her youngest son, Emanuel."

"How many sons does she have?" I couldn't help asking.

"Five of them. Elias was the eldest, and he's the one who was killed by Marshal Warren. Then there's Marco."

"I believe he is Hernan's father," I said.

"Mario is next."

I nodded. "That's Pascual and Emilio's father."

"Then Jorge, but he died a couple summers ago when we had that cholera outbreak."

"That was so dreadful," I sighed.

Angelina tapped a pencil thoughtfully on the desk. "And the youngest, Emanuel. He's a widower with no children. So he lives at home and supports his mother."

"Then Mrs. Mendoza would have known if her son went out at night."

Angelina shook her head. "I'm afraid she wouldn't. Her bedroom is at one end of their rooms and her son's on the other end. And she's so deaf in one ear that she sleeps very soundly."

I frowned. "I suppose I shall have to find some time to talk to him. Do they have a farm or does he work here in the pueblo?"

"He's the shoemaker, the one with the shop on Calle Primavera, next to the schoolhouse."

"Ah. I do know the place." I didn't say so to Angelina, but I generally had my shoes made for me specially at another establishment that happened to be connected to my dressmaker's. But I did know that the different families on my rancho preferred the work of Mr. Mendoza.

There seemed to be little else to discuss, so I made my excuses and, walking Daisy, headed toward the center of the pueblo in search of Mr. Mendoza. However, I was delayed in my mission by the appearance of Deputy Dye, who was standing in front of the market at the Clocktower Courthouse. I reined Daisy in, made sure she was tied fast to the hitching rail and made my way over to the market.

My conceit was to have been the usual pleasant remarks one makes with one's fellows at the market. I had spoken to Mr. Dye before, although I confess, the conversation had been limited to the usual greetings. I was not sure how I was going to inquire as to the dealings of his fellows. However, I had usually found a way to ask questions that could be considered awkward. I had no reason to believe that this occasion would be any different.

I contrived to accidentally bump against Mr. Dye on the side I knew to be hale and hearty, as opposed to the side with his wounded limb.

"What do you think you're doing?" he snarled at me.

He had dark hair and a thick curl over his forehead, and blue eyes that were utterly arresting in their lightness and intensity.

"Pray forgive me, Deputy," I said, smiling. "I merely stumbled. It's good to see you up and about after that terrible affray with the marshal."

He harrumphed but said nothing further.

"I hear you've received many good wishes on your behalf?"

He harrumphed again.

"I understand your friends have been offering you a great deal of support." I smiled with what I hoped was a winning smile.

His arresting eyes narrowed as he glared at me. "What are you talking about?"

"Your friends. I have heard they've been offering you all kinds of bon mots in support of your claim against the marshal."

His language deteriorated with an amazing rapidity and he pushed toward me, his icy, pale eyes flashing in deep ire.

"What are you after, Miz. Wilcox?" he demanded in between language so foul I could scarce believe my ears. "I know dagnabbed well you think there was something funny in the marshal's death. Well, I didn't do a dadblamed thing about it!"

"Pray forgive me, Deputy," I said, uncomfortably aware that I'd been pushed up against a wall and that there was no place else for me to go. "I was not suggesting for a moment that you had. I was merely asking after your companions, hoping to—"

"You leave my friends out of this!" He put his face in mine, his fetid breath spilling over me. "You dadblamed nosy parker! You don't know a dagnabbed thing about my friends. And you'd better just keep that long nose of yours out of my affairs. You hear me?"

I swallowed. "Quite well, Deputy."

"I mean it!" he screamed. "You don't go nowhere near anybody I know. You hear me?"

His hands landed on my shoulders, and in retrospect, I suppose I should have been glad that he hadn't drawn his gun. However, at that moment, I was truly afraid for my personal safety.

"Joe, old pal." A hand landed on Mr. Dye's shoulder from behind and I worried that the deputy would draw on the one who had come to save me.

But the intervention, fortunately, served to interrupt Mr. Dye's fury. He turned to face Deputy Lomax and began to calm down.

"Oh, it's you, Walter," Mr. Dye said. "What are you doing here?"

"Just saying hello," Mr. Lomax said, smiling. "What brings you out on this fine day?"

"I'm taking the air. It's been awful slow, being all cooped up in my rooms, you know." Mr. Dye shifted his gun belt and smiled.

Mr. Lomax nodded, then shifted toward me and slightly tipped his hat. "Mrs. Wilcox. How do?"

"Quite fine, Deputy Lomax," I answered, still shaking inside, but offering a pleasant smile nonetheless.

"Well, I'll be moseying along now," Mr. Dye said, with a fleeting smile.

He aimed a rather terrifying glare at me, then shifted his gun belt again and limped off down the street.

I leaned back against the wall and got my breath. Mr. Lomax fixed a pensive gaze on me and I knew I had to answer it.

"I saw him here and thought I might inquire after his friends," I said simply. "It is possible that one of them thought to seek the revenge that Mr. Dye wanted."

"Mrs. Wilcox, do you know the definition of the word foolhardy?" Mr. Lomax asked, and for all I knew he was chiding me (with good reason, alas), his eyes glinted with a spark of amusement.

"Mr. Lomax, your concern is warranted," I said, smiling faintly. "However, I have cause to believe that one must occasionally take advantage of the moment. I saw Mr. Dye and my only thought was to engage him in friendly conversation."

Mr. Lomax quirked that odd half smile of his. "No such thing with Joe."

"Mr. Dye has made that manifestly obvious."

I moved to the sidewalk and Mr. Lomax accompanied me.

"So, you think Joe Dye knows something?" Mr. Lomax asked.

"Not necessarily," I said, straightening my bonnet and shifting my leather bag into place. "I was more curious about his friends."

"He doesn't have many of them."

"But I was given to understand that there was considerable support for him in the pueblo."

Mr. Lomax shrugged. "That's more the folks who think the marshal got what he deserved." He looked at me. "There's almost as many folks wanting to string Dye up right here and now."

I gazed down the street where Mr. Dye had gone. "I don't doubt it. This morning, Mr. Wilson, Mr. Glassell, and Mr. Judson all came to call on me to ask me not to find the marshal's killer. They want Mr. Dye to be convicted for it."

Mr. Lomax frowned and shook his head. "That's what I don't understand. It was as plain as day that it was a case of self-defense. I may not like Joe Dye, but that's not a reason to hang him."

"I wholeheartedly agree. However, the idea behind convicting Mr. Dye was to find a way to get rid of him without getting shot in the process. And I must say, I am somewhat in sympathy with that, especially after this latest encounter. He is something of a menace."

"Can't say he isn't. But it doesn't seem right to convict him of something he didn't do."

"He did provoke the marshal and one could almost make the argument that the marshal drew to defend himself against Mr. Dye."

"That's what I'm told Judge Tafford decided."

I sighed. "I know. It would be a gross miscarriage of justice if Mr. Dye were to hang for the marshal's death if he didn't cause it." I frowned. "I don't know that I want to make the true cause of the marshal's death common knowledge. Or that he was clearly murdered, though not by Deputy Dye's bullet. But if certain leaders in this community try to hang Mr. Dye without just cause, then we shall have to come forward."

"I'm afraid so."

I looked out at the street. "I am glad for this meeting on another account. Your brothers in arms, Mr. Redona and Mr. Brooks. Why were they watching that night?"

Mr. Lomax nodded. "I had street duty that night, and I pulled Navarro and Smith on duty, as well. Didn't want any more trouble. So Brooks and Redona were all that were left. They both swore they were okay."

"I know," I said, sourly. "And both of them fell asleep while they were watching. Mr. Brooks almost took sick from his wound." I paused. "But that also means they each had the opportunity to kill the marshal."

Mr. Lomax's eyebrow lifted. "Don't know that Brooks had cause, although the marshal was pretty hard on him. But Redona was getting pretty sore about the commissions.."

"So I've been told. And since Mr. Redona was the last on watch and it seems probable the marshal was killed closer to dawn than not, he would seem to be the most likely to have done it."

Mr. Lomax nodded. "Except that I can't see either one of them killing the marshal, especially that way. I've seen Redona nearly get himself killed trying to break up a fight without shooting anybody. And Brooks is about as mild a fellow as they come. One of the reasons the marshal was so hard on him."

"I see. Do you know anything about a Jorge Villega? I saw him at the trotting races."

"He's a foreman at the wool mill. Likes to gamble and sometimes gets into fights over his debts." Mr. Lomax looked at me. "He's one of Dye's friends. Is that why you're asking?"

"Mr. Brooks said that they were afraid he and a Mr. Bonner might have wanted to finish what Mr. Dye had started."

Mr. Lomax shrugged. "I was more worried that folks would continue the fight and we'd get a riot. If the marshal were done for, and it certainly seemed like he was, it wouldn't make sense to worry about finishing the job."

"But it might make sense to make sure the job was done," I said. "Also, it's possible someone was listening at the windows to the house and may have found out that we were expecting the marshal to live.

Mrs. Warren told me that someone seemed to be doing just that the next day, and you know what happened yesterday morning."

Mr. Lomax nodded. "I'll see to keeping an eye on the place."

"Thank you, Mr. Lomax." I smiled and shifted my leather bag. "Now, I'm afraid I must be on my way."

"Good day." He smiled and tipped his hat and we went our separate ways.

I went next to the shoe shop owned and run by Emanuel Mendoza, it only being a few paces away from where I was. It was a medium-sized shop, located on the bottom floor of a brick building that also housed several offices belonging to attorneys and land agents. In fact, Mr. Glassell's office was among them. There was an apothecary on the other half of the bottom floor, although not the one I preferred. This fellow specialized in all manner of patent medicines, many of which were worse than useless.

The shoe shop, however, was a pleasant place, smelling of leather and wax. While Mr. Mendoza could, and often did, make shoes bespoke, he mostly sold shoes and boots that had been assembled at a factory up north, which he then finished. He also did considerable business repairing boots and shoes.

Mr. Mendoza was of medium height and of fairly round shape, perhaps abetted by his stooped over posture. His dark hair was speckled with gray, as was his full beard, and he peered at me over his eyeglasses.

"I wasn't sure if it was going to be you or Mrs. Sutton," he said, coming to the counter of his shop.

I couldn't help sighing. "Mr. Mendoza, it is not my place to accuse you, nor to assume your guilt."

He shrugged. "But you know about my uncle. My nephews will have told you that they are innocent. But me. I have a good reason to hate the marshal. So if there was something that helped him to his death, then you should ask me. Not that it will help. I was out celebrating that night."

"By yourself?"

He looked away. "With my friends."

I could not ask more, as a young boy had entered the shop, with some coins tied into a handkerchief and a woman's shoe dangling from one hand.

"It needs a new heel," he said. "Mama said to wait."

Mr. Mendoza glanced at me, then took the shoe from the boy.

"Well, good day, Mr. Mendoza," I said. "I appreciate your candor."

I left feeling somewhat nettled but realized that my reputation and mission would continually precede me. It had made speaking with Mr. Mendoza somewhat easier. In addition, brooding and worrying about what others thought of me had never done me any good. It was my duty to behave as kindly and righteously as possible, and if others failed to see my charity, at most, I should examine my conscience to see where I had erred and then beg forgiveness, or simply recognize that I could not possibly please everyone, and, indeed, seldom did.

I also had one other errand to undertake, a visit to Mr. Mahoney. His saloon was quite close, but instead of approaching it from Calle Primavera, I went around to the back of the property and knocked at the kitchen door. As a woman, I was not allowed in the front of the saloon. The only women who appeared in saloons were women of ill-repute, plying their noxious trade, and Mr. Mahoney had banned them from his place of business as they caused too many fights, he claimed.

Mr. Mahoney's daughter Annie showed me to his small office behind the saloon proper. He was a tall man, with bright blue eyes and graying dark hair. He seldom wore a suit coat over his shirt and vest, nor did he wear a collar, although he did button his shirt to the top. That day, gray stubble covered his chin as it usually did.

"I'm glad you're here," he told me, staying standing just long enough for me to perch myself on the less rickety of the two chairs in the cramped space littered with papers and crates. Mr. Mahoney took the chair in front of the large kneehole desk. "I need to order two more barrels of angelica and a case of claret."

"Very well. I'll have Sebastiano send them to you right away. However, I do have one other matter to take up with you. I have it on good authority that you were abroad the night of Marshal Warren's death."

He glared at me. He knew who had told me of this but would not mention her name.

"I see." He pursed his lips together. "And I assume this person of good authority told you why?"

"I see no shame in your visiting her." I smiled softly. "You obviously care for her a great deal, even if it is difficult for you."

He nodded.

"However," I continued. "That does mean that you were abroad the night the marshal was killed and may have seen or heard something, even if it didn't seem particularly remarkable."

Mr. Mahoney's eyes gleamed at me. "You're not thinking I was the culprit, are you?"

"I suppose it's possible," I said, shifting carefully. The chair was quite rickety, but my discomfort was acute and I couldn't help myself. "However, you seem to be one of the few people in the pueblo who bore the marshal no ill will."

"None." Mr. Mahoney shook his head. "He even paid for his drinks, which is more than some of those deputies will do. And if there was a fight, I was always glad to see him. It didn't matter how drunk a fellow was, Marshal Warren could stop that fight faster than anyone in the pueblo."

"I suppose there is some benefit to having everyone afraid of you."

Mr. Mahoney chuckled grimly. "It wasn't just that. Everyone is afraid of Joe Dye, but when he comes, the fight almost always gets worse."

"Oh, dear," I said. "He is quite the menace, indeed."

"I don't hold with stringing people up without benefit of a trial, but I could almost make an argument in favor of stringing up Joe Dye," said Mr. Mahoney, scratching his chin again. "If there was something odd about the marshal's death, then I wouldn't put it past him to have done it."

"Except that he was in jail," I said, then thought. "Did you see him that night? Or any of his friends?"

"Nope." Mr. Mahoney tilted his chair back on its rear legs. "Only fellow I saw, well, I didn't see him that well, not so as to recognize him. It was in the wee hours as I was coming home. He was ranting about how the most upstanding citizens of the pueblo are the worst sinners. Then he started singing The Battle Hymn of the Republic."

"Good Heavens! It's almost as though he were asking to be shot," I gasped.

Many of us have now forgotten, but at the time of which I write, the Americans in Los Angeles were mostly Confederate sympathizers. Indeed, at the news of General Robert E. Lee's death earlier that week, a group of the town's society women decided to create a committee to build a memorial to Lee. If ever anything could be compared to waving a red flag in front of a bull, then it would be singing that old Yankee hymn popularized by the Union soldiers. Being a Yankee, myself, and a dedicated abolitionist, the war years here had been very hard for me.

"Where did you see this fool?" I asked.

Mr. Mahoney shrugged. "Not far from here. I don't entirely recollect where."

My brow creased. "I wonder. You did hear about what happened to Mrs. Warren's house the day after the marshal's funeral."

"I heard somebody splashed it with red paint."

"There was also a sign that had been made from a large piece of paper, counting the marshal's sins."

"That is interesting."

"They got it down fast enough that I don't think

anyone saw it. Still, I can't help wondering if this fellow might have done something related to the marshal's death. After all, there are several in the pueblo who have family members the marshal killed, justly or not."

Mr. Mahoney shrugged. "I have no idea. At least you'd know you're looking for a Yankee."

"Possibly." I stood and Mr. Mahoney got up, as well. "Well, I'll take my leave now. You've been very helpful. Thank you, and thank you, also, for the order."

"You're very welcome, Mrs. Wilcox."

I slipped through the back, and once on the street, I began to debate my next move. Remembering Mr. Mahoney's order, I went also to the American Hotel and then the Pico House, where I received orders for still more claret and angelica. I even made a note of them, so as not to confuse the orders.

In any case, I returned to the rancho feeling well pleased with myself, never mind that I was little nearer to finding the marshal's true killer. The weather being quite fine, although there were a few clouds coming in, Maria and Olivia had set up the tables for a mid-day dinner in the courtyard of the adobe. My maid and confidante, Juanita Alvarez, helped me change into a work dress, and we sat down to a most pleasant meal.

However, as we finished, Juanita gave me a note that had arrived earlier that morning.

"I'm sorry about not giving it to you when you got in," Juanita said, completely unrepentant. "But you did say that you wanted to change as soon as possible so as not to hold up dinner."

As the note was from Regina, I suspect Juanita thought there was dire news and wanted me to have a pleasant meal before dealing with whatever crisis the note portended. I am reasonably sure she'd read enough of it to know that I was not urgently needed somewhere else.

And, as it happened, I had barely read the note when I was called away to tend to a ranch hand on one of the local ranchos who had fallen off his horse.

His injuries, fortunately, were mostly minor, except for the bump on his head. I applied some arnica to his bruises and instructed his fellows to keep waking him every hour and left him some laudanum for his headache. I then spent the next few hours patching up and soothing the various other aches and pains among the other hands.

By the time I had returned to the rancho, I had only a few minutes to spare to read Regina's note again. She went over her meetings with the purported friends of Mr. Dye, namely Mr. Villega and Mr. Bonner. The latter had, indeed, been the ranchman in the new suit that I'd seen the day before. She noted that Mr. Villega was a foreman at the town's wool mill and had considerably more money with him than one would have thought a laborer of his station would have, even if we were to assume that his luck at whatever gambling he'd been doing was exceptional. As Regina pointed out, no one is that lucky, and he had, in fact, lost heavily on the last two races of the day. Mr. Bonner, however, was considerably harder for her to speak with.

"He would not let me near him," Regina wrote. "And after overhearing him, I was quite happy not to speak with him. Somewhere between the second and third races, he began to rant on the End Times and how all sinners were going to be revealed. I cannot imagine what he was doing at such a festering pit of sin as the trotting park unless he'd been compelled to drive someone there. Worse yet, I fear he may be of the Temperance type, as I saw him drinking only water. His chief complaint seems to be how so many of the pueblo's upstanding citizens are the worst of sinners. Well, everyone knows that. At least, he seems to be practicing what he preaches. I think. Odd how the ones most bent on condemning the rest of the world are so often steeped in even more sin."

I looked at Juanita, who was tidying up my bedroom. "Where's Maria?"

"In your study, I believe." Juanita's eyes twinkled.

"So, Mrs. Medina's note has helped you?"

"Not necessarily. If what I recall is happening tonight, I may have to leave after supper."

"Oh, the revival meeting."

My eyebrows rose. "You know about that?"

Juanita began pulling out my brown visiting dress and brushing it. "Everyone knows about it. They all say Reverend Bennett is the most amazing preacher."

As she said that, I realized I had heard the same from various ladies of the pueblo's society but had chosen to ignore it. There was enough condemnation flowing from Reverend Elmwood's pulpit and I had no interest in more hellfire and brimstone. But what I'd heard from Mr. Mahoney and from Regina led me to believe that I needed to see who was at that meeting.

Even with the clouds starting to roll in, it was a fine, cool night, so I was not entirely surprised that the revival meeting was held outside in a corral near where Aliso Road meets Alameda Street. I found it quite ironic that someone had chosen the site, as it was also a popular spot for the occasional lynching.

But I could also see why it was also a good spot for a revival. It was a fairly large lot with a solid fence around it. Torches had been lit and were on poles tethered to the fence posts, making it possible to see in the dark. As I stepped down from my buggy, I could see that at one end, a platform had been erected and Reverend Bennett sat at one end, waiting for his moment. Armando, who had been driving me again, pulled off to find a place where he could tie Daisy up.

I had been told that the first of Reverend Bennett's revivals had been overflowing with the faithful. Since that time, however, while the crowd filled most of the corral, it seemed that a good many of the earlier faithful had found other amusements and attractions for a Friday night. There were the usual hymns, led by Mr. Hill, who had come to fix my buggy wheel earlier that week. He had on his Sunday suit and played a rickety old spinnet that someone had placed on the

platform. Many of the women carried tambourines
and banged them with vigor in time with the piano.
As I looked at the crowd, I was not entirely surprised
to see that it was exclusively American. The Mexicans
in the pueblo were Catholic and the Negroes preferred
worshipping amongst themselves. As for the Chinese,
they weren't even Christians, and apart from the few
businesses that catered to such, did not mix with the
Americans at all.

After one last rousing chorus, the reverend slowly
stood and a hush fell over the crowd.

"My fellow sinners," he intoned. "Yes, we are
all sinners, and I am perhaps the worst among you.
But it has been laid upon my heart to share what a
sinner I am. Earlier this week, we were reminded of
the shortness of life as a great man of our community
was cut down. He lived by the sword and died by the
sword. As have I. Yes, even I have taken a life or two
in my time. But I heard the glorious Word of the Lord!
I heeded the call to repentance, and now I stand before
you, freed, in the blessed name of Jesus, of the burden
and stain of even the worst of my sins. That blessed
night, when in my wretchedness, I saw the light of a
loving and forgiving Lord, who beckoned to me and
called me out of sin."

And so it went on, and on. I found the lesson rather
boring and repetitive. However, I must say that the
Reverend's presentation of it was quite affecting. I did
not doubt that he had grappled with some very heinous
sins in his past and his relief at finding salvation
was quite palpable. I was standing at the side of the
corral, listening and watching the crowd. Mr. and Mrs.
Glassell were there, she being one of the ladies with a
tambourine. Mr. and Mrs. Hewitt were standing right
next to them. Dr. and Mrs. Skillen were also there. I
saw Mr. Bonner across the corral from me, waving his
hands and shouting amen with the best of them, and
pondered how it was that he was a friend of Mr. Dye,
someone I would have considered an obvious sinner.

Near Mr. Bonner, Mr. Wills, the notary, trembled with religious fervor. Deputy Brooks stood near the gate to the corral, but I wasn't sure if he was there as one of the faithful or merely keeping an eye out for any potential trouble.

I was truly tiring of it all when I felt my skirt twitch. Behind me, on the other side of the fence, a young Mexican boy looked up at me plaintively.

"My mama, she is sick," he whispered to me in Spanish. "Please come."

I nodded and made my way along the fence to the gate.

"I have to find my buggy," I told the lad as I slipped through the gate.

Apparently, Armando had been close enough to see me leaving the corral and he quickly pulled up. I helped the boy into the buggy's seat and got up onto the seat next to him.

"I'm Jaime Gutierrez. We live up on Calle Toma."

The house he directed us to was, indeed, up at the far northern edge of the pueblo, and it was little better than a shack, being a small one-room adobe. It was crowded with small children, many of them sniffling and coughing, and a couple men, both apparently relatives of the woman who lay on the one bed. She, too, was coughing and burned with fever. I sighed. There wasn't much I could do. I did mix a plaster with oil of turpentine and some other herbs and put it on her chest, then got a bucket of water and a couple clean cloths. I wet one and made a compress for the woman's forehead, and after wetting the second, I wiped her arms and legs.

"You'd best fetch the priest," I told the man I'd taken to be her husband. "Take my buggy."

He looked at his wife with an agonized frown, then hurried off. I refreshed the compress on Mrs. Gutierrez's head, then pulled some tonic from my bag and dosed all the children with it. Only one had a fever, but I feared it wouldn't be long before all of them did.

I was grateful that there weren't any signs of diarrhea or vomiting that would indicate cholera or the muscle aches that meant typhoid. I'd read in the newspapers that there had been some outbreaks of each further north.

"Jaime, has anybody been traveling of late?" I asked the boy who had brought me.

"No. We work on the farm, that is all."

"Anyone visit here?"

He shook his head again. That didn't eliminate the threat of those two dread diseases, but it did make it more likely that we were dealing with influenza.

Father Jimenez, himself, arrived in good time. He blessed all the children and gave Mrs. Gutierrez the Last Rites. After that, we waited. Knowing that it would be a long night, I sent Armando back home in the buggy. I could walk home easily enough.

Shortly before midnight, I wandered outside to the front porch of the home to get some air and ease the crick in my neck. Mrs. Gutierrez was asleep, but I still feared the worst. Father Jimenez was outside, also, smoking a small cigar. He smiled softly.

"Paco tells me Jaime found you at the revival meeting." He spoke in English, his tone gently teasing.

"I feel terrible that it was so hard to find me," I said, the guilt consuming me. "But I can't stay at home all the time."

Father chuckled. "I didn't mean to fault you. Of course, you can't stay at home. I know how you feel about that kind of religion, though, and it seemed odd to me that you would be there."

"Unless I were looking for whomever splashed red paint on Mrs. Warren's home?" Relief flooded through me to know that he hadn't meant a criticism.

"Exactly." His cigar glowed as he puffed.

"Yes, that's why I was there," I said, beginning to pace. "And so were a great many other people. I have found that there is at least one man in this community who has a grievance with the certain others who appear upstanding but are, nonetheless, committing all manner of sins, but I could ascertain nothing from the meeting. It's probably just as well that I was called away. Although I must say, Reverend Bennett is quite affecting as a preacher."

"I know. I went to a meeting after several of my parishioners commended him." Father Jimenez frowned. "It seems as though I've met him somewhere else than here. I can't say where, but there is something about his face that I have seen before, and it was not connected to any revival meeting."

"What an odd coincidence." I looked back at the adobe.

Father snuffed his cigar and we went back inside. Mrs. Gutierrez failed to rally. Instead, the fever burned on and after another hour, she finally succumbed to it.

By then, at least two more children had fevers. I dosed and plastered for the rest of the night, and was sadly grateful when only one of the children died.

CHAPTER SEVEN

As happened so often, when my household realized that it was coming on for dawn and I was still not at home, they sent someone after me. I had barely started down Toma Street when Sebastiano pulled up in the buggy. He reined Daisy in, then got off the seat to finish helping me up.

"Did you sleep at all, Maddie?" he chided, although he knew well why I hadn't.

"I'm afraid not."

"It did not end well?"

I shrugged. "We saved four of the children. But poor Mr. Gutierrez will be raising them by himself. And we lost one of the little ones."

"Not a good night for you."

"I'm trying to remind myself that it could have been a great deal worse." I shivered. "It was probably influenza, which means I shall have to alert the other doctors."

Granted, as diseases go, influenza was usually the least of our concerns. In addition to typhoid and cholera, we had to worry about malaria, whooping cough, measles, lockjaw, the consumption, scarlet fever, all manner of ills for which we had no cures beyond hope that the victim would prove stronger than the disease. However, influenza was extremely contagious, and while most people survived it, it could turn deadly, especially if it infected a child or old person. That Mrs. Gutierrez was neither of these worried me a great deal. I hoped it did not mean a bad year for the disease.

Still, I did not have long to brood on it. As soon as I stepped down from the buggy, Juanita and Olivia whisked me off to my bedroom and put me to bed. Fortunately, the sun's rays had yet to creep over the horizon, which meant I got at least a few hours of sleep before being roused again, this time by Councilman Wilson. Or his messenger, rather.

Olivia had already sent the lad back home once to tell the councilman that I would be there as soon as I could. But, alas, the councilman refused to wait and I was awakened by the frantic pleading of the boy. Juanita helped me to dress in my best riding habit and Olivia insisted that I eat a pan dulce and drink a cup of strong coffee before Armando took me in the buggy.

Mr. Wilson lived in a three-story white clapboard house on Calle Segundo. Like many of his fellows on the council, he'd apparently made some deal with the Zanjero, or Water Overseer, because his yard was filled with green plants. But most of them had been obliterated by the pools of red paint all over them and over the large porch that ran across the entire front of the house. Mr. Wilson was waiting for me in the street, pacing angrily with a large piece of paper in his hands.

"What do you know about this?" he demanded before I'd even had a chance to alight from the buggy. "I heard you were asking questions about the Warren house. What do you know about this?"

I stifled a yawn and finished getting safely to the ground. "As much as you do, I would imagine." I nodded at the sheet of paper in his hand. "Was that posted on the front of the house?"

"Yes!" he snapped. "Drove a nail into my beautiful latticework and shattered it. Do you have any idea how much latticework costs these days?"

"May I see the paper?" I was holding onto my temper as best I could.

He shoved it at me. Like the one that had been posted on the Warren house, it was a large piece of brown paper and had been painted with a similar message.

"A sinner lives here!" proclaimed the red paint. "These are his sins: Lust - as he chases all manner of women, paying them unwanted attention, whether married or not. Greed - as he finds all occasions to cheat those he does business with."

"Well?" he demanded. "What do you think of that?"

"Having never done business with you, I can't speak to the latter accusation," I said mildly. "However, the writer seems reasonably astute as to your behavior with women."

"What?" Wilson's face began turning red. "I have never paid a woman unwanted attention."

"Oh. So you believe that all of your attentions have been welcomed?" I glared at him.

"Of course!"

"That's odd because Mrs. Warren was quite adamant that she did not care for the way you paid her attention. Nor did Miss Gaines look as though she welcomed your company."

"That's ridiculous. You're just jealous that I've never—"

"I am profoundly grateful that you haven't." My temper finally snapped. "Indeed, Mr. Wilson, you are not in any way as attractive as you like to think yourself. In fact, almost any woman I've ever heard mention you has said what a grave nuisance you and your attentions are."

He snorted and pulled himself up straight. "And what are you going to do about this?" He gestured at the paint-spattered porch.

"What do you mean, what am I going to do? The way you are behaving right now, I couldn't care less who did this to you. My only interest in this attack is in how it might help me better protect Mrs. Warren. Now, good day."

I climbed back into the buggy and nodded at Armando.

"You might as well take us back to the rancho," I

told him, trying and failing to stifle another yawn.

Back home, I tried and failed to get another couple hours of sleep. My mind pored over all the possible people who could have killed the marshal, and then begun attacking others this way. At least, it seemed as though I had a reason why someone wanted to help the marshal to his death. But with the marshal in his grave and the supposed vengeance completed with the first attack of paint, it didn't make sense that the attacks would continue on other people. I supposed it was possible that I was looking for two different malefactors, one guilty of the vandalism and the other guilty of murder, but that the first attack had been on the marshal's home.

It was close to mid-day when I gave up and had Juanita help me again into my best riding habit and sent one of the children to have someone saddle up Daisy.

I was able to find where Reverend Bennett was living after a couple of inquiries. He was renting a room from Mrs. Marshland, whose husband had died some years before, but, alas, not before he'd spent most of the money he'd made. Fortunately, he did leave her with a huge house on the east side of town, which Mrs. Marshland had turned into a very respectable boarding house for gentlemen. It was an almost perfect arrangement for an itinerant preacher, except that I did not know how he was paying her rather steep fees. I could only suppose that any collections he made at his revivals were sufficiently generous.

I was admitted by the maid and shown to the front parlor. Whatever excesses her husband had indulged in, Mrs. Marshland had exquisite taste. The furniture was of the best quality and there was even real art on the walls. Mrs. Marshland, herself, was tall and imposing, with medium brown hair piled on her head. She looked at me with some disdain as I explained my purpose in being there, but did not argue. A few minutes later, the reverend appeared and greeted me warmly.

"Thank you, Reverend," I said politely as I settled myself on the green velvet sofa.

"Did I not see you at the meeting last night?" he asked with a smile, settling himself into a matching armchair across from me and leaning forward.

"You did, indeed, sir. I am sorry that I was not able to stay for the whole meeting. I was needed urgently elsewhere."

He must have seen me blink, for he cocked his head curiously.

"I take it, it did not go well?"

"No. I'm sorry it didn't entirely. But it could have been a great deal worse."

"The workings of the Lord can be most mysterious, indeed."

"That they can. Nonetheless, that is not my purpose in coming here." I swallowed as I watched him.

He leaned back, but his face looked apprehensive.

"Say on," he said.

"You will have heard about the attack on Mrs. Warren's house the day after the funeral. There was another similar attack on Mr. Wilson's this morning. Both times, there was a sign posted that enumerated the sins of the men who lived there. Now, I do not wish to accuse you or anyone else. But given your preaching, it would be unwise, at best, if I did not consider the possibility that one of your flock was responsible."

I had braced myself for an angry retort or denial. Instead, the reverend relaxed and smiled.

"Naturally. You were right to come to me." He spread his hands. "I am afraid, however, that I know nothing of these matters."

I looked at him carefully. I remembered that when I had asked him whom he'd seen at the Warren house on that fateful day, he'd been annoyed. However, we had been at the marshal's graveside service at that moment and it seemed entirely plausible that he had found my questions inappropriate for that time. Heaven knows, I would have been annoyed, myself.

"You spoke most eloquently last night," I said, for lack of anything better. "It's quite a change to hear about redemption for our sins rather than just being repeatedly accused of them."

"Thank you. Salvation is my preferred theme." He leaned forward. "I find it's easier to encourage people to do good, in gratitude for this greatest of gifts, than to chastise them."

"I do wish more men of God felt that way." I smiled and rose. "I'm afraid I must be on my way. Thank you so much for speaking with me."

I did not wait for Mrs. Marshland's maid but left quickly. I couldn't help believing the reverend when he'd said he didn't know who was behind the paint attacks. If salvation and forgiveness truly were his preferred themes, it did not seem logical that he would encourage men to vandalize and post the sins of others as a warning. As I rode slowly toward Calle Primavera, I pondered who else might be involved, and could not help but wonder about Mr. Bonner. He seemed like such a contradictory fellow, spouting bible verses, yet holding in friendship one who, to all appearances, was one of the worst sinners in the pueblo.

The difficulty would be in finding a way to talk to the man. There were few respectable forums in which I could speak to a complete stranger. That there were those who believed that would hardly stop me meant only that they did not understand me at all. I only abandoned respectability to come to the aid of another, not to question people because I thought they might have information. After all, there is almost always a respectable way to get done what one needs to do.

To that end, it happened that a respectable way to speak to Mr. Bonner presented himself at that very moment in the persona of Deputy Ernesto Navarro. I realize that in these pages of my memoirs I seldom mention him. There are many good reasons for that which are neither here nor there. I would ignore him completely were it not for the fact that to tell my story accurately, I have to acknowledge the small role he played here.

He was a younger man, in his middle twenties, with dark, gleaming eyes and a happy demeanor that hid just how hard his heart was. There was many a young girl in the pueblo whose heart had been broken by him, although one had to concede the devil was very charming and the very image of innocence. His grandparents had been among the first settlers of our little pueblo nearly a hundred years before. And at that time, I still considered him a friend.

He was riding a black stallion that was surprisingly calm. He greeted me with his usual charm and I smiled back.

"So, who's sick along this street?" he asked.

"No one today, thank Heaven," I replied. "You have heard about the attack on Mr. Wilson's house?"

"I have and I have been told that you are on the hunt for the villain who has done this."

"You have?" My eyebrows raised. "Well, I am, more or less."

Mr. Navarro's eyebrows lifted impishly. "I have also heard that you don't entirely believe that Marshal Warren died of his wounds."

"From where have you heard this?" I said, trying not to glare at him.

"It's gotten about," he replied with a shrug. "Mr. Wilson asked me about it."

That worried me, but there was little I could do about it. It was a small community, so it was not entirely surprising that the secret had spread. It was aggravating, but there was little I could do about it.

"Sadly, the marshal was not killed by his wound, Mr. Navarro," I said, rather severely, then remembered that there was something he could help with. "And I need to speak with Mr. Sam Bonner. Do you know him?"

Mr. Navarro shrugged. "Not well. He's a friend of Joe Dye's, isn't he?"

"Yes. And he may have something to do with these red paint attacks, but I can't say one way or another until I've spoken with him."

Mr. Navarro bowed from his seat on his horse. "Then allow me to accompany you. We'll go out to the Stonefield ranch and I'll let you ask all the questions."

And so we went. It took a few minutes to find Mr. Bonner, but we eventually found him in the ranch barn, where he was tending to a horse that had gone lame.

"Mr. Bonner, allow me to present you to Mrs. Wilcox," Ernesto said with a small flourish.

Mr. Bonner was immune to Mr. Navarro's charm, which was understandable. Mr. Bonner, instead, looked at me and nodded, even though he remained seated on a three-legged stool as he massaged the horse's front leg.

"Excuse me for not standing, Mrs. Wilcox." he said. "This here mare is real skittish and I can't stop right now. How can I help you?"

"I am curious what you might know about the attacks on the home of Mrs. Warren and, now, Mr. Wilson," I said. "They would appear to be the work of a very religious person."

Mr. Bonner looked away. "'Tweren't me."

"Yes, I suspected that," I said, even though I hadn't. "But do you know who it was?"

Mr. Bonner shrugged.

"You seem to be a good friend of Mr. Joseph Dye," I asked.

"So?"

"Well, I've heard that some of those who are supportive of Mr. Dye now are not actually friends of Mr. Dye, but just did not like the marshal, and then there are a few who are actually Mr. Dye's friends," I said. "I am curious as to which you are."

Mr. Bonner shrugged. "You don't have to be a good friend of Joe Dye to know he got a raw deal from the marshal. And he wasn't the only one who was angry at the marshal. You might even say I was."

"Oh?" I forebore to say more in the hopes that Mr. Bonner would continue.

He did. "Marshal Warren promised me the next position as a deputy when one came open. Instead, he hired that petunia Brooks. That weren't fair. It weren't fair at all."

"I dare say it wasn't." I smiled at him. "I saw you at the revival meeting last night."

"That I was, ma'am."

I nodded. I was going to point out how contradictory it seemed to be professing that kind of faith and still being friends with Mr. Dye when I realized that I couldn't possibly do so when my own friends were equally contradictory. I liked to think that I was friends with the likes of Regina out of true Christian charity, but I could well understand that there were those who would not understand that.

"Well," I said, instead. "It was very kind of you to speak to me, Mr. Bonner. Would it be all right if I visited again in the future?"

He shrugged, then nodded. "If the bosses don't mind."

"I will keep that in consideration, Mr. Bonner. Good day."

Mr. Navarro insisted on accompanying me back to the pueblo and I found myself complaining about the marshal's murder.

"But maybe Mr. Dye did kill him," Mr. Navarro said.

"No, he couldn't have. He was in jail that night," I said.

"Are you sure? It's not that hard to get out of that jail, especially if you have the keys."

"Of course it wouldn't be if you had the keys," I said impatiently. "But those aren't kept with the prisoners. Mr. Lomax has assured me that they are kept in the front of the office."

"But Mr. Lomax doesn't know that Joe Dye had a set made for himself." Mr. Navarro's grin was particularly charming.

I gaped in spite of myself. "That couldn't be. Why on earth would Mr. Dye have done that?"

"To get the jump on Marshal Warren." Mr. Navarro shrugged. "I've been told those two were thick as thieves when Mr. Dye first came on the force. But then they began to fall out and Mr. Dye didn't trust the marshal to do him right. So he made a set of keys to the jail."

"I can't see how that would help him," I said.

"Who knows? And does it really make any difference? Mr. Dye had a set of keys, which means he could have gotten out of that jail as easy as you please. And I, for one, don't believe he stayed there that night."

"Do you have any evidence that he didn't?" I asked, frowning at him.

"No. Just my gut feeling about Joe Dye. But it should be fairly easy to find out."

I thought. "He was wounded in the affray. His forehead had been grazed and there was that hole in his nether limb."

"But he was walking the next day," Mr. Navarro pointed out. "And he didn't take sick from it, so it couldn't have been that bad."

"That's true."

We were nearing the center of town, so I bade farewell to Mr. Navarro. I checked to see if Mr. Wills, the notary whose brother had been killed by the marshal, was in his office and was gratified to find that he was. He was wearing his marigold-colored vest again and adjusted it, then polished his pince-nez as he bade me enter.

"I haven't much time today," he announced even before I was seated.

He was such a pompous and persnickety fellow, I knew of few in the pueblo who actually liked him. I only did business with him because he was the notary that Mr. Judson most preferred, and since I had my account at Mr. Judson's bank, I was forced to cater to his preferences, including dealing with the odious Mr. Wills.

"I will endeavor not to take too much of it," I replied. "I expect you've heard about the attacks on Mrs. Warren's and Mr. Wilson's houses. There seems to be a religious motive behind the attacks, and since I saw you at the revival last night—"

"I had nothing to do with that!" Mr. Wills trembled and glared. "Nothing at all! How unkind of you to come in here and accuse me."

"I'm not accusing you, Mr. Wills," I said, holding for dear life onto my patience. "However, it is possible you know something about who did these acts without even knowing it. The man or men behind the attacks appear to be angry that certain well-respected members of our pueblo are not as respectable as they should be."

Mr. Wills took his pince-nez off, then put it on again, his hands visibly shaking. "This is ridiculous. Why are you here bothering me? I am as likely a target as any of them. Why aren't you trying to find this monster before I'm attacked?"

I sat up straight. "That is precisely why I am here, Mr. Wills. To try to prevent another attack. Now, have you heard anybody complaining about upstanding members of the community?"

"No. No, I haven't. The only member of our community I have heard someone complaining about is you. If you hadn't insisted on caring for our good marshal, he might be alive today."

I stood. "He would most likely be alive if someone hadn't murdered him while he slept. He was on the mend, which is why I find it very curious that you assumed he was on his deathbed and shared that with Mr. King, especially after you had been so insistent that you get his statement that evening."

Mr. Wills puffed himself up but fidgeted with his papers. "That's what you said. That he was asleep and would not be answering any questions."

"I did not say that he would be asleep forever. You

made that assumption. Or maybe you helped him to his death after finding that he was likely to live."

"Another vile accusation! I shall bring suit against you."

I fixed my eyes upon him. "Please do."

I turned and walked firmly from the office, although I was hardly feeling such confidence. Indeed, I was shaking almost as badly as Mr. Wills had been. The worst of it was that I knew there was a reason I'd challenged him, but couldn't think why.

I have always prided myself on the sharpness of my mind. It's one of the reasons why I've been able to diagnose illness and other problems so well. However, no one's mind is at its best when one is exhausted, and I was certainly very tired that day, thanks to my sleepless night and inability to nap. And if what Dr. Freud and Dr. Jung have been writing about the unconscious mind is true, then it would account for my strange retort to Mr. Wills. In short, there had been something odd about Mr. Wills' responses, but I could not immediately put my finger on what it was.

There seemed little point in dwelling on it, especially as I had another errand of some import to accomplish that day. I went to Dr. Skillen's home and office, on Calle Tercero, just above Calle Forfin. He was, fortunately, in, and agreed to see me in his front parlor. His wife brought us tea and biscuits, then left. It was a comfortable room, with a battered brown sofa, and spinnet piano in the corner. The two upholstered chairs were newer but had slightly threadbare pillows on them.

"I thought I'd best alert you," I said, as soon as we'd gotten our cups and settled. "There's been an outbreak of influenza on the north side of the pueblo. We lost two of the family last night."

Dr. Skillen shrugged sadly. "It does seem that we are coming into the season for it."

"Indeed, but I fear it may be a bad year. One of the deaths was a young mother, in her twenties, according to her husband. They would not consent to an autopsy, so I do not know if there was some other condition that had weakened her. However, according to her husband, she had already cared for him and one of the older boys before getting sick, herself. So it is possible that she had weakened herself caring for her family."

"As we see all too often." Dr. Skillen shook his head. "Nonetheless, we could be dealing with a bad year for it. Thank you for alerting me. I'll mention this to the others."

"Thank you, Doctor." I sipped, then looked at him. "I was surprised to see you at the revival last night."

"Oh, yes." He leaned forward. "The wife's idea. I go to please her."

"Ah. Well, at least the reverend's lesson was on redemption and forgiveness."

"It does seem to be one of his preferred themes, which is the only reason I indulge my wife by going. I do not hold with hellfire and brimstone." He looked at me. "And why were you there?"

"The attack on Mrs. Warren's house, and now, on Mr. Wilson's house. There seems to be a religious theme to the attacks. Also, there is someone in the pueblo who has been loudly complaining of the perfidy of citizens who claim to be and are regarded as upstanding people, but who, in fact, are not."

"I can certainly see why they chose to attack Mr. Wilson." The doctor chuckled.

"Oh?"

The doctor cleared his throat as he suddenly realized that he was speaking to a woman. "Well, it's all rather indiscreet."

"The attentions he pays to women in the pueblo." I sighed. "I'm afraid I lost my temper and disabused him of the notion that those attentions were, in any way, wanted."

The doctor laughed. "Good for you! So many women have complained to my wife about him." He sighed. "And I have heard rumors that he is not entirely honest in his business dealings. I believe Mr. Crumb was unhappy that his claim was not paid. But Mr. Wilson insists that the issuing company denied the claim and that he had nothing to do with it. I don't know the particulars, however."

"That is interesting. I purchased my fire insurance from Mr. Handley and it seems to be in good standing, fortunately."

Dr. Skillen smiled. "I have heard nothing but good things about Mr. Handley. Alas, I cannot say the same for Mr. Wilson."

I stood and he rose with me. "Well, I appreciate your observations, Doctor. And if you hear of any more influenza cases, I would thank you to alert me."

"Of course, Mrs. Wilcox. The better to hopefully contain the contagion," he said.

"I will alert you, as well," I added.

He let me out the front door, and I untied Daisy from the hitching post outside his small house.

It was a neat little house, with only one floor, but made of whitewashed clapboard. There were a good-sized chicken coop and yard attached to it, not surprising as doctors were often paid with gifts of chickens. There was also a small stable for his horse and his buggy. I had heard that Dr. Skillen lived rather better than the other doctors in the pueblo because his wife had inherited some money and I believed it. I had to concede that it was probably just as well that my living was not dependent on the fees I received from my patients, who were generally even more impecunious than those of Dr. Skillen.

However, the doctor's observations regarding Mr. Wilson began to gnaw at me, as well as my earlier conversation with Mr. Wills. Actually, Mr. Wills began to become uppermost in my mind, as I was finally coming to see what it was that had bothered me as I'd left that place. Or perhaps it was that Dr. Skillen, an upstanding citizen of the community, was not worried about becoming a target for the vandals. Mr. Wills, on the other hand, was convinced that he would be.

CHAPTER EIGHT

Saturday nights were usually very busy for me. Saturday was when wages were generally distributed, in advance of the Sabbath rest day, and that meant the saloons and brothels were filled with customers who, inevitably, got into various and sundry fights. Which, likewise inevitably, meant that I would be summoned to dig bullets out of various limbs and stitch up knife wounds, in addition to babies wanting to be born and illnesses that needed attending.

After I left Dr. Skillen, I returned to my rancho, ate a very early supper, and went promptly to bed in anticipation of another sleepless night. Fortunately, it was a relatively quiet night with only three knife fights and a shooting. I was summoned to care for the combatants in two of the knife fights. So while I did end up working rather late, I was able to go to bed several hours before the cock crowed.

The other blessing was that church services were held at nine in the morning, which allowed me yet another hour or so of precious sleep. That I was rather reluctant to go to church had a great deal to do with our pastor, Reverend Elmwood. Most of his sermons were rather mild, but when he got the wind up, the hellfire and brimstone flowed. I had been the target on more than one of these occasions, although I had given him such an extraordinary piece of my mind on the last occasion that he had yet to target me again. I suppose I could have gone to the Methodist/Episcopal church, but I'd heard Mr. Miller could be even worse, and I was a

Congregationalist by training and by choice. Given the events of the past week, I could not help but be worried that Reverend Elmwood had his dander up again.

I am often amazed at how many times, as a younger woman, I got caught up in worrying about matters that turned out to be of no consequence whatsoever, while events that turned out to be enterprises of great pitch and moment failed to stir the least flutter in me. Perhaps it is the wisdom of hindsight. I cannot say. Nonetheless, my fears regarding that Sunday's lesson turned out to be completely unfounded. Indeed, the reverend's sermon was so tame that I almost fell asleep. However, as I greeted him while leaving the church, I again caught the smell of oil of turpentine on him.

"I trust your catarrh is feeling better?" I asked him kindly.

He was of bookish mien with light brown hair and whiskers that he kept neatly trimmed. He hadn't seemed particularly hoarse that morning, but that didn't mean he didn't have what we now call a cold.

"I do not have a catarrh," he said, haughtily.

"Pray forgive me, reverend," I said with a smile. "I merely smelled oil of turpentine, which I often use in a chest plaster for catarrh or influenza."

He cleared his throat, which did not sound all that congested. "Indeed. No. I'm merely having my house painted and the idiots doing the work have repeatedly failed to alert me to which surfaces are still wet."

He snorted and looked up. I was among the last to leave the service and we were now alone.

"However, Mrs. Wilcox, I would like a word with you," he said quietly.

"Yes, Reverend."

He moved somewhat closer to me than I would have liked. "The paint attack on Mr. Wilson yesterday morning. He came to me yesterday and told me that you had no interest in helping him find the culprit. In fact, he suggested that you had done it yourself."

"That would have been very hard for me to do, as

I was caring for the Gutierrez family on Toma Street all that night." I frowned, trying to remember what, exactly, I had told Mr. Wilson the previous morning. "And, yes, I did tell him I had little interest in helping him, mostly because of how heinously he was behaving at the time. Indeed, why should I help someone so full of braggadocio?"

"He said you were very unkind to him."

I couldn't help it. My eyes rolled Heavenward in search of aid. "Isn't it more unkind still to allow such a fool to continue wading in his delusions?"

"Mr. Wilson has never paid unwanted attention to any woman." Reverend Elmwood sniffed in high dudgeon.

"Have you asked your wife about that?" I retorted. "Mr. Wilson expressed the same surprise to me when I assured him in no uncertain terms that his attentions were very much unwanted by many women in this pueblo, if not most. The very arrogance of the man to assume that he was immediately desired by every woman he met!"

"But the painting was done by a Yankee. And you are a Yankee."

"As are you." I glared at the reverend. "And why do you say it was a Yankee?"

"Everyone knows that. It's all over the town."

"That is hardly proof that will stand up in a court of law." I glared at him again. "Honestly, Reverend. I am hurt to the quick by your suggestion that I am responsible for these attacks simply because I coincidentally share a common homeland with some poor drunk fool outside a saloon, a homeland that you and I both share. It makes absolutely no sense that I would do such a thing. What benefit could I possibly expect to achieve by it? Not to mention the fact that I hardly have the time. It would make as much sense as you having done it."

"You're not accusing me!"

"Of course not. Did I not just say that it makes no

sense that you would have? Now, if you will excuse me, Reverend, I'd like to go back to my rancho and enjoy my day of rest."

I walked off. I generally walked on Sundays and was very glad that I had that day. I was, not surprisingly, quite furious with Reverend Elmwood. I was even less likely to have committed the vandalism than the reverend. If anything, he had more reason than most. And as my furor stilled and my ire cooled, I began to consider that perhaps Reverend Elmwood had committed the vandalism. It wouldn't be unlike him to hide his actions in that way.

But what benefit could he expect to achieve? Or, as I thought about it, would anyone, for that matter? It was very puzzling.

I arrived home in quite a stew, but it was time for our Sunday dinner, so I put my rancor aside and focused on enjoying my time with my household. It was a most pleasant day. The children were, once again, filled with energy, and while I would have thought playing quietly was more in keeping with it being the Sabbath, I found their chatter and running about quite refreshing and calming.

Later, just after supper, I went to my study only to be called back to the parlor where Wang Fu waited with another Chinese man. Mr. Wang was scarcely older than me, and only somewhat taller, and usually wore American clothes. Like most of the Chinese men, the sides of his head and forehead were shaved and he had a long braid, which he usually tucked up under his hat to keep it out of the way. However, that night, he was wearing his odd Chinese coat and full pants, and his braid hung down his back. Mr. Wang's companion was similarly dressed and even younger, although he was taller and his face was rather long. They both bowed to me and I bowed back.

That surprised Mr. Wang's friend. Mr. Wang said something to him in Chinese and his friend nodded. I bade them sit down on the sofa and they did. Maria came in with tea and pan dulces. The men accepted the tea and sweet breads.

"Mrs. Wilcox," Mr. Wang said in his halting English once we were alone. "This is Lon Cao. He is brother to Lon Yu, the woman the marshal brought back."

"Mr. Wang says that I might know something that would help you," Mr. Lon said. Although his accent was, not unexpectedly, pronounced, he spoke with an ease that meant he was fluent in our tongue.

"You speak English," I said.

Mr. Lon looked slightly frightened, then nodded. "I learned as a child from American missionaries. Both I and my sister, Lon Yu, did. We do not want Sing Lee to know. We are all but enslaved to him as it is."

"And your sister?"

"Her owner Sing Lee took her from me. She is pretty and has good manners, not like a common peasant. She is worth a great deal to him. Sing Lee said I sold her to him, but I did not."

I thought. "I was told that she was kidnapped last summer, then escaped last month."

"Yes. I helped her escape. We were caught in San Buenaventura while we were waiting for her lover. He is American and could not leave right away."

"Do you know his name?"

Mr. Lon shook his head. "She will not tell me and I do not want to know until we are well away from here. I do not want to give her away by accident. Sing Lee is very powerful and does not like to be crossed. The American will be able to protect her, but only if we leave this city. They want to marry, but if he does and he stays here, everyone will know that he is married to a Chinese and that she is married to an American. The Chinese will reject her for marrying a barbarian, and the Americans will reject him for marrying a Chinese. If we go someplace where we are strangers, then the Americans will think that she is his concubine and will not bother him. But his family is here and he cannot leave easily, my sister says." Mr. Lon frowned.

"He's married?" I asked.

"She says she would be first wife." Mr. Lon paused. "That usually means he has no other. In China, wealthy men often have more than one wife. I know it is frowned upon here."

"It is, indeed." I looked over at Mr. Wang, who was smiling softly. I sighed. "You do realize that this gives you a good reason to have killed the marshal. Or for your sister to have done so."

Mr. Lon looked downcast and anxious but pulled himself together. "I did not kill the marshal. I am Chinese. I would have been seen had I come near the house. And my sister was returned to Sing Lee, of course. She was locked in her room and forced to work all night, even with the beating she was given. Sing Lee will be watching her very carefully so she cannot get away. Besides, what good would killing the marshal do me or my sister? If she escapes again and Sing Lee swears out another bounty, the new marshal or one of the deputies will again chase us."

"You could have done it out of anger."

Mr. Lon nodded. "I could have, but I did not. It is not the marshal who is our enemy. It is Sing Lee."

"And you say that you are enslaved by him, as well. How?" I asked.

"I have a small grocery. I must give him food and pay him rent for my space." Mr. Lon sighed. "I had hoped to buy a farm here, to grow my own vegetables to sell. But I must buy from Sing Lee's farms and sell those vegetables and pay rent."

I nodded. I didn't doubt that this Sing Lee had found other ways to make money than brothels and opium dens.

"And your sister's affianced," I said. "Could he have killed the marshal in anger, perhaps?"

Mr. Lon shrugged. "I have no idea. My sister says he is a kind man, but the men she is forced to be with, anyone who does not beat her must seem very kind."

"That, alas, is true." I looked at him again. "And you have no idea who this man is?"

"No. Only that he has family in the city."

"Can you write and read in English?" I asked.

"Yes. Both my sister and I can. I think that is how she contacts her lover."

"It would make it easier." I thought it over again. "Does Sing Lee know how to write and read English? He must speak some."

Mr. Lon nodded. "He can read, but not always well. It is why I do not wish him to know that I and my sister can. I would be forced to write and read for him. And it would be even harder for her to escape. She would be more valuable."

"I see." I thought for another moment, then looked at Mr. Lon. "Is there anything else?"

"If you could help her to escape," Mr. Lon said. "Perhaps you can hide her."

"I might be able to, at that," I said. "Her name is Lon Yu?"

"Yes, only she is called Sing Yu by Sing Lee."

I stood and the men stood, as well. "Well, thank you, Mr. Wang, for bringing Mr. Lon to me. We'll see what we can do to help his sister."

"Thank you," Mr. Wang said with a short bow. "I know you of good heart."

I bowed after them and went to bed musing. Could it be I was searching for two different malefactors? If Miss Lon were, indeed, the reason behind the murder of Marshal Warren, whether by her brother or her American lover, then there would be no reason to connect the vandalism to the murder. But who could be this mysterious lover? I was somewhat inclined to discount Miss Lon's assertion that her lover was not married, as it was not unknown for a man to lie about such things and for naive young women to believe them. However, if she'd been forced to sell her flesh, I couldn't imagine her being that naive. On the other hand, Regina had often commented how naive her girls could be about affairs of the heart, and certainly many did believe that a man would come and carry them away from their terrible fate.

It was all too confusing and I woke up the next morning feeling even more out of sorts. It did not help that yet another urgent message arrived later that morning.

Mrs. Carson waited for me in her front parlor, wearing her favorite pink lawn dress, which sadly, did not compliment either her coloring or her round figure. She had once admitted me to her home through the back door to avoid letting anyone see me there. This time, I was again admitted through the back because the front of the house had been drenched in red paint. In addition, one of the front parlor windows had been broken. Needless to say, she was in considerable agitation. Her husband, who was just as round as she, with white hair and whiskers, was sneering, as usual, and pacing even more than his wife. Upon my arrival, they had also shoved a large and familiar piece of brown paper into my hands. Mr. Carson's sins were the rather obvious gluttony, wrath in that he yelled at and struck many in his employ, and envying his neighbor's goods.

"I do not see how you could have let this happen to us," Mrs. Carson sniffed. "As kind as we have been to you."

I glared at her. "I did not let this happen to you. And I have been earnestly looking for the malefactor in question. But I cannot be everywhere in the pueblo, nor can the deputies."

I forebore to suggest that she had, in fact, been less than kind to me many times, as well.

"Mr. Wilson seems to think you've been utterly lax." She picked up a fan and began fanning herself, never mind that it was a rather coolish day with clouds covering the sky.

I caught the small beads of perspiration on her brow and wondered if I could find a way to ask her about her condition at some point. It is not an uncommon effect of growing older as a woman, and if there has been precious little inquiry into the causes and possible means of relief even these days, there was even less then. However, musings on Mrs. Carson's state of health would have to wait.

"Mr. Wilson took offense when I told him his attentions were not nearly as well received as he imagined," I said.

Mr. Carson harrumphed.

"Well, it's about time someone did," Mrs. Carson snapped at her husband. "Good heavens, he was utterly brazen and relentless."

Mr. Carson harrumphed again, although given Mrs. Carson's glare at him, I would have thought suggesting that her charms were sufficient to be worthy of such attentions might have been more politic.

I looked at the paper again and smiled. "Actually, Mr. Carson, as terrible as it is that you've been attacked, this could actually be a help to finding the person who did it."

"How?" he growled.

"Look here at this sin, that you envy your neighbor's goods," I pointed to the spot on the paper. "Anyone could have seen you yelling at your employees or cuffing them. But envy is not something that is readily visible to all and sundry."

You'll note that I did not mention his gluttony. Thanks to his girth, that was somewhat apparent, although I was well apprised of his eating habits. I had been called to treat his dyspepsia on any number of occasions and while I did have more success than most of my colleagues, I was also of the opinion that his dyspepsia had more to do with the vast quantities of food that he ate rather than a lack of the right tonic. I had suggested the same to him more than once, a suggestion that was quite patently ignored.

His sneer turned into a curious frown. "What do you mean?"

"If one envies someone, does one announce it to

everyone?" I asked. "No. If you envy another his goods, you might express a desire to own something similar, but you don't go about telling him and everyone else that you should have what he has and not him."

"No. One doesn't," said Mrs. Carson. "Except my husband."

"What are you talking about?" Mr. Carson roared.

"The tremendous umbrage you took last month when Mr. Carter obtained that bit of land down near Wilmington that you had your eye on."

"I did not announce to all and sundry that I should have that land and Mr. Carter shouldn't."

Mrs. Carson shook her head and turned to me. "They are quite competitive, those two. What one has, the other must have and better."

I nodded. "But the important part is who knows this about your husband? Is it common knowledge?"

"Of course not," he sputtered. "It's not even true!"

"Could someone have heard you say something and misinterpreted it?" I asked.

That gave him a moment's pause. "That is possible. But what could I have said and to whom?"

"Well, I shall have to find out, I expect," I said. "It would not necessarily be obvious to you, especially if someone misinterpreted something. But it does give us something to ask about." I looked at the window. "Are you sure you did not hear it breaking?"

"I'm afraid we were both sound asleep," said Mrs. Carson. "I'd taken a short walk sometime after eleven to help me sleep, so I have no idea what time this was done."

"I might have heard something," Mr. Carson said finally. "It was an hour or so before dawn. I wasn't sure if I'd heard anything or not. I listened for several minutes and heard nothing more, so I went back to sleep."

"That's very interesting," I said. "So now we can make a guess as to when this person is abroad. I'm sorry this had to happen to you, but it may yet be for the best. Thank you for being so forthcoming."

I left trying to make sense of it. I also wondered how much effort I should put into finding out who was behind the vandalism, especially when it seemed possible that it wasn't connected to the marshal's death. And I did need to find out who killed him. However, each vandalous attack had gotten increasingly worse, with more and more paint, which also made me wonder where it was all coming from.

I was riding that day and decided to attempt to find Deputy Lomax. I debated heading to his farm on the north side of the pueblo, but thought I would try at the police office behind the Clocktower Courthouse first, and, indeed, that is where I found him. He agreed that it would be worth trying to find who was buying large amounts of red paint or if any was missing and said he would ask around, himself, that very day.

I headed back to my rancho, intent on writing down everything I had learned and possibly getting some of my own work done, but there was a note from Regina waiting for me that made me rush back to my horse.

Regina's house was on New High Street, not far from Mr. Mahoney's saloon. To all outward appearances, it was another nicely built white clapboard house with a small turret on one side. It was close enough to the commercial district that the fine, upstanding citizens weren't too offended by its presence. It was also far enough away from the brothels on Bath Street and the Chinese brothels on Calle de los Negros to cater to a more refined clientele, if you could call it that.

I did not. Regina knew well that I did not approve of her trade, although I agreed she had little other option, as did many of her girls. It was a travesty that if a young woman was turned out by her husband, father, or brother, she had little recourse to support herself but to turn to prostitution. There were shop girls, of course, and the occasional nurse. But few of the Americans would hire other Americans to serve them, preferring Negroes, Chinese, or Mexicans. And women were still barred from working in offices. Women managed, of course, some taking in laundry and sewing, others finding work in more masculine pursuits. But there were a goodly number who found selling their flesh their only chance to survive, and far too many men willing to buy it for an hour or more.

As was my normal custom, I entered Regina's house from the back so as not to be seen by the neighbors. The house was built at the foot of a steep brush-covered slope, and actually had two other entrances discreetly screened from prying eyes. However, those entrances led to the front parlor and dining room respectively, and those were generally occupied by one or more clients, most of whom would prefer not to be seen. Sybil, a young Negro woman who had started as Regina's maid and had taken over Regina's accounts as her clerk, showed me to Regina's study. I was a little surprised, as I had assumed that one of her girls was sick or injured.

"Oh, I'm so glad you're here!" Regina gushed as she hurried over to greet me. "I was afraid I was going to have to ask questions of the little worm all by myself."

"What worm?" I was even more puzzled.

Regina seldom had an ill word for anyone, indeed, she often displayed more Christian charity to her fellow man than most Christians I knew. So her angry words shocked me. Then she led me to one of two small "cooling off" rooms where the occasional client could be put should he become unruly, or obstreperous or drink far too much and pass out. Regina's discretion was absolute and had to be as it was the cornerstone of her business, which meant that I seldom saw the inhabitants of these rooms. I can think of only one or two other instances in which someone was so badly incapacitated that his need of my services was greater than his fear of discovery

The greatest shock, however, was when Regina led me into the small room and I found Mr. Wills sitting disconsolately on the small cot on the far wall.

"He's not a client," Regina said. "I can assure you, he doesn't have enough money."

"I do so!" whimpered Mr. Wills.

Regina leaned over and put her face in his. "Then why were you cheating at faro in my parlor this noontide?" She straightened and looked at me. "One of my clients had invited Mr. Wills for lunch and some gaming. Mr. Wills not only cheated but could only offer a note for his debt after he lost, and we almost had a full-on fight. Thank Heavens my boys were able to put it down before someone pulled a gun. I would not be surprised if dear Leander owes money elsewhere, too."

Mr. Wills trembled and sniffed.

"No wonder you fear being targeted by our vandal with the red paint," I said. "A fine, upstanding notary who's in debt up to his ears? It might also account for your strange behavior on the afternoon of the marshal's death."

"Oh, that," said Regina with a frosty smile. "How did it go? I heard you were quite forceful about taking the marshal's statement until Mrs. Wilcox came down and told you the marshal would not be awakened. Oh, and then suddenly everyone believed the marshal was on his deathbed. How kind of you to tell them, not to mention convenient for you, Mr. Wills. No one would question it if the marshal suddenly died, after all."

"What? I didn't kill the marshal. Joe Dye did!" Mr. Wills almost began crying, he was so frightened.

"No, he didn't," I said. "The marshal was not ready to expire after all, Mr. Wills, no matter what you were hoping. Did you owe him money?"

"No. He didn't gamble." Mr. Wills nervously licked his lips. "I know who did want to hurt him. Jorge Villega. He's got even more gambling debts than I do. But he steals to cover his losses. I can't." Mr. Wills stopped and whimpered a little.

"I wouldn't place a wager that you don't," I said. "Or if you don't steal, you find other dishonorable ways to find the money you need. But I suppose I would have to find someone to bring a lawsuit against you to find out."

Regina chuckled. "That would be fun. I wonder who we could ask to do it."

"I suppose I could do it, myself," I said. "Being a widow, I would have a better chance at succeeding, and I do business with Mr. Wills often enough. Of course, Mr. Judson will be terribly disappointed in you, Mr. Wills. A dishonest notary? Can you imagine the fit Mr. Judson would have?"

"No! No!" Mr. Wills begged. "Mrs. Wilcox, I swear, I did not kill the marshal. But ask Mr. Villega. He was a good friend of Joe Dye's and was very angry with the marshal for cheating Dye yet again. Ask him. He's the one who killed the marshal. I'm sure of it."

Regina looked over at me and I shrugged. She reached over and, with one hand, pulled the man to his feet.

"All right, you little pest. Leave now and do not darken my door again." She pushed him out the room's door and nodded at somebody on the other side.

I looked at Regina. "I suppose this eliminates him for both the marshal's murder and being the vandal."

"You don't think he would lie to save his own miserable skin?"

"I am utterly convinced that he would," I replied with a grim smile. "I just don't think he'd be very good at it."

Regina laughed. "I dare say you have a point."

"So, how do we speak with Mr. Villega? If he's as prone to fighting over gambling debts as Mr. Wills and Mr. Lomax have hinted, I'm not sure you'd want to invite him to a faro game in your parlor."

"No, indeed. I suppose we could ask Angelina. She may have some idea of how to gain an interview with him."

I nodded. "That is an excellent idea. I suppose we could have a meeting, perhaps at the rancho tonight after supper?"

"I should be able to make myself free. Actually, now that Sybil has been doing the accounts, there's very little I need to do besides make sure the girls aren't hiding anything and set up the appointments." She led me back to her study and checked a ledger. "Yes, I believe we're fully booked for the evening, and I should be back in time to make matches for any later guests."

I shivered. I did not like to think about what that might mean, nor did I care to censure Regina. She already knew how I felt about her profession, as it were.

"I will stop at Angelina's house before I go home," I said. "I have to go that way, in any case."

"Excellent. I shall see you tonight."

As I left, I hoped greatly that Olivia had a nice hearty stew or joint or some other nice, filling offering for supper that night. With Regina and Angelina both coming over to discuss the murder and the vandalism, I was going to need it.

CHAPTER NINE

After arranging for the meeting with Angelina but before going home, I did realize there was one other stop I could make, and one that might bring me closer to speaking with Mr. Villega. The wool mill was near the corner of Alameda Street and Calle de Colejio. It was the perfect location in that the mill had been owned by a former Zanjero, or Water Overseer. Water being scarce in Los Angeles at the time, the Zanjero was possibly the most powerful person in the pueblo. He would be one of the few people who could get away with putting a mill almost right on top of the Zanja Madre, the ditch that came from the Porciuncula River to provide water for the pueblo and irrigate our fields and vineyards.

The wool mill was a terribly noisy and dirty place, filled with Mexican, Negro, and Chinese laborers and mostly American foremen overseeing them. The machines clacked and roared in a most fearsome way, and over this noise, the shouts of the men rose. But I must say, that the wool produced by the looms and the spinners was quite fine, as was the bombazine, a very popular fabric for dresses in our little pueblo, as it was not nearly so warm to wear as pure wool. Cotton was also popular, but we did have to import it from the Southern states, which were still rebuilding after the War.

I found the young owner, James Rivers, in his office in a loft that was built over the main floor of the building. He was tall, broad-shouldered and very fair.

Indeed, I would have been surprised that some sweet young lady had not already caught his eye, but that the young man's father had died the previous spring and had left his affairs in a considerable mess. Young Mr. Rivers was all of twenty-two years of age but was managing quite well in spite of the chaos he had been left.

"Mrs. Wilcox!" he crowed when he saw me in his office doorway. He leaped up from his desk, his dark suit neat and very new. "How good of you to come by. And what brings you here? I have news, too, just arrived this morning."

He bustled me into the office, which mostly featured his large wooden desk, littered with papers and two small wooden chairs. I gravely feared the chair would not be big enough for my second best brown riding habit, but I somehow managed my hoops, nonetheless.

"I am so glad you came by," Mr. Rivers said as he settled himself behind the desk. "I just got a letter from Mother and she bade me tell you all that has happened since her last letter."

I must here make mention of the events of the previous spring which had concerned the death of the elder Mr. Rivers. He had, in fact, been murdered. Mrs. Mae Rivers had remained in the pueblo with her sons for only a month after the murderer had been executed, then had decided to take two of the children with her and return to her father's family in Philadelphia. James, her eldest, had elected to stay in Los Angeles to manage his father's interests. We'd had one letter from when she'd arrived with the good news that everyone had survived the arduous journey and that they had been well-received by her brothers. Or rather, James had gotten the letter but had been instructed in it to share those particulars with me, as Mrs. Rivers and I had become friendly over the troublesome events surrounding her husband's death.

"That is most kind of her," I said, mentally adding

a note to make sure I wrote her back. "Does she have an address yet?"

"Oh, yes. I was planning on giving it to you." James pulled the letter from a corner of the desk, then got his pen, flipped the inkwell open, and found another piece of paper and tore a corner off of it. "Here it is. I hope you can read my writing."

It was a neat, but bold, script and I was able to reassure him that I could read it quite easily.

"Now, let me tell you the best part." James winked at me. "She wrote that her former suitor has contacted her again and they had the most pleasant meeting."

"Indeed." My eyebrows raised. "That sounds very promising for both of them. You seem happy about this turn of events."

Mr. Rivers shrugged and grinned. "Why not? Ma deserves some happiness after all she's been through. If this fellow can give that to her, why should I object?"

"Then it sounds like a most satisfactory turn of events all around."

"There's even better. Steven is studying with a real artist and George, if he passes his exams, will be accepted to university to become an engineer."

"Oh, that is wonderful. I am so happy for all of you." I looked at him. "But you, young Mr. Rivers. How are you doing?"

He shrugged. "Well enough, I suppose. I never thought I'd like my father's business all that well, but I don't mind it at all. If it makes enough money to keep Mother comfortable and pay for George and Steven's schooling, then I'm happy enough."

"That's more than a lot of people can ask for," I said with a smile, then frowned. "Alas, my purpose here is considerably less than happy. Do you have a foreman named Jorge Villega?

He sighed. "Yes."

"Would it be safe to say that he has caused some trouble for you before now?"

"Indeed he has. Or actually, I have suspected him

of such. But I have no proof."

"And since your mother has exhorted you to kindness in the face of your father's lack thereof, you feel obligated now to be kind, even though he does not appear to deserve it."

Mr. Rivers smiled in relief. "That's it exactly, Mrs. Wilcox. I hadn't thought of it that way, but that's exactly how it goes." He slumped in his chair slightly. "Do you have any thoughts on how I should handle this matter?"

"That is up to you," I said with a small shrug. "However, I have been given to understand that he has amassed a considerable amount in gambling debts and had expressed great enmity toward Marshal Warren, whose killer may actually be someone other than Deputy Dye."

"I'd heard something about that." Mr. Rivers sat back in his chair and thought. "There is money missing from the company safe, and it is possible that Mr. Villega has obtained the combination somehow. Whether that makes him the man who killed the marshal, I cannot say."

"But it does give me a reason to speak with Mr. Villega. Is there some way that you can arrange an opportunity for the two of us to have a conversation?"

"I think that could be arranged." Mr. Rivers got up from his desk and went to the edge of the loft, where he looked down at the manufactory floor. "I can't see Mr. Villega. It doesn't mean that he's not around, but he does often go on errands." Mr. Rivers smiled at me. "Would tomorrow suit for the examination?"

"It will do very well." I got up and stood. "Thank you, Mr. Rivers."

I took Daisy at a nice trot on the way home, and stayed on Alameda Street with the intent of avoiding the central part of the pueblo. However, as I neared my rancho, I saw that Mr. Lomax was riding up to the gate on his horse.

He tipped his hat as he saw me. "Mrs. Wilcox. I

was hoping to find you at home."

"I'm not quite there, I'm afraid, but why don't you follow me in and we'll speak in my parlor?"

He smiled and nodded.

His news, however, was not what I wanted to hear.

"As near as I can tell, no one has been buying any red paint except the Hewitt factory, and nobody seems to be missing any, either," Mr. Lomax said from his seat on my front parlor sofa.

The Hewitt factory made buggies and other conveyances and would, naturally, be the largest buyer of red paint in the pueblo. As white was the easiest and most economical color to buy, most houses in the pueblo tended to be white-washed. Red was saved for barns, the trim on buggies, mostly, and for signs. There were probably some other uses for red paint and I simply cannot remember them now.

"How grievously annoying," I exclaimed. "Then where, in Heaven's name, is this vandal getting the paint? There were great pools of it on the Carson home and yard, even more than on Mr. Wilson's home. It must have taken buckets."

"One or two, at least. Once you splash it out, it doesn't take that much paint to cover a fair piece of landscape," Mr. Lomax said.

I sat back and considered. "You may be right. Still, red is not that common a color to not go noticed when it's missing."

"There is something else." Mr. Lomax frowned. "When I went to the Hewitt factory, Mr. Hewitt was indisposed, so I spoke with Mrs. Hewitt."

"I'm sure you did," I said, not willing to reveal, even to Mr. Lomax, what I knew of how the manufactory was actually run.

Mr. Lomas fidgeted with his hat, which he'd kept on his lap. "I do not know why, but I think Mrs. Hewitt was lying."

My heart froze. There could be any number of very good reasons why Mrs. Hewitt had lied to Mr.

Lomax, none of which meant that she was behind the vandalism. But I had seen her at the revival meeting.

"I suppose I shall have to pay her a visit," I said, feeling annoyed. "I hope it can wait until tomorrow."

"I'd think it could," Mr. Lomax said with a shrug. "And I almost forgot. Joe Dye was not in the jail the night the marshal was killed."

"So he was right," I muttered.

One of Mr. Lomax's eyebrows lifted.

"Oh, nothing," I said in response. "I'd just heard that Deputy Dye had made a set of keys to the jail for his own use. It makes it a great deal easier to get out of jail when one has the keys."

"I know," Mr. Lomax said. "Even the marshal knew about those keys. Didn't seem to bother him."

"Except that now it is possible that Deputy Dye did kill the marshal after all."

"Seems unlikely to me," Mr. Lomax said, again fidgeting with his hat. "Dye isn't that subtle or that quiet. How'd he get in and out of that house without waking anyone?"

"That would be a good question." I pondered for a moment. "Perhaps someone was awakened and didn't realize there was something wrong. Maybe I'll ask Mrs. Warren. Even if no one saw anything, it might give us an idea of what time it was that it happened."

Mr. Lomax agreed and took his leave almost immediately after.

Supper that night was a good hearty chicken stew, for which I was grateful. After supper, Regina arrived first, then Angelina, and we settled ourselves in my study with angelica and pan dulces. I went first, giving my accounting of all I had learned, then Regina said her piece. Angelina was just about to start telling us her findings when there was a loud knock on the door and I went to get it, Maria and Magdalena having gone to the barracks for the evening.

Constable Brooks was there.

"It's my sister's time, ma'am," he told me.

I sighed. Of course, it was. "Come in and settle for a moment while I get my things."

I went to the study and asked Regina and Angelina to show themselves out when they were ready, explaining that I was being called away.

"Why do the little devils always seem to want to be delivered at the most inauspicious times?" Regina asked. "Why can't they show up on a nice, quiet afternoon?"

"Don't ask me," Angelina said. "It's at the wrong end of life for me."

"And I get both ends and everything in between," I grumbled. "I'll meet with you in the morning, Angelina, assuming I'm awake."

"Any time you like. None of my projects are likely to be going anywhere."

Chuckling, I went to my bedroom and got my bag. I was glad I'd changed to one of my work dresses before supper. Mr. Brooks was standing in the parlor, with his hat in his hands.

"Is your hand healing well?" I asked as we walked quickly along the dark streets.

"Well enough, thank you."

He certainly did not seem to be favoring it, and his bandage still looked clean.

When we entered the rabbit warren that was the Lawrence home, Mrs. Lawrence was in her room, in possibly the only bed in the place. Mr. Lawrence had been holding her hand, but once he saw me, he left the room.

As deliveries go, this latest was not particularly complicated but merely time-consuming. Mrs. Lawrence and I talked of this and that between her pains. At one point, as the pains were getting very close together, Mrs. Lawrence lay back on her pillows and began to weep. I took her pulse, which was holding up quite nicely.

"I know we're getting to the hard part," I told her. "But you're doing quite well."

"It's not me," she said softly. "It's Bobby."

"Your brother?"

She took a deep breath and looked toward the ceiling. "He's in love. But he's worried about leaving us. And he won't bring her here."

It was not hard to imagine why, given the state of the house and all those children.

"We're poor, you know,"

"Yes," I replied, anticipating what usually came after such a statement. "But do not fret about my fee. You have other business to concentrate on."

And just then, the next pain took hold and we worked through it.

"It's not me," she gasped as the pain subsided. "It's Bobby. I want him to be happy."

"Of course, you do. I'm assuming you would be happy to welcome his beloved."

"Oh, yes. I've told him so many times. It's not that."

Another pain wracked her and after that, there was little time for chatter. Another two hours later, I wrapped an infant girl in swaddling clothes and laid her in Mrs. Lawrence's arms. I did truly like Mrs. Lawrence. She was one of those rare beings who was genuinely filled with the grace of Christian piety and love. It was just like her, even at the worst of her labor, to be more worried about her brother than about herself. I was quite happy that all had gone well and even though it was quite late, I was happy enough that I shrugged off any offers to accompany me back home.

"It's not that far," I told both Mr. Brooks and Mr. Lawrence. "And at this hour, I'm not likely to find anybody abroad. I know. I've walked these streets often enough."

Mr. Brooks looked as though he were about to say more, but demurred at the behest of his brother-in-law. Both were quite tired, as was I. Still, I smiled with a great deal more energy than I would have thought, adjusted the leather bag across my shoulder and headed out.

It was a cool, crisp night. In fact, it was the kind of night that was endlessly extolled as the kind of perfect weather that made our little, benighted corner of the world so wonderful. I had yet to see the glory of it, although I did appreciate not having to slog my way through four months of snow every year. That night, I smelled rain on the horizon and was glad of it.

I was walking along Alameda Street, having avoided Bath Street, where the worst of the brothels were, when rough hands grabbed me from behind. I gasped as I felt the sharp edge of a knife against my throat.

"What do you want?" I gasped. "I have morphine in my bag. You can have it."

"No!" hissed an angry voice.

I could feel the heat of his breath on my ear.

"Say nothing," the man whispered again. "I do not want to kill you. I want to be done with killing, but dagnabbit, I will kill you if I have to."

"I'm quite happy not to be killed," I said.

"Then let Joe Dye take the credit for killing Marshal Warren. Do not seek after another killer."

"But that wouldn't be just to Mr. Dye."

"Nobody cares about Joe Dye. And nobody cares who really killed Marshal Warren."

"Mrs. Warren does."

"Just keep your dadblamed nose out of it, Mrs. Wilcox! For God's sake, keep your nose out of it. For the first time in my life, I have found a place to call home. I will not let you take that away from me!"

The anguish in the voice was quite real, although his identity was obscured by his whispering.

"Mrs. Wilcox?" a voice called from down the way.

The man who had grabbed me pushed me forward and I fell to my knees. A moment later, Mr. Brooks came running up from the direction I'd come along Alameda Street.

"Mrs. Wilcox, are you all right?" Mr. Brooks gasped as he helped me up.

"Well enough, Mr. Brooks," I said, working very hard to sound a lot calmer than I actually felt.

"Who was that?" he gasped.

"I have no idea, but he wanted me to stop looking for Marshal Warren's killer."

"But you said it wasn't Joe Dye, that something else had killed the Marshal." Mr. Brooks face, from what I could see of it in the light of an almost full moon partially obscured by clouds, creased into a frown.

"He was murdered, Mr. Brooks. I do not want to say how, but someone stole into his room that fateful night and killed him."

"How terrible. Oh, my God. When I was asleep!"

I put my hand on his shoulder. "Calm down, Mr. Brooks. It most likely happened under Mr. Redona's watch and I did say that neither of you were fit to be watching. I understand from Mr. Lomax that you were only there because there was no one else, so there is no fault to be laid on you."

"This is terrible, Mrs. Wilcox." He was mere seconds away from breaking down in sobs. "Completely terrible."

"Pull yourself together, Mr. Brooks. I need to consider who that man might have been and I cannot with you falling into pieces." I took a deep breath to steady myself and ran my hand along my throat where the blade had rested. There was no blood and I thanked God for it. "One good thing. Assuming my attacker killed the marshal means that you can't have. Now, I'd best make my way back to my rancho."

"I'll walk with you," Mr. Brooks said, showing some admirable aplomb. "It's not safe for you. I wish you'd waited for me to walk with you."

"It can't be helped now and I often walk alone at night," I said. "This is the first time I have ever been accosted."

It was, indeed, the first time I'd ever been accosted, and it troubled me deeply. I got back to the rancho and thanked Mr. Brooks for seeing to my safety, then sent him back to his home.

But as I later lay in my bed, all I could think of was that warm breath and the cold steel next to my throat. And the anguish in the whisper, "For the first time in my life, I have found a place to call home. I will not let you take that away from me!"

CHAPTER TEN

I did sleep somewhat later than normal the next day. It was hard not to. The rain I'd smelled the night before had, indeed, arrived, although it was mostly a mist with fits and starts of heavier downpours. I did so want to stay under my lovely warm blankets and rugs. Indeed, I almost did. I knew I had to visit Angelina as soon as possible but riding in the rain is most assuredly not among my preferred pastimes. And then, as if the Heavens knew that I was wavering in my purpose, the rain stopped and the clouds parted.

Rain in Los Angeles is annoyingly fickle. Back home in Boston, if it was raining, it did just that, usually for some days. True, there would be the occasional Nor'easter and those were nasty. But more often than not, there would be a nice, steady rain, with a few thunderstorms in the late spring and summer. Here in Los Angeles, the clouds build and can either provide anywhere from a full-on downpour of several hours all the way to a light sprinkling here and there, and it was next to impossible to tell what was going to happen.

However, there is one saving grace to rainy weather here. Once the clouds clear, they leave behind a sky and landscape of radiant brilliance. What colors there are in the brown of the hills become more vivid, and the relentlessly blue sky all but glows. It is as though one can pick out each individual leaf on the oak trees dotting the barren slopes. One can smell things better, too, usually horse muffins back then. But the roses that had been planted along the fences of my rancho gave off a rich scent, as did any small blooming flowers along the streets.

I wore my third best, and actually oldest. riding habit. It was a faded cotton and blue wool, and the skirt was a bit rounder than current fashion decreed. But that was because it was several years old by that point. Still, I was not going to risk getting my best riding habit dirty and it was going to be quite a mucky day in the streets.

Angelina's preparation room was unusually empty of corpses, but we went to her small study anyway.

"I have all my lists there," she explained.

We settled in, I on the sofa and Angelina in her favorite chair, and she pulled her little desk around. We went back over everything I and Regina had said the night before, then Angelina gave me her news.

"I have found out that Emanuel Mendoza was not celebrating with his friends on the night of Marshal Warren's death."

"What? How?" I asked.

Angelina shrugged. "I talked to Arturo Sedonez. He works behind the bar at that big saloon on Calle Principal, near Calle Alta. Mr. Mendoza was drinking, all right, but he was alone in the saloon."

"How did you happen to speak to Mr. Sedonez?"

Angelina shrugged. "The usual. He brought in a body. We buried it yesterday"

"But there are dozens of saloons in the pueblo. What made you think to ask Mr. Sedonez about Mr. Mendoza?"

"We were talking about the affray between the marshal and Deputy Dye. Mr. Sedonez said there were lots of people celebrating and I asked about Mr. Mendoza and Mr. Sedonez said that Mr. Mendoza was there but he was alone."

"Well done, Angelina." I thought about it. "But why was he lying?"

"That I can't tell you. We should talk to his mother

again, though. It's possible she heard something and didn't recognize it for what it was."

"I agree." I suddenly sighed. "And it seems as though we'd better find Marshal Warren's killer sooner rather than later. I was accosted last night."

I told Angelina the whole frightening experience.

"What did Sebastiano have to say about that?" she asked, a worried frown on her face.

I shuddered. "I haven't told him yet."

"Oooooh!" Angelina's eye grew wide. "He is not going to like that. He'll probably yell at you."

"Perhaps. But if I'd told him, he'd be dogging my every step and he has other work to do." I stood. "In any case, the incident certainly serves to remind us that we must find this killer before he kills again, however much he may not want to."

"Indeed." Angelina got up and found her bonnet, which was hanging from a peg near the door to the preparation room, and wrapped a shawl around her shoulders. "We may as well go to visit Mrs. Mendoza together."

I put my bonnet back on and the two of us walked over to the Mendoza home, which was above the shoe shop. Mrs. Mendoza opened the door to the rooms she shared with her son and eyed me suspiciously, then spoke to Angelina.

"It's good to see you," she told Angelina in Spanish. "But why did you bring her?"

She obviously did not know I spoke Spanish. In fairness to her, however, most Americans, especially the women, did not.

"Señora Wilcox is here to help us," Angelina said, also in Spanish. "And she speaks very good Spanish, too."

Mrs. Mendoza smiled a little awkwardly at me but let us enter. She was a medium-sized woman with a rounded figure and hair that was dark gray. Her brown eyes were somewhat clouded over, which was not surprising for a woman of her considerable years. Her hands were bent and the joints on them swollen, and she moved as though she were in considerable pain. Nonetheless, none of her obvious infirmities made her any the less imposing.

"So, why are you here?" she asked in Spanish, still glaring at me. "How are you going to help me and my son?"

"I am not going to make any wild accusations," I told her. "I am going to insist on real proof before making any accusations at all."

One of her eyebrows slowly lifted and she considered me. Angelina told me later that she was impressed by my accent. If I do say so myself, it was better than most Americans'. That being said, it was still quite thick and I worked almost every day to make it better.

"I have already told Señora Sutton everything I know, which is not much," the old woman said to me, finally.

"Sometimes we do not understand that we know something," I said. "Perhaps you awoke that night and did not know what it was that woke you. I was speaking with a man yester morning who had been awakened by a window in his house breaking, but had not realized that was what had awakened him."

"Of course, I am awake many times in the night," she said with a fatalistic shrug. "When you are old, you do not sleep and there is always the necessary."

"So I've been told," I said.

She was right, of course, but I was much younger then.

"And I do not check Emanuel's room. Why should I? He is a grown man and supporting me."

"He is a good man to do so," Angelina said.

Mrs. Mendoza suddenly blinked her eyes, then sank onto a sofa. It was a small room that we were in, simply furnished with good furniture, including the sofa and a couple of chairs. Light from the windows over the street filled the room with brightness.

"They are proud men, my sons," Mrs. Mendoza said, tears beginning to creep down her cheeks. "I am so afraid that Emanuel did something terrible. And because my ear is so bad, I cannot tell when he comes or when he goes. I did wake an hour before dawn that day. I thought I heard Emanuel stumbling about, but I cannot be sure. I had no reason to worry about him then. He closed his shop that day. He does not do that often. But my sons, they know they were not to hurt the marshal. They were not to go near him."

"We have been told that he was in a saloon that night," I said with a glance at Angelina. "But I am afraid that he did lie about being with his friends. Do you know why he would do that?"

Mrs. Mendoza shook her head. "I do not know. Señora Wilcox, he is a good man. His brother's death, it was hard for him. But he listened to me and promised not to hurt the marshal. Why would he break his promise to me?"

"That we cannot say," said Angelina, sitting next to her. "And it does not mean he did. But we do have to ask the questions. It is the only way to be sure he is innocent."

Mrs. Mendoza nodded. I was in a bit of a quandary because if Emanuel Mendoza was guilty, it would break his mother's heart and I did not want to do that. But it was true that I did not have to remind her of that, and if we offered her some hope of his innocence, it was simply kindness to do so.

To be honest, as I thought about it, I did not believe that Mr. Mendoza was the guilty party. For one thing, the man who had held me at knifepoint the night before had had no trace of an accent, and to the best of my knowledge, Mr. Mendoza had spent his entire life in Los Angeles, rather than recently having found himself a home. That would seem to have eliminated Mr. Mendoza, whose speech, like most of the Mexicans in the pueblo, carried the accent of his heritage, never mind that they spoke English at least as well as most of the Americans did (and in many cases, spoke better English).

I looked at Angelina and she nodded. She spoke softly to Mrs. Mendoza and after a few minutes, the older woman also nodded and Angelina rose from the sofa. I offered some balm for the older woman's rheumatism, which she accepted with effusive thanks. The two of us left the small room and went downstairs.

Mr. Mendoza was in his shop, as we had expected. He looked at Angelina and me with a wary glare as we approached him. I, too, felt a moment's apprehension.

"Ay, Señor Mendoza," Angelina said in Spanish as we walked into the shop. "We do not want to accuse you, but we know you have lied about being with your friends the night the marshal died."

"And how would you know that?" Mr. Mendoza asked, glaring even more fiercely at Angelina.

"We have talked to Señor Sedonez," Angelina said as if she didn't care a whit for the angry glare she was getting.

Mr. Mendoza looked over at me, then seemed about to say something to Angelina. So, I broke in to prevent him from embarrassing himself.

"If you were in the saloon all night, it would mean that you didn't harm the marshal," I said, in Spanish.

Like his mother's, his eyebrow rose.

"I didn't go near the marshal's place," he said, finally. "Why would I? Everyone said he was dying."

"To gloat, perhaps?" I suggested.

"And what good would that have done?" Mr. Mendoza asked, then blinked and shook his head. "Mama was right. It would not raise our brother from the dead to get our necks stretched by the Americanos. I went to celebrate and all I could think was how much I missed my brother. So his killer was dying. It did not make me feel better. All I did was get very drunk." He looked away and sighed deeply. "I did not want Mama to know. So I told you I was with friends, like I told her. I think she knew anyway."

"Do you remember what time you got home?" Angelina asked.

He winced. "Sometime in the early hours before dawn. I think. I remember Mr. Sedonez waking me up and telling me I had to go. I think I walked home. I remember I was sick in the street somewhere, but I don't remember if anyone helped me or not. Wait. There was someone else. An Americano. He was singing a hymn about grapes of wrath."

"The Battle Hymn of the Republic," I said.

Mr. Mendoza shook his head. "He helped me. Told me I should be on guard against drunkenness. That the Lord is coming like a thief in the night and some other religious nonsense. But he got me home all right."

"Do you, by any chance, remember what he looked like?" I asked.

Mr. Mendoza snorted. "He was an Americano. What do you want?" He glared at me. "I have been shamed by my behavior that night. Do you think I want to remember it?"

"No, I'm sure you don't," I replied. "But there is a killer abroad who kills by stealth, and as such, threatens quite a few people in this pueblo. We must find him before he kills again."

"It wasn't me. I have not killed anybody, even a few who might have deserved it."

"We weren't saying you have, Mr. Mendoza," Angelina said quickly. "But if you were abroad that night, well, early morning, maybe you saw something."

He sighed deeply. "No one but that Americano." Mr. Mendoza stopped and thought about it. "Could he be the one who is painting all the houses?"

"We have reason to believe he might be," I said.

"Then maybe I can help you," he said thoughtfully. "He did say something else about how one expects Mexicans to be drunk."

"What a terrible thing to say!" Angelina folded her arms across her chest.

"He's an Americano," Mr. Mendoza said, waving

her off. "What else can you expect from them? But he said I should be glad I'm not an Americano. If I were, he would have to do something about me being drunk in the street." Mr. Mendoza suddenly frowned. "I think he also knew where I live. I don't remember telling him that. But he helped me home."

"Do you remember meeting him in the saloon?" I asked.

"No. He was not there. Lots of others were. A lot of them were celebrating. I could have sworn Deputy Dye came in, but I was so drunk by that point, I would not credit it. He would have been in jail, no?"

"He should have been," I said, glancing over at Angelina.

She held her tongue and it seemed that she agreed with me that there was little point in making Mr. Mendoza aware of the fact that we knew that the deputy had not, in fact, been in jail that fateful night.

Angelina and I made our goodbyes and left the shop. We walked toward her house.

"He could have killed the marshal," Angelina said. "I would swear that the marshal had not been dead very long when I saw him. It was cool that night, but not so cold that it would have kept the marshal from stiffening for any length of time."

I looked at her. "You know, you ought to make a study of that. I could see where knowing all the circumstances of rigor mortis would be very helpful in determining when someone died, for just such cases as this."

Angelina giggled. "I've already started."

"I would greatly enjoy seeing what you've found."

"Mas tarde, Maddie." Angelina's eyes glowed with mischief, then turned somber. "We have other work to do, first."

"Indeed," I said. The Courthouse clock tower began grinding out the hour. "I'd best make my way to the wool mill. Young Mr. Rivers said that he would make Mr. Villega available for me to speak to."

"Very well. We'll speak again soon."

Angelina went off to her home and I headed down the Calle Principal to the mill.

Mr. Rivers was waiting for me rather anxiously. He came down almost immediately after I had knocked on the mill's entry door.

"I have Mr. Villega in the foreman's office," he told me. "He seems like such a nice man. I hate to think that he's been stealing from me. He says he hasn't, of course."

"I don't doubt that part," I said, feeling somewhat cross. "Do you know how much money is missing?"

"Yes, my accountant has the figures for you in his office."

"Let me speak to him, first."

The accountant was named Mr. Hugh Davis. He was a tall, thin man with a narrow face and dark hair. He wore spectacles and looked down through them at me with an air of vague disgust.

"I don't expect you to understand the intricacies of accounting," he said slowly.

"I can't imagine you expecting me to understand anything of consequence," I replied, sniffing. "Yet, there is a great deal that I do understand, including how money might disappear in a busy manufactory such as this one."

His was a small office, featuring a large roll top desk backed up against a wall and a large safe in the corner. The safe hung open.

"Mrs. Wilcox, I do not appreciate base accusations without evidence. Moreover, I have the full confidence of Mr. Rivers."

"Mr. Davis, I did not make any accusations." I pulled myself up straight and folded my arms. "However, as soon as one of my employees or any other man to whom I've entrusted the handling of my money or goods tells me not to worry my pretty little head about something, more often than not, I find that something untoward is going on that I should, indeed, worry my pretty little head about. Now, I do not doubt that you have Mr. Rivers' full confidence. However, it remains to be seen whether that confidence is misplaced or not and the way you have immediately jumped to the conclusion that I was accusing you of some sort of malfeasance makes me wonder if there is not some sort of malfeasance on your part. There clearly is on somebody's part, as there is money missing. We have observed at least one of your employees spending far more money than might be expected given his wages. I will be speaking with him momentarily. However, my conversation should be considerably more fruitful if I know ahead of time how much money is missing and how it might have been stolen."

Mr. Davis stepped back. "I, eh, don't have an exact figure for you. I am, ahem, still going over the clerks' work. But it is several hundred dollars over the past month or so. How far back it goes, I do not yet know."

That did not surprise me, nor did I bother to ask how it might have gone missing, as I had the answer right in front of me, not in the person of Mr. Davis, but in the fact that the safe sat open whilst he had his back to it.

"Thank you, Mr. Davis." I turned to Mr. Rivers. "And now to Mr. Villega?"

"This way, Mrs. Wilcox." The young man's eyes were gleaming with relief and some amusement. As soon as we were alone, he laughed. "What a tongue lashing you gave old Davis! I must admit, I find it hard to believe that he would be behind the thefts. He is always so correct and so worried about every penny we spend here."

"I actually suspect he's honest," I said. "That officious kind usually is. Although it wouldn't hurt to hire an independent accountant to go over your records, just in case. That being said, you shouldn't let him bully you."

Mr. Rivers sighed, his broad shoulders slumping. "I know."

"Dear, Mr. Rivers," I said gently and smiling kindly at him. "I fully understand how much you do not want to carry on your father's legacy of meanness. That is a very noble thing. But there is a world of difference between being kind and letting everyone use you as their doormat. You can and, indeed, should be firm. It's not kindness to let your employees run amuck."

"No, I suppose it is not." Mr. Rivers sighed. "I still have a lot to learn, don't I?"

"You've already learned a great deal in a very short time and the business does seem to be prospering."

He smiled. "It is, indeed. Now, onto Mr. Villega."

The latter person was waiting nervously in the office. It was a fairly large room, above the manufactory floor, with several desks scattered about, and large windows letting in air and light. The roar of the looms below was somewhat muted. The man was wearing his vest over his still-dirty shirt and smoothed his full, dark mustache as he glared at me. However, he addressed himself to Mr. Rivers.

"Are you here to accuse me of stealing?" Mr. Villega said.

I glanced at Mr. Rivers and stepped back. The young man nodded and took a deep breath.

"Mr. Villaga, there is money missing and Mrs. Wilcox has informed me that you've been observed gambling with far more money than your wages would account for."

Mr. Villega shrugged. "So I'm lucky."

I couldn't help chuckling.

"Apparently you're not," said Mr. Rivers with considerably more aplomb than I would have thought.

It didn't really do, but I felt the pride swell in my chest.

"You can't say that," Mr. Villega snapped.

"Oh, yes, I can. We've had fellows come by to collect from you more than once," Mr. Rivers said. "And Mrs. Wilcox has verified that you have several gambling debts about town. In addition, there is considerable money missing from the safe."

Mr. Villega nodded at me. "And why does she care what happens at your factory?"

"Apart from a general concern for Mr. Rivers' welfare, I don't," I said with some asperity. "My interest in this matter is strictly focused on finding out who murdered Marshal Warren."

"It wasn't murder," Mr. Villega snarled. "Joe Dye shot the marshal in self-defense."

"I am well aware of that, Mr. Villega," I said. "As it happens, I was a witness to the affray. However, Marshal Warren was murdered early the next morning by someone operating in stealth and I am determined to find this person before he kills someone else. Which means, Mr. Villega, unless you are more forthcoming with information that I can verify elsewhere, a charge of theft from this manufactory will be the least of your worries. Unfortunately, having the debts you do would make it very easy to manipulate you into doing something you wouldn't otherwise."

"You can't prove it was me who took the money!" Villega wailed. "It's easy. Mr. Davis leaves the safe open all day long and he's always being called away from the office. All anybody has to do is wait. You can't prove it was me."

"And the marshal? Mr. Dye is one of your friends," I asked.

"I didn't kill the marshal. Why would I bother? He was about to die anyway, and it was exactly what he deserved, the way he cheated Joe all the time. You might as well ask Mr. Redona what he was doing that night. The marshal cheated him, too, you know."

"And where were you that fateful night?" I asked.

"I had a drink or two at the saloon, then went home to bed." He glared at Mr. Rivers. "I have a job to go to in the mornings."

"Yes, you do," said Mr. Rivers. "But only because I cannot prove that you took money from the safe. However, if anyone else tries to extort money from me to cover one of your gambling debts, then I will be forced to dismiss you. Do you understand?"

"Yes, Mr. Rivers." Chastened, Mr. Villega hung his head.

"Now, please go back to work. We've a mule train that needs loading."

I waited until Mr. Villega had gone back to the manufactory floor.

"Well done, Mr. Rivers," I said with a smile.

He shrugged. "Now all I have to do is convince Mr. Davis to keep the safe closed at all times. Better yet, I think I'll have it moved to my office." He looked at me. "Do you think Mr. Villega killed the marshal after all?"

I looked toward the staircase Mr. Villega had headed down. "I can't say for certain, but I think not."

"I most sincerely hope not," Mr. Rivers said. "Even apart from the scandal if he did, he really is a very good foreman. He's one of the few people in the town who can keep the teamsters in line."

"And that is no small accomplishment," I said.

And with that, Mr. Rivers escorted me to the street. We said our good-byes quite congenially, but I was not well settled by the conversation. Oddly enough, it was not Mr. Villega that concerned me, but young Mr. Rivers. It was understandable that he'd want to avoid a scandal, and keeping on a man of dubious honesty might, indeed, prove well worth it if the man could keep teamsters in line. But at the same time, one could buy the loyalty of someone of less than honest character if one knew that person's terrible secret.

CHAPTER ELEVEN

My fears regarding Mr. Rivers, however, did not deter me from seeking out one other person I did not care to confront, namely Mrs. Hewitt. As I have said, she and I had become friendly since the previous spring, when I had found out her secret that it was she, and not her husband, who ran their successful buggy manufactory. Both of us commiserated fairly frequently on the difficulty of being women doing man's work, the difficulty not being in the work, itself, but in having to deal with men and even women who thought we should not be doing it.

At the manufactory, I was met by Mr. Frank Hill at the door. I asked if Mrs. Hewitt was in and Mr. Hill deferred to his foreman, a large, sturdy fellow named Ellsworth, I think. The foreman went to see if Mrs. Hewitt was receiving and left Mr. Hill to keep me entertained.

"I believe I saw you at the revival Friday past," I said. "You were playing the piano."

"Yes, ma'am," Mr. Hill replied, a little nervously. "It's a great honor to play for the reverend."

"You must know a great many hymns," I said, wondering how I was going to bring up the Yankee hymn.

"I do, indeed, ma'am. I love a good hymn, and my granny taught me a whole lot of them."

"How wonderful for you. Do you have a favorite?"

He sighed. "I do, but I'm not allowed to sing it, as it upsets folks in these parts."

"Oh?"

"Mine eyes have seen the glory." Mr. Hill swelled with the joy of it. "I love that hymn, so full of the Lord meting out his marvelous justice."

"Ah. Yes." I smiled. "I understand what you mean. Sadly, people in the pueblo are more apt to think of General Sherman meting out his justice."

"I know, ma'am. That's why I do not sing it anymore." He smiled weakly.

The foreman returned and admitted me to the main office. He shut the door and I greeted Mrs. Hewitt. She was actually a rather tiny, mousy-looking little thing but she had the heart and temper of an angry lion when she was roused. Given the stresses she endured trying to keep her husband's business afloat without letting anyone know why, she became roused rather frequently. There were many who pitied Mr. Hewitt because of her temper without realizing or considering that Mr. Hewitt's drunkenness was actually the cause of it. It was most unjust.

The office I was in was more of a sitting room, with elegant sofas and an antique writing desk in one corner. Windows overlooked the street below and the infernal noise of the manufactory below us were somewhat muted.

"Mrs. Wilcox, so good of you to stop by," Mrs. Hewitt said, coming forward and gesturing towards a laden tea-tray on a low table. "I've just had these tea and biscuits brought in. Please have a seat."

"Thank you so much, Mrs. Hewitt," I said, availing myself of one of the sofas. "The biscuits look lovely." I took the cup she'd poured me and looked at her. "Thank you. And how are you, dear?"

"Well enough," she said with a small sigh. "And you?"

"Well enough." I smiled. "I saw you at the revival the other evening."

"Oh, yes. I never thought I'd appreciate hellfire and brimstone, but the good Reverend Bennett doesn't spew all that much of it. Better yet, Mr. Hewitt has enjoyed going. I can't tell if it's helping, but he was asking if I thought he could be forgiven yester morning."

"That is a hopeful sign, indeed. Although, it is a difficult habit for men to break."

"Especially one as weak-willed as poor Mr. Hewitt." She shook her head. "You didn't stay long."

"No. I'm afraid I was called away to care for the Gutierrez family. I believe it was a bad case of influenza. We lost one of the children as well as Mrs. Gutierrez."

"Oh, dear. I hope it's not a bad year for that. I was reading the other day that they've found a couple cases of cholera up north, and also typhoid somewhere else."

"I read the same." I smiled, although I was dreading the possibility that we would have outbreaks of either in the pueblo. Both were and are terrible, terrible diseases. "Fortunately, we haven't had any consumption of late, but I don't expect that to last."

Mrs. Hewitt sipped her tea, then smiled at me conspiratorially. "I hear you're on the hunt again."

"I'm afraid so. In fact, that's why I'm here."

"No." Mrs. Hewitt put down her cup.

"I'm not accusing anybody," I said a little icily. "But I must gather information if I am to find Marshal Warren's killer."

"Oh. That's what you're looking for." Mrs. Hewitt smiled.

I looked at her, puzzled. "Of course. There's another killer loose, acting in secret. You know better than most how dangerous that can be."

"I do, indeed." She shuddered at the memory. "So it's true that Marshal Warren wasn't killed by the affray."

"Not directly, no. I'm afraid I can't say more than that."

"No, no, you can't."

I smiled at her as winningly as I could. "And yet, you seemed afraid just now that I'd come to accuse you of something."

"Well, I..." Suddenly, Mrs. Hewitt burst into tears. "It's the red paint. Everyone is looking at me and I haven't done anything. I swear it!"

"I'm not looking at you, nor is anybody else that I've spoken to."

"But they are. They have to be wondering. But there's no paint missing. Of any color."

I sighed. Mrs. Hewitt was painfully conscious of what others said about her, and I was not surprised that I and Mr. Lomax were not the only people in the pueblo who had realized that she had ample quantities of red paint in her stores.

"I really wish you'd leave it alone," Mrs. Hewitt snapped. "I have enough problems, what with getting an insurance claim paid, running a factory. I can't afford a scandal. Not now when Mr. Hewitt might actually be getting better. I have to protect him, you understand."

"I do, but the attacks are getting worse with each one. Besides, there may yet be a connection to Marshal Warren's murder."

Mrs. Hewitt bounced to her feet. "Then let the deputies catch this madman! Please do not look at me or my business. I need you to let it alone!"

Her voice had risen in pitch and volume.

"I'm sorry, Mrs. Hewitt," I said, setting down my cup and standing. "I did not mean to alarm you. I only came to gather information, information that could prove that you had nothing to do with anything and help you to avoid scandal. I shall take my leave now."

I left to the sound of Mrs. Hewitt's moans and sobs, feeling decidedly out of sorts. I could well understand her histrionics, as her position in the pueblo was very precarious. I could even appreciate her tender concern for her husband, never mind how little I thought he deserved it. Weak-minded men such as he were and are the plague of far too many good women. I have never supported the Temperance Movement, firmly believing that prohibiting something only makes it more attractive, especially to the weak-minded (and it certainly seems to be working out that way in these days of Prohibition). However, I am certainly in sympathy with its aim of protecting innocent women and children from the effects of wastrel men who think nothing of wasting themselves away on drink rather than supporting their wives and children. Instead of Prohibition, I think it would be far more effective to provide more opportunities for women to support themselves. Faced with the threat of swiftly losing his beloved wife and all he holds dear, I suspect many a man would suddenly find the strength to turn aside from demon rum. At the very least, a woman would not feel she had no choice but to live with the bum and accept his weaknesses.

That, however, is neither here nor there. I did have a killer to find and it didn't matter how out of sorts I was, I still had to do it. Heaven knows that apart from the few friends I could count on, no one else would be trying. Our police force was too inadequate and they had no understanding of the concept of investigation. But that was, in fact, a rather happy thought, in that I knew that I could and should discuss things with one of those very friends.

I found Deputy Lomax coming out of Mr. Mahoney's saloon chatting amiably with Mr. Judson. Mr. Judson tipped his hat my way and went on toward his bank.

"What was that about?" I asked Mr. Lomax as we ambled along the street.

"Mr. Judson stood me to a lunch," Deputy Lomax said. "He was offering me condolences on not being made City Marshal."

"Have they appointed somebody already?"

"Yes. Sheriff's Deputy Frank Baker."

"I don't believe I know the fellow."

Mr. Lomax offered me his odd little quirked smile. "You will soon enough. He lives out in the Anaheim Colony but wants to move here. Has quite a reputation as a real tough hombre."

"Oh, no," I sighed. "You'd think they'd have learned their lesson with Marshal Warren."

Mr. Lomax shrugged. "This is a pretty tough town."

"Well, for what it's worth, I do think you would have made an excellent City Marshal."

Mr. Lomax chuckled. "The thing is, I didn't necessarily want the job. It's a mite dangerous."

"There is that," I said, nodding. "I have just come from visiting Mrs. Hewitt."

"Really." Mr. Lomax winced and I strongly suspected he'd fallen victim to her temper, as well.

"I'm inclined to agree with you that she is lying about the paint, but there doesn't seem to be any way to prove it. Poor thing. She has plenty of good reasons for lying, if she is, and innocent reasons at that."

"I see. Now, what do we do?"

"I haven't the faintest. It's not as though we can watch every house in the pueblo."

"No. But maybe there's a house or two that would be a more likely target."

I considered. "Well, let's consider those whose homes have already been painted. The first was Marshal Warren, then Councilman Wilson, then Mr. Carson."

"All fine, upstanding members of the community," Mr. Lomax said.

"You're right. And our painter seems to have a grievance with those who appear to be upstanding but, in fact, are not." I frowned in thought. "Actually, I think most of us knew that none of those people were all that upstanding."

Mr. Lomax nodded.

"So, I guess then, we should try to figure out who might be in a similar category," I said.

Mr. Lomax laughed. "Mrs. Wilcox, you are not insensible to just how great a task that might be."

"No. I am not, alas," I said. "I should be a fool not to acknowledge the hold hypocrisy has on much of our citizenry. That being said, there are those whose hypocrisy rises above the normal level to the point where one might take more than the usual umbrage. For example, Reverend Elmwood, who claims to be motivated by Christian charity, but is, in fact, hardly that."

"I don't know him," Mr. Lomax said. He was, in fact, a Morman, of sorts, in that he had practiced, but had since fallen away from the faith of his fathers. "Still, I don't see the painter being the sort who would attack a man of God, even if imperfect."

"That seems likely." I thought. "Mr. Wills appears to be honest. However, I've just recently become aware that he has considerable gambling debts. And when I spoke with him last, he seemed to believe that he would be a target of the painter."

Mr. Lomax's gaze settled on Mr. Judson's bank. "There's also Mr. Judson."

"I would think not," I said with a chuckle. "He genuinely is upstanding, much to the dismay of his fellow councilmen."

"Mr. Wilson is among them," Mr. Lomax pointed out.

"But Mr. Warren was not, and Mr. Carson has not joined that august body, nor does he have any plans to that I've heard." I paused. "You may have heard differently."

"Nope." Mr. Lomax tapped the toe of his boot for a moment. "Why don't we watch Mr. Wills and the rest of the councilmen?"

"That should be manageable," I said. "The good news is that we won't have to wait up all night. It would seem that most of the attacks are happening in the hours just before dawn."

"That makes sense."

"I can watch Mr. Wills' house."

Mr. Lomax shook his head. "I'm afraid, you're not watching anybody tonight or any night, Mrs. Wilcox."

"What do you mean?" I did not mean for it to, but

my ire rose quickly and fiery hot. I was so shocked by Mr. Lomax's pronouncement.

"Mr. Brooks told me how you were accosted last night and by the very man who apparently killed the marshal."

I sniffed. "I have walked the streets of this pueblo time and time again and the first time I am accosted, you want to mew me up like a babe in swaddling clothes."

"No. I want you to stay alive." His hand grabbed my arm as I attempted to stalk off down the street. "I would not be worried, but that there is a killer loose and one who has set his sights on you."

"And how am I to get to my patients?"

"We'll find someone to go with you." Mr. Lomax let go of my arm. "I've already talked to Mr. Ortiz and he doesn't think it's a good idea for you to walk alone, either."

My heart sank utterly. I was very much afraid of the tongue lashing that would be waiting for me at home.

"You spoke with Mr. Ortiz," I said, glumly.

"Am I wrong to be concerned with your well-being?"

"No," I drew myself up with all the authority and hauteur I could manage. "However, I do believe that I am the best judge of what constitutes my well-being."

Mr. Lomax chuckled. "I'm sure Mrs. Ortiz will have plenty to say about that."

Unfortunately, there was no possible way to answer that. So I held my head high and made my way home.

It was worse than I imagined. Sebastiano was not enraged. He was sulking.

"So this is how it is to be," he said when he met me in the yard. "You said we were partners. But now you treat me as a servant who does not deserve to know what his mistress is about.'

"That is not in the least bit fair, Sebastiano."

I blinked back tears. I had not intended to hurt his feelings, but they had plainly been hurt. "Is it not possible that I did not want to worry you so that you could continue your work without interference from me?"

"And what about friendship? Eh? You say we are friends. Do friends keep such secrets from each other? You think I cannot take care of you?"

"I do not care to be taken care of. I am not a babe in arms!"

"No. You are a woman who makes people want to kill her."

"This is only the second time it's happened. And I can't stop. This is important to the pueblo."

"I know. But we work together. It is important to work that way. Otherwise, you get killed. You are my friend. You made me your partner. I don't want you killed."

I sniffed. "I don't want to be killed, Sebastiano. But I don't want to be trailed after as if I were a toddler who can't be trusted to stay out of trouble. Would you like being treated like that?"

Sebastiano stopped, then glared at me. "I'm a man."

Pointing out that I was a full-grown woman would not have helped. As far as most men were concerned back then (and even now, sadly), women were little more than foolish children.

"All the more reason why you would resent someone following you around to protect you. Even if you needed it." I glared right back at him. "For whatever reason."

He muttered something under his breath in Spanish, which I suspect was foul, then glared at me again.

"The next time." He put his finger up to stave off my response. "The next time you start searching for a killer or other outlaw, you will tell me what is going on. And you will keep telling me what is going on."

"Very well," I said, pulling myself up straight.

"And together, as grown-up people, we will decide whether I need reinforcements. Is that fair?"

He sighed. "Yes. That is fair."

The poor thing. He was such a dear friend and one who had the grace to concede that I was a fully intelligent and sensible human being. It may have been all those years when he was my servant, and that during that time, he had come to respect me. But Sebastiano was also a very intelligent man in his own right, and open to new notions and ideas, as was his brother. It's not a very common trait, but it is why we all got on so well together.

If, however, Sebastiano had been hard to face, the delegation that awaited me in the front parlor was no less ready to let me know how badly I had erred in my silence over the events of the night before. Olivia, Magdalena, and Juanita stood with their arms crossed, glaring furiously at me.

The ensuing tirade was loud, in two languages, and came at once from all three women. It is impossible to recount all that was said, but the gist of it was that I had no right to keep secrets from Sebastiano, especially when such secrets could quite easily get me killed, and that I was absolutely to stop walking alone at night, even if there wasn't anybody out there trying to kill me, as the pueblo was dangerous enough. And why did I have to keep making people angry enough at me that they wanted to kill me? It was ridiculous that I didn't have the sense to stay away from such dangerous situations, and that I was no better than a colicky infant.

"I can take care of myself," I protested once I could get a word in.

This, alas, set them off again. After all, I couldn't be trusted to even feed myself, let alone get enough sleep, not to mention the state of my clothes, because it was certain that I had no idea how hard it was to get out bloodstains and brush adobe mud off of skirts, and so forth and so on.

In truth, I must concede that the ladies had the right of it. I was horribly dependent on them for my daily functioning. My mother had taught me how to oversee a household, but because we had been of that particular social class that always had servants and expected to always have them, I did not know how to cook, clean, or sew. Indeed, my beloved mother could not have conceived of a situation where I would need to learn how to do those things. I have since learned the basics, largely because of this lecture. I desperately did not like the idea of being so dependent on others that I could not clean my clothes or prepare a simple meal for myself. I have never actually needed to do so, which is fortunate because I was not interested in the art of housekeeping and, as such, made a terrible student. Juanita, however, seemed particularly pleased by my efforts, possibly because I was much better at sewing than anything else. There isn't that much difference between sewing up a tear in a skirt and suturing a wound closed.

However, for the rest of that afternoon, I dealt with annoyed sniffs and baleful stares. I ate my lunch obediently and was allowed to go to my study and write my journal notes. At supper, we all discussed my need for reinforcements, which I conceded I probably did need, and Enrique announced that Armando's new job would be to accompany me at night and, until this latest hidden killer was caught, during the day, as well. I suppose I should have been more nettled by this latest turn of events, however, I could see that it was born out of their deep caring for me. Furthermore, I probably shouldn't have been walking the streets of the pueblo by myself at night. It was a very dangerous place, with all manner of drunk and disreputable sorts out on the streets. That I hadn't come to some misadventure was perhaps the best sign of intervention from the Divine that there is.

Sebastiano, Enrique and I all went to bed very early that night. I may have been banned from keeping the actual watch that night, but I was going to be awake and ready to hear whatever news came. Mr. Lomax arrived as the clock struck three of the morning. He took the Ortiz brothers with him and I paced in the front parlor. I tried reading. I tried writing in my journal. I even almost hoped for a fight in a saloon or that some woman would go into labor that I might occupy myself while waiting for the sun to come up.

The men came back sometime after six-thirty when the sun was just peeking over the eastern horizon. I heard the dogs barking and went to the door of the adobe. Sebastiano was fastening the gate shut behind himself and Enrique. They looked over at me and shrugged. Nothing had happened.

CHAPTER TWELVE

I could not have conceived of a more aggravating turn of events. According to Enrique, even the Calle de los Negros, where most of the Chinese brothels and opium dens were, had been quiet. Worse yet, no house had been painted. There wasn't the least hint of paint red or otherwise, and nary a shred of paper, let alone one brandishing the sins of the supposed righteous.

Not that one wants trouble, but when one is looking for the source of such trouble, it is immensely frustrating when it suddenly stops for no apparent reason. One doesn't know if it has stopped for good and one can breathe a well-deserved sigh of relief, or whether the troublemaker is merely biding his time and the trouble will erupt again.

Fortunately, a message from Regina arrived shortly after noon-time with some good news. Sing Lee, who owned Lon Yu's contract, had agreed to meet with Regina and me that very afternoon. Enrique was beside himself, not wanting either me or Armando anywhere within breathing distance of Calle de los Negros. And, indeed, it was understandable. Mothers used to frighten their children into good behavior by threatening to send them to that dank alley.

However, I reminded Enrique that Regina would be there, so we would hardly be alone, and shortly thereafter, Armando and I walked off.

There really was very little to distinguish the small street from any other in Los Angeles, except that the houses were built very close together and many of them needed painting. There were a couple of doorways out of which spilled crates of vegetables, presumably for sale, as each small collection of different vegetables had its own sign written in that curious Chinese script. But otherwise, the street was deserted. Regina had met me at the end of the alley and had sent Armando to wait over by the Pico House hotel, which was a few short blocks away.

She looked particularly imposing, even for her, in a midnight blue walking suit and matching hat, with black gloves and parasol. We were admitted to one of the larger houses, which had two floors stacked on top of each other with no porch or turret or any other architectural interest. It was simply a plain box of white clapboard. I was surprised that there weren't any of those curious swooping eaves one sees on Chinese houses but then realized that the Chinese in the pueblo at the time did not care to distinguish or otherwise call attention to themselves. Unfortunately, American sentiments toward the Chinese were decidedly harsh, which was hardly fair. The Chinese, as a people, were no more or less honest than their American counterparts. I had been taught by my mother's excellent example that all people were God's children and equally deserving of respect as such. Mother had been a Transcendentalist, and while I do not know if it was common among her fellows to extend such ideas and respect to Indians, Negroes, and Orientals, my mother most certainly did, and as a result, I did, as well.

The room to which Regina and I were admitted looked decidedly ordinary, with several sofas and small tables scattered about. There were several long painted scrolls hanging from the walls, bearing images, I presumed, from China, along with more of the script running along the vertical edge. There was no other sign that this was a place where Chinese people lived, let alone a rather notorious brothel.

Sing Lee was a slender man who wore the front part of his hair partly shaved and the rest in a long braided queue down his back, as most of the Chinese men did. His robe, however, was an elegant blue silk with gold-colored silk embroidery. He did that odd bobbing bow that was traditional among his people. Regina and I did likewise, although Regina's bow was just barely deep enough to be polite. I could tell she'd dealt with Mr. Sing before. Mr. Sing, for his part, waved us to an empty sofa and smiled just briefly.

"How can I help you ladies?" he asked pleasantly. His command of English was excellent, in spite of the heavy accent.

"We've come for information," Regina said. While she'd wanted me present, we had agreed that she would ask most of the questions. "As you know, Marshal Warren was shot during the affray over your girl and we wonder if there was any other business going on that might have led to the marshal's eventual death."

"What other business is there?" Mr. Sing asked. "She ran away. Marshal Warren caught her. I paid the bounty." He shrugged. "I know you say someone else killed the Marshal in the night, but it was not I."

"We don't know that you would have, Mr. Sing," Regina said with a smile. "I can't imagine doing so would have been all that good for your business. Yet, there was some hint that your girl had help when she escaped the last time, perhaps by a lover?"

Mr. Sing frowned. "It does not matter. I have her now and she will not escape again."

"Or rather, you hope she doesn't," Regina said. "You know as well as I do, Mr. Sing, that once a girl gets a taste of freedom, it's almost impossible to keep her."

"Impossible for you, maybe, but not for me." Mr. Sing smiled, as well.

"Ah, yes. I suppose I could terrify my girls into keeping their place, but I find it doesn't help my business very much. A happy girl is far likelier to satisfy my clients."

"My clients take what they get. They have no

choice."

"They have Ah Chen's place."

Mr. Sing snorted. "Ah Chen has no advantage over me and I will not give him one any more than he will give me an advantage. You run your business as you like, Mrs. Medina. Trust me to run mine."

"Very well, then." Regina rearranged her purse on her lap. "I guess you would not be interested in a lucrative offer for Lon Yu."

"She belongs to me. Her name is Sing Yu."

"Whichever," said Regina.

"She makes good money for me. Why should I give her up?"

"Because she's costing you money by not being available when you've had to beat her for escaping."

"Then why do you want her?"

Regina's smile suddenly resembled that of a serpent. "Let's just say I have a couple clients who want a taste of something unusual. And wouldn't throwing a girl to the barbarians be more frightening to your other girls than simply killing her?"

I could see that caught Mr. Sing's attention, even though he kept his face passive.

"You write offer. I will think about it," he said, finally. "As for Ah Chen, you may want to talk to him about the marshal. He complained often that the marshal was asking for larger and larger bounties."

Regina rose and I with her. "Perhaps I'll find out if he's looking to sell a girl, as well."

As we left, I trembled with utter distaste.

"What a miserable business that was," I grumbled.

"It's about to get worse," Regina said, grimly. "Mr. Sing's house is, by far, a nicer place."

She pointed out Mr. Ah's house, which looked much like Mr. Sing's, although it needed painting badly. But as we approached the door, it opened and Reverend Bennett stepped out. We stared at each other.

"What are you doing here?" I asked, finding my voice at last.

"What are you doing here?" he asked. He looked at Regina.

"I'm going to speak to Mr. Ah, whose house this is, regarding particulars on the murder of Marshal Warren. Mrs. Medina, here, is graciously providing me entée." I held my head up, daring him to question my associations.

"I'm here ministering to the poor unfortunates within," the reverend replied, also pulling himself up. He looked again at Regina, whose eyebrow had quirked up skeptically. The reverend bent forward toward us. "I would not mention such a thing, but you should know that there is an opium den in the back of this establishment. Mr. Ah has lured more than one poor unfortunate into its evil clutches.

"Then turn him in to the law," I said, feeling quite shocked.

Reverend Bennett shrugged. "What good with that do? Someone else will merely come along to take his place. No. If we are to save these poor souls, then we must help them turn away from the evil elixir." He smiled and glanced again at Regina. "Much like you, one sometimes must dance around the demons to save our fellows."

I swallowed. "To be sure."

He nodded and tipped his hat and I nodded back and he left.

I looked at Regina. "That was... Surprising. Should we believe him?"

Regina looked after the reverend thoughtfully. "There is no reason not to."

"Is there an opium den in this house?"

"Oh, yes," said Regina. She pursed her lips, then blinked her eyes. "Nasty stuff, opium. Once you get a taste of it, you can't let it go until you've wasted away to nothing. It's worse than watching the consumption."

I put my hand on her arm. "You know from personal experience, don't you?"

She nodded. "Thomas and I lost a brother to opium.

There was nothing we could do." She looked down at her feet, then back at where the reverend had gone. "The reverend was right about that much. It doesn't do any good to shut the vile places down. My father tried and tried. He'd get the police to shut down one den, then two more would spring up after it. John always found them, too."

It was a rare event for Regina to share anything about her family and background. To this day, I'm not entirely certain where she was raised, her slight accent notwithstanding. Thanks to my native curiosity, I often wanted to find out more about her. But Regina was hardly in a position where it would have been wise of her to be more forthcoming. So I chose not to pry, even as I treasured those rare moments when she did reveal something. Mr. Mahoney found it incredibly difficult to talk about her at all, and he and I were not on terms of sufficient intimacy that it was reasonable to expect him to do so.

She looked at me and smiled wanly. "It's only one of many reasons why I find Mr. Ah a most odious little fellow. So I guess we'd best get this over with."

She knocked on the door and took some minutes convincing the young Chinese man on the other side that it would be in Mr. Ah's best interests to let us in.

Again, the front parlor was not particularly notable, although something about the disheveled state of the sofas made me somewhat leery of sitting on them, but sit we did. Mr. Ah was a small man, wearing his hair in a long queue, and the traditional jacket and full pants, both made of a green and gold silk brocade.

"We've come to ask for particulars regarding the murder of Marshal Warren," Regina said.

"I do not care about Marshal Warren," Mr. Ah said. "He bad man. He make my life very difficult, charge too much to catch runaway."

"Then you had a good reason to kill him," Regina said.

Mr. Ah laughed loudly. "I no kill. Sing Lee, he say I

do. Right?" He laughed. "Sing Lee, he will say anything to get rid of me. But no get rid of."

Regina's eyebrow lifted. "How is that Mr. Sing and you do not get on then? I thought your Company worked together."

"We from different Companies. And he not like that I sell opium to Americans. And that I sell my girls to Americans. He think it cause trouble." Mr. Ah shrugged philosophically. "I don't care. Chinese money is good. American money is good. As long as I make money, I am happy."

"You might not be so happy if you are arrested and hung for the marshal's murder," Regina said severely.

Mr. Ah laughed again. "If Americans going to hang me, they hang me no matter if I am guilty or innocent. I am Chinese. They do not need excuse to hang me. I do not want to be hung, but as long as I am here, there is always chance it will happen. It is like gambling. But I am lucky. I have many businesses here. I sell jewelry, hardware, dry good, laundry."

"Do you sell paint?" I asked suddenly.

"Of course. You want? I get you very good price."

"Do you sell red paint?" I asked.

"To Chinese, but Americans don't want. You want?"

"I don't understand," I said, glancing at Regina.

"Americans not want red paint. Only Chinese."

"There's an American in the pueblo who has been using quite a bit of red paint," I said. "Are you sure you've not sold any to an American? Or perhaps sold it to a Mexican?"

Mr. Ah shrugged. "No. Only Chinese."

"Have you been selling more than usual?"

He shook his head, then looked at me. "Why do you want to know?"

"I suppose you haven't heard about the person painting up houses in the pueblo," Regina said, smiling calmly.

Mr. Ah laughed again. "Oh, that. But I not sell

much red paint this month and only to Chinese." He stopped again. "But I know American with red paint. Mr. Mahoney. Monday, I go to courthouse. On the way back, I see empty buckets behind his saloon. They have red paint in them."

Regina and I kept our faces passive. It seemed very unlikely that Mr. Mahoney was behind the vandalism, although he would have occasion to see our best citizens at their worst. Instead of questioning Mr. Ah further, we chose to leave. I had thought Mr. Ah a rather jovial little imp until I remembered his opium den and how conveniently he had planted the icy glare of suspicion on Mr. Mahoney. I wondered briefly if Mr. Ah knew Mr. Mahoney's and Regina's secret, but couldn't imagine how he would have found out. It certainly was not commonly known. In fact, it was not really known at all. Besides Mr. Mahoney and Regina, I knew of only one other person who knew the two were siblings and that was Angelina. What Mr. Ah had said about Mr. Mahoney and the paint was most confusing and probably a coincidence. Regina, as usual, held her own counsel and I did not care to ask her.

"I shall have to speak with Mr. Mahoney," I said, however, as we reached the end of Calle de los Negros and entered the Plaza.

"Of course, you must." Regina shrank back into the alley a ways. "You go on, darling. I'll watch until you get to the Pico House and Armando."

"It's broad daylight," I said.

"Even more reason for me to stay back." She flicked her fingers at me. "Go on."

I sighed. It seemed Regina had somehow managed to join the conspiracy to keep me safe. I couldn't fault her and decided that I should be grateful for her caring, even as it irked me that I needed such watching.

As I thought about it, it really wasn't that my friends thought I was incapable of taking care of myself, it was that there was a madman looking to harm me. And thus, if I were to be annoyed by having to keep

Armando at my side and otherwise be cautious about where and how I went about the pueblo, my ire should be directed at the madman and not my dear friends who only cared to see me live a long and healthy life, which, thankfully, I have. Thus resolved, I found Armando talking to his cousin Ramon in the restaurant's foyer.

We made our way to the back of the saloon. If there had been buckets of paint there, they were gone, although I did see several drops and one solid smear that attested to their former presence. I was not surprised. Mr. Mahoney did like to keep a clean saloon and would have gotten rid of the buckets, even had their presence not been so incriminating. Indeed, it seemed very unlikely that he would have left them there if he were the vandal, something I had a great deal of trouble getting him to understand when I asked about them.

"I didn't do anything!" he exclaimed for the third or fourth time as he tried to pace in his tiny office.

"I know. You would not have left the buckets right there behind your saloon," I said, for the third time, at least. "I promise you, I understand that."

"Then what makes you so certain they were there? They're not there now."

"No, but when I looked, I saw drops and a few smears of paint. Mr. Mahoney, will you please sit down and see sense? I'm not making an accusation of any kind, nor do I believe you are the vandal. However, to find the vandal, I need to know when those buckets first ended up behind your saloon and what happened to them."

"I burnt them," he said quickly. He looked at me. "I burnt them as soon as I saw them. Mrs. Wilcox, I can't afford the least scandal. You know that. I have my girls to think of."

"I do know, Mr. Mahoney. But those buckets could have led us to the vandal. Do you remember seeing any mark or indication of where they came from?"

He shook his head. "They were just buckets, like

any other."

"How many of them were there?"

"Four of them."

"When did you find them?"

"Monday afternoon."

That was just after the vandal had attacked the Carson home.

I thought it over. "Can you think of anybody who has something against you?"

"Plenty of people." He shook his head miserably. "Don't you think I haven't been asking myself the same thing? Who is it out to ruin my good name? What have I done to deserve this?"

"Probably not much of anything," I said as soothingly as I could. "What about Ah Chen? He said he saw the buckets when he went to the courthouse."

"Why would a blasted Chinaman give me more than a second thought?" He shook his head. "I treat them decently, not as some around here. I don't kick them. I can't let them have a drink at the bar, of course, but they can't get a drink anywhere else in town, either. Why single me out? It doesn't make sense."

I looked toward the back of the house, thinking. "But it does make sense if you're looking for a quick place to hide something. The alley behind your saloon is quite dark at night. It's entirely possible that the vandal has nothing against you personally and may not even know that it was your saloon that he'd hidden the buckets behind."

Sadly, that did not seem to make Mr. Mahoney feel better. It was not surprising. After all, it was as likely that the vandal saw Mr. Mahoney as yet another target as it was that mere chance had resulted in the buckets being where they were.

I got up and Mr. Mahoney bounced to his feet with me. "I'd best be on my way, then," I said. "And, if you find any more buckets, please feel free to hide them, but do make sure I see them before you burn them. We might find something useful."

"Aye, Mrs. Wilcox." Mr. Mahoney nodded at me, then sighed. "I want you to know that I truly appreciate your help in this matter. You're very good to us."

"You're a very good customer," I said, smiling, even as I hoped he wouldn't get any more fulsome.

There is often a tendency among those of the Irish race to get sentimental in the most unseemly ways. Nor have I ever been very good at dealing with fulsome gratitude. I hurried from the office and back to the alley. Once there, I paused to look around. It was well within reach of the Carson home. Armando was waiting for me but chose not to say anything.

It was still possible that Mr. Mahoney was the vandal. I tried to remember if I'd ever heard him sing the Battle Hymn of the Republic. While I didn't know where exactly he and Regina had been raised, I did have good reason to believe it was solidly within the Northern states, rather than the South. Still, he was my friend, or at least, I considered him such, and he appeared to reciprocate the sentiment. I knew from bitter experience not to let friendship cloud my thinking, however, and so was left in considerable turmoil as I left the alley behind the saloon.

I did realize that I had one other person to speak to: Mrs. Warren. I did want to confirm that the vandal, at any rate, was abroad in the early hours right before dawn, rather than later at night. It would make watching for him much easier.

She was at home and chose to receive me, but was still wearing her widow's black. She greeted me most cordially, as well. We were seated in her front parlor and tea with biscuits and jam were served.

"It is so good of you to come by and visit," Mrs. Warren said. "I'm glad to be free of my social obligations, but it does make it almost too easy to brood about..."

Her eyes filled, but the tears did not spill over.

"I know," I said simply. I had been driven near to distraction during my year of mourning for my husband, mostly because I hadn't been mourning his passing all that deeply.

"It's good to talk to somebody who has also known this loss," Mrs. Warren said.

"I'm sure it is." I took a sip of my tea, desperately hoping I was not going to be subjected to an extended discussion of mourning and lost husbands.

Fortunately, Mrs. Warren was made of sterner stuff. She spoke briefly of how much she missed the marshal, then smiled.

"The good news is that I am left well off. Our girls will not want for anything. Mr. Warren did have his affairs in order, which is a great blessing, indeed."

"It is very much a blessing," I said, my sigh escaping me in spite of myself. Mr. Wilcox's affairs had been in no order beyond a letter promising me all his goods should he die before me. That letter, and the fact that he had no relatives beyond those on the other side of the continent, saved my life. I put my cup down. "Mrs. Warren, as much as I do not want to increase your grief, you did ask me to find out who killed your husband and why."

"And there was that terrible attack on the house," she added.

"There is some good news about that. It would appear that the vandalism visited upon your house and your husband's death are probably not related. I had a very uncomfortable encounter with someone who claimed to be behind the murder and he did not mention a word about the vandalism. Based on the later attacks, it would seem that he would have done so."

"But what did the killer say to you?" Mrs. Warren asked, her face going a bit pale.

"He seemed to feel more enmity toward me rather than you, which is also good news for you. That does not mean he must not be caught, but it should ease your mind somewhat."

"As much as it can be," Mrs. Warren said, again blinking her eyes. "Mrs. Wilcox, you are so kind to take this on. And so brave, too."

"That's very kind of you to say so, Mrs. Warren," I said, hoping to forestall the fulsomeness. "However, I need to ask you more about the night your husband died. Do you remember what time it was when you last saw him alive?"

"Oh, yes. It was just after a quarter after two. The clock in our bedroom had chimed, and I heard it from the girls' room, where I was, so I thought I would check on him. He was breathing well and did not have much of a fever at all."

"Did you awaken again at all that night?"

"Oh, several times, but I went right back to sleep each time." She frowned suddenly. "There was one time, perhaps around half past four, when I thought I heard something, but there was nothing more, so I went back to sleep."

I nodded. "That would make sense. The day before the funeral, you told me that someone seemed to be listening in at the windows and sneaking around the house."

"Yes. That's stopped, thank the heavens."

"But the night after the funeral, did you awaken, think you heard something, then go back to sleep?"

She thought for a moment, then her eyes grew wide. "Yes! I thought I heard some tapping, but then the clock chimed four and I didn't hear anything after that." She sighed. "I have not been sleeping well. I keep waking up all night long."

"That is, sadly, quite normal," I told her. "You'll eventually start to sleep better. When I can't say. It seems to vary from widow to widow."

She smiled softly. "Still, you are kind to reassure me, Mrs. Wilcox."

"You're very welcome, Mrs. Warren. I appreciate you taking the time to speak with me."

"Please feel free to visit at any time. It helps with the tedium."

"I'm sure it does."

I left as quickly as I could do so and still be polite. But I still had to admire her staunch attitude in the face of great grief, and I do confess that I rather liked her and we eventually became good friends.

In the meantime, however, I wanted to get back to the rancho before supper time. Olivia was still prone to sniffing and I did not want to worry her. I did get a lovely supper with the entire household in recompense and we had a very fine evening, although we went to bed early. Not only were Sebastiano and Enrique meeting Mr. Lomax to watch for the vandal, but we'd added Hernan and his cousins and Rodolfo to the team. I got up with them and saw them off.

They returned around dawn, not having seen a thing. I, however, was pondering a message that had been delivered shortly after the men had left. I'd heard the dogs barking and went out and found it on my doorstep, even as I saw a shadowy figure running off into the night.

CHAPTER THIRTEEN

As soon as Wang Fu and the Wei brothers arrived for work that morning, I pulled Mr. Wang aside.

"Yes, Mrs. Wilcox," he said quietly.

I read aloud to him the note I'd received. "My brother says that you can help me. This life is too terrible and I long for release. If I do not receive aid soon, I fear I will take the only release left open for me. If you can help, send for my brother. I must escape. Signed, Lon Yu."

Mr. Wang's eyebrow lifted. "We must help her."

"Of course, we must help her. But how to hide her so that Sing Lee does not find her again is what I need to know."

"Mr. Sing will claim she stole something then swear out a warrant," Mr. Wang said. He shook his head. "It will not be easy."

"She has a lover in the pueblo, an American."

"Yes. I do not know who he is."

"We must find out." I looked at Mr. Wang. "I would imagine a woman at your home would stand out quite a bit."

"What do you mean?"

I paced the room in irritation. "There are no Chinese women in the pueblo except for the prostitutes. If Miss Lon came to stay at your home, people would notice, wouldn't they?"

"Mrs. Wilcox, that is not kind," said Mr. Wang, looking rather annoyed with me. "You assume that because the only Chinese women you see are prostitutes that they are the only Chinese women here. But there are honorable women here, properly married. There is woman who works in the wash house with her husband where I live. That is why we go home at night instead of eat here at the rancho. We go to live with proper Chinese family."

I felt my face growing hot. "Mr. Wang, I owe you a great apology. I should have asked."

He shrugged. "Lee Ma is good woman. She would hide Lon Yu, but she cannot. Reach of Sing Lee is very long and even though wives are kept at home, there is little the Companies do not know. But you should be able to hide Lon Yu here for a while. Until her lover can take her home."

"If we can find her lover," I growled. I looked at him. "Thank you, Mr. Wang. I see that I still need to learn a great deal about your people."

He smiled. "But you are learning. That is better than most Americans."

"Thank you, Mr. Wang."

He bowed, then ambled his way back to the fields or the herb garden, I do not remember which.

It was too much. I had enough to worry about, what with trying to find Marshal Warren's killer, and then the vandal currently terrorizing the pueblo. I only hoped that everyone else would find a way to stay well and whole for the time being.

I did not have time to brood on this, however. A young Chinese boy arrived at the adobe, begging me to follow him to his master's home, which it turned out had become the site of the next vandal attack. It also turned out to be the home of Robert Gaines, father of the young Lavina Gaines, who'd been introduced to me by Councilman Wilson at the opening of the race track. Mr. Gaines, a tall man with a florid complexion and angry mien, was pacing about front parlor. He was a particularly successful land agent in the pueblo and had amassed considerable holdings of his own, in addition.

"This is an outrage!" he declared quite forcefully. "An outrage, I tell you!"

His daughter, Miss Gaines, quite gently handed me the all-too-familiar piece of brown paper. This time it took issue with Mr. Gaines' greed, in the form of his miserly behavior toward his clerks, and with his wrath, in his unkind and miserly treatment of his only daughter, Lavina. I knew I'd recognized her name when Mr. Wilson had presented her to me, and now, I remembered how. In the morning newspaper, there had been a notice for more than a month or two proclaiming that Mr. Gaines would no longer pay for any debts against his credit incurred by Miss Gaines. I had suspected from the first that there had been a lawyer behind the notice. I never did find out one way or another. What did seem clear was that there was someone in the pueblo who had taken umbrage over the public notice. Miss Gaines, herself, stood modestly by.

"I am not a miser!" Mr. Gaines proclaimed loudly. "I am careful with my money, as well I should be. So what if I expect an honest day's work from my clerks? Any reasonable man would."

I held my tongue, especially as I did not know what Mr. Gaines considered an honest day's work, although I did not doubt his clerks would not agree with their employer's definition of such. I also found it odd that he did not take umbrage at being taken to task for his treatment of his daughter.

Their home, like most other homes of the well-to-do in the pueblo, was white clapboard, with two stories and all manner of gingerbread trim over the front porch and dripping from the upstairs windows. The red paint had been generously splattered over the porch and front windows, none of which, by the way, were broken.

"Did you hear anything in the early morning hours, before dawn?" I asked.

"Of course not!" Mr. Gaines snarled. "I am a good Christian man. I am in bed at that hour, sleeping the sleep of the godly."

"Did you wake at all?" I asked.

He turned on me. "Did you not hear me? I slept the sleep of the righteous. I always do."

"I did hear you, Mr. Gaines," I said quietly. "But just because your sleep was not disturbed by your conscience does not mean that it was not disturbed by something you heard outside your house. If it was, it might be critical to finding who it was that did this thing."

Mr. Gaines harrumphed and chose not to answer.

"Mrs. Wilcox," Miss Gaines said softly. "I did hear something this morning. It could have been the person who vandalized the house. There was a tapping sound."

"Do you remember what time?"

"It was in the hours before dawn," she said, shaking her head. "I cannot be more specific. I heard the clock chiming the quarter hour shortly after I heard the tapping, but did not know which hour it was."

Mr. Gaines coughed, then pulled out his handkerchief and blew his nose quite loudly.

"And what do you intend to do about this?" he demanded of me.

"We will continue watching," I said. "However, we cannot watch every house in the pueblo and can only make guesses as to who is doing this. Do you know of anybody who would be taking umbrage over your treatment of your clerks?"

"I treat my clerks perfectly well."

I offered a smile I did not feel. "I'm sure you do. However, as clerks sometimes will, they might not agree. I wondered if there were anyone who could have heard them complaining about your so-called miserly habits?"

Miss Gaines smiled again. "Papa, isn't there a saloon where your clerks like to go of an evening? Perhaps they met someone there."

"I do not encourage the practice of drinking in saloons," Mr. Gaines said. "It is a licentious practice and should be banned."

"Then there is little that I hope to discover here," I replied.

Miss Gaines showed me out.

"I will ask some of Papa's clerks about where they spend their time," she told me quietly before letting me out the back door, the front still being impassible.

"That's very kind of you, Miss Gaines," I said. "I truly appreciate it."

I left feeling more than somewhat overwhelmed. It did seem possible that clerks and other employees of fine, upstanding citizens that had been targeted had, indeed, been complaining about their lot and that the vandal had chanced to hear. But that meant finding them all, asking where all of them had been and their habits regarding complaining about their employers and then hoping to find a common thread among the complaints that would lead to the vandal. I had a more important and more critical venture, namely searching out Marshal Warren's killer.

Armando had the buggy ready and I climbed in. Yet we had no sooner turned into the yard at my rancho when I discovered that I had another summons awaiting me, this time from Mrs. Judson. I sighed but directed Armando to drive me to the Judson home forthwith.

Mrs. Judson was an average-sized woman with gray hair whose pink skin was complemented by the yellow gowns she almost always wore. She was wearing a poplin day dress that morning. With Armando waiting on the front porch, we settled ourselves in her large front parlor with tea, jam, and biscuits.

"I wouldn't wish you to think that I am accusing you," she began slowly. "However, this terrible vandalism has frightened quite a few people."

"I don't doubt it," I said. "The deputies have been looking for the vandal, but it's not easy, and we can't watch every house in the pueblo."

"To be sure," Mrs. Judson said. "But I have some

information that might help you. It seems as though the vandal might be a Yankee."

"So I've been told." I looked at her, then sipped my tea. "And what is your information based upon?"

"Last night, one of Mr. Gaines's neighbors heard someone whistling that song. You know the one, that dreadful Yankee one. It was in the early hours before dawn. She came to me immediately."

I sighed. Now, it looked as though I was going to have to speak to all the neighbors around the houses that had been attacked about the vandalism, and I had a killer to find.

"I know you come from Boston," Mrs. Judson said, somewhat hesitantly. "Perhaps you know the person responsible."

"I do not know every Yankee in the pueblo," I said, trying not to sound as annoyed as I felt. "We've already spoken with Reverend Bennett and Reverend Elmwood. There are probably others. You know as well as I do how often people come and go in these parts. It's impossible to say who it might be simply because we hear someone singing The Battle Hymn. Our current course is to watch those we think might be targets. In fact, there were several people watching last night. It couldn't be helped that the vandal targeted someone we did not think of."

"That would be difficult." Mrs. Judson frowned. "I've heard that the vandal posts a list of sins on each house."

"Yes. It seems he is taking umbrage with those who appear to be upstanding citizens, yet are cheating others and otherwise behaving in an unbecoming manner." I smiled at her. "Which is why we do not expect your home to draw the vandal's attention."

Mrs. Judson drew herself up, clearly pleased. "I should hope not. Mr. Judson's rectitude is widely known. Perhaps you should look at what else the vandal's victims had in common. Perhaps there is a singular sin among them."

"I don't believe there is," I replied, even as my mind raced through the possibilities.

There was not much else to be said, although we did chat briefly about other goings on, including the new committee to erect a monument to General Lee. It did not surprise me that Mrs. Judson was leading it. I was quite relieved when she did not ask me to join.

However, she had put another idea into my head, that I should be looking at what the victims had in common besides being less upstanding than we had previously thought. We now had four. Marshal Warren seemed to be something of an anomaly, in that he was a public servant and the others were all businessmen. In addition, his home had been attacked after his death. The others were clearly all living.

There was only one thing to do, consult Angelina. Her talent for making lists would be indispensable. The only problem was that, when I arrived, Angelina had three bodies to prepare, including a young child who'd died in an accident the day before and whose viewing was that night. I agreed that the matter of the vandal was not so terribly urgent and went off to find Deputy Lomax.

He found me, as it turned out, and asked me to come to the marshal's office and jail. Armando was sent off at the deputy's behest, as it was pointed out that Mr. Lomax was perfectly capable of keeping an eye on me. The office was a long room divided by a counter that ran almost the length of it. Behind the counter were a couple of desks, including what had been the marshal's desk. It looked untouched. At the back wall, also behind the counter, was the door to the jail cells.

"I'm expecting Joe Dye to come by shortly," Mr. Lomax explained to me once we were alone. "That's why I didn't want your buggy hitched anywhere around here. I can hide you in the jail and I can ask Mr. Dye where he was the night the marshal was killed."

"But will we be able to trust his answer?" I asked. "He's not likely to say he was at the marshal's house suffocating him."

"Nor is a pillow Joe's way of dealing with things," Mr. Lomax said. "If it were to hand, I wouldn't put it past him, but Joe's far more likely to draw a gun or use his fists or a club."

I thought of the cane in Mr. Dye's hand. "I dare say you're right, Mr. Lomax."

Mr. Lomax looked out the window. "I don't see him yet."

"I was speaking with Mrs. Judson earlier," I said. "She gave me an idea about the vandal. Perhaps we should be looking at what the four victims had in common."

Mr. Lomax nodded, then waved me toward the jail cells. "He's coming."

I slid through the door to the cells and pressed my back against the wall. Mr. Lomax left the door ajar, letting it cover me. I could hear everything that was said in the office. I just hoped that Deputy Dye would not find cause to go back to the cells.

I heard the deputy enter, then expectorate into the spitoon near the door.

"Hello, Walt," he said to Mr. Lomax. He sounded reasonably cheerful, although I'd seen how fast that could change. "Good of you to get the council to give me my back pay."

"We don't want you begging in the streets," Mr. Lomax said. "You might be hearing that they were not happy about it, though."

The spitoon echoed again with another hit. "I could not care less about them."

"Some of them think you didn't spend the night in jail like you were supposed to."

Mr. Dye laughed. "I didn't. I was out celebrating."
"Where?"

"Uribe's place. You know the big saloon where Arturo Sedonez is barkeep. A couple of the fellows had to drag me to my rooms." Dye laughed again. "I was lucky I could get to the examination the next day."

"Do you know who posted your bail?"

"Jim Judson."

I tried not to gasp. Why would Mr. Judson have paid Mr. Dye's bail? It was a tremendous amount of money to risk for someone he wanted to see convicted or otherwise away from the pueblo.

"Don't worry," Mr. Dye continued. He explained in particularly foul language(which I would not repeat even if I could recall his exact wording), that Mr. Judson had his own interests in Mr. Dye's affairs such that Mr. Dye was completely under his control. "Well, I'd best be ambling on. Thanks again, Walt."

Mr. Lomax waited until he was sure Mr. Dye was gone, then came and pulled me from behind the jail door.

"Mr. Judson?" I gasped again.

Mr. Lomax. "Had to be somebody with money. Wonder what his hold on Mr. Dye is."

"I shall have to find out," I said with a sigh. "I guess we'll have to leave looking at the vandalism victims more closely until later."

"Mrs. Wilcox, are you going to be talking to Mr. Redona again?"

"Quite probably. Why?"

Mr. Lomax frowned. "I talked to him the other day. I just don't think he killed the marshal. He was angry, but he's not the sort of fellow to fly off the handle. Besides, even with the marshal wounded, it would have taken some strength to have smothered him and Mr. Redona had that bad arm."

"That is an interesting point," I said. "Very well. Why don't you walk with me to Mr. Judson's bank? I do have some business to transact, in any case. We can send someone to fetch Armando and the buggy, and then I will speak to Mr. Redona."

We found a young urchin waiting at the marketplace, which was on the other side of the jail. I gave him a couple pennies and a note and he scampered off.

"I'm curious," I began as we walked toward the bank. "What house did you watch last night?"

"Mr. Wills." Mr. Lomax said. "Actually, he does not have his own house, but rooms at a place near his office."

"Were there any other houses under observation?"

"About five, including the Judson place. We don't have that many men and it was a busy night last night."

"I know. I visited Angelina earlier."

Mr. Lomax nodded. "That was the knife fight on Bath Street. We had about five men die. The Suttons took two of them."

"I didn't see anybody in the jail."

"According to the witnesses, the main parties were all dead."

I nodded. There was little reason to question the event. Heaven knows, it was quite common in the pueblo, although we didn't usually have so many dead all from a single event.

At the bank, Mr. Lomax saw me inside then left to do whatever else it was he needed to do. Mr. Judson agreed to see me readily and I was quickly escorted into his office and offered a seat in front of the impressive oak desk. We quickly transacted my business and Mr. Judson seemed quite ready to dismiss me when I paused.

"Mr. Judson, I do have a question or two for you," I said slowly. "Regarding the marshal's murder, I mean."

"Oh?" His eyebrows lifted, but he did not seem alarmed.

"I have just learned that you were the one who posted Mr. Dye's bail," I said. "This seems very much at odds with your stated aim when you came to visit last week, of finding a way to get rid of Mr. Dye. I would have thought you'd want him to stay in jail."

"It would have been preferable," Mr. Judson said, shifting uncomfortably in his seat. He looked at me closely. "You are probably one of the few here in town that would understand. I could not, in justice, allow Mr. Dye to stay in jail. However guilty he was of initiating the affray, it was very clear that the marshal drew first. The others, they were ready to string Mr. Dye up without benefit of trial." Mr. Judson winced and sighed. "We've seen far too many lynchings around here. If we are to suspend the most basic tenets of our justice system even for the most odious, then we shall soon be suspending them for all and sundry. That is not civilization, something we are desperately in need of around here. You heard about the knife fight on Bath Street last night?"

"Just now, yes."

"As I understand it, a couple negroes were walking down the street, mostly minding their own business, when they stumbled onto a fight between some ranch hands. They pulled knives, the ranch hands pulled knives, and soon the negroes and five others are dead."

"I thought only five men had died," I said, trying to remember if the two bodies in Mrs. Sutton's preparation room had been negroes or not.

"Yes, five men," Mr. Judson said, looking at me as if I were being purposefully obtuse.

That's when I realized he was not counting the two negro men among the dead. It wasn't surprising, but it seemed rather harsh.

"That's quite terrible."

"Something must be done," Mr. Judson said. "Marshal Warren may have had his faults, but he knew how to put down a fight. I have advocated for adding more men to the police force here, but I fear my colleagues are more concerned about whether we can collect enough taxes to pay them first. I suppose that it is a matter of being fiscally responsible. However, I would think we could find a way to raise the money. We found enough when we needed to buy a new safe for the city funds."

"Why would you buy a new safe?"

Mr. Judson snorted his disdain. "Because the other one wasn't very secure." He shuddered. "Imagine having a safe that anyone can break into."

"Were you one of Marshal Warren's supporters?" I asked.

"Not really. I couldn't abide the man, actually. Couldn't trust his temper. The only person who was worse was Mr. Dye."

"Which makes it all the more surprising that you would risk two thousand dollars on Mr. Dye's bail," I said.

Mr. Judson chortled. "It wasn't much of a risk, and I am the only person who could have done it. You see, I hold the notes on Mr. Dye's land in Santa Barbara. There's an oil seepage near there and I believe he has hopes of drilling for more."

"But I've heard California oil does not make good kerosene."

"Tar is still very useful. And I think we'll find a way to distill the stuff into something at least as good as kerosene. There are quite a few fellows working on the problem, you know."

"I didn't, actually." I smiled. "This is all very interesting. So, I guess you've added the bail money to Mr. Dye's loan."

"I have, indeed. Mr. Dye may be a hothead, and his temper is not to be trusted, but he's a reasonably astute businessman. I am not worried about getting my money back."

"But if he fears conviction, perhaps he'll be more worried about being hung than saving his land interests."

Mr. Judson harrumphed. "Mrs. Wilcox, I, eh, have no worries about him being acquitted. You are looking for the true killer and even if we let the impression continue that Mr. Dye did kill the marshal, it was very clearly a case of self-defense."

Mr. Judson looked somewhat perturbed, nonetheless. I suspected that he had some inkling that justice for Mr. Dye was being aided by some less than honorable means. It was not something he would have countenanced easily.

However, I had finished my business and I could not find some way to ask Mr. Judson if he'd been involved in the marshal's actual murder, so I made my goodbyes and left the bank. Armando was waiting with the buggy.

We made our way to the Redona residence and I was happy to find Mr. Redona in. He was still on leave from his duties as deputy, thanks to his injured arm. I took a few moments to look at it. It was healing well enough, but it would be a few more weeks before he would be able to use it normally.

He sighed deeply when he heard me say that. "A few more weeks? How am I going to keep my family?"

"You have a farm, do you not?" I asked.

"Yes. Fifty acres."

"Well, we're coming on for winter and you've presumably had a good harvest, as the rest of us have had. I would imagine that you'll manage."

"There's work to be done on the farm, still."

"Some of which you'll have to do one-handed for the time being," I said.

He knew I was right. True, most of the deputies had other jobs or farms and used the money they made as deputies to fill out otherwise meager incomes. So I could understand Mr. Redona's concerns. Still, he and his wife would not starve while his arm healed.

"I am actually here to ask you again about the day the marshal was killed," I said, then continued quickly as he began to protest. "I've been told you were angry with the marshal about him not giving you your share of the bounties."

"We were out all night chasing that China girl," Redona grumbled. "I rode all the way down to Wilmington to track her, and then to Anaheim. I brought in the man she'd hired to help her, and the Marshal questioned him that Saturday. That's how we found out she was in San Buenaventura. We left Saturday afternoon right away and got to San Buenaventura on

Sunday. We got the girl and rode straight home. The marshal said he was going to split the bounty with me."

"When did he say that?"

Mr. Redona frowned. "On the way back from San Buenaventura. He was laughing a lot, too. Said he was going to get a really big bounty once he got back to the pueblo."

"Did he say who he was after?"

"No. Just that no one would believe it and he was going to have to be careful to get the fellow."

"I wonder if it could have been Mr. Dye."

That made Mr. Redona laugh. "Would you be surprised to find that Joe Dye had a bounty on him?"

"No. You're right. No one would be surprised at that." I thought it over. "So, it would appear that the marshal saw something in San Buenaventura that made him believe that he would be able to collect a sizable bounty by catching someone here in Los Angeles, someone who would not be expected to have a bounty on his head."

"Yes..." Mr. Redona's eye grew wide as he recollected. "He must have seen something in the sheriff's office, there. They'd held the girl for us. The marshal was looking at a bunch of notices and started laughing."

"That's very interesting, Mr. Redona. Now, the night he died..."

"I didn't do it, Mrs. Wilcox," he said quickly.

"I can't prove you did. However, you were in the house when he presumably died and you were angry with him."

"But I didn't do it. He must have been stabbed or poisoned because I didn't hear anything, either. And if he was stabbed, I couldn't have done it." He raised his injured arm. "This is my knife hand."

"Someone else has made that point," I replied. "I pray you'll forgive me for asking, but I must if I am to find who did this terrible thing. Now, did you awaken at all after you fell asleep, maybe thought you heard something and dismissed it?"

He shook his head sadly. "Not at all. I'd gotten quite a lot of whiskey."

"Doc MacKenzie is rather popular that way," I said with a sigh.

There seemed little more to be gained, and I left the house shortly after.

CHAPTER FOURTEEN

Armando took me back to the rancho, where I had high hopes of at least getting some dinner. It was later in the afternoon, but not that late. Olivia had some soup ready for me and served me with a minimum of grumbling about the hour. I ate two bowls to appease her.

After that, I went to find Sebastiano and Enrique to ask whose houses had been watched the night before. None of them had been anywhere near the Gaines house. I retreated to my study to write down the names of all who had been victims and everything I knew about them to try to find some common thread. I couldn't find one.

Shortly before supper, I received a curious visit from Mr. Brooks, who asked me to come to his sister's house around seven o'clock. I hoped Mrs. Lawrence and the new baby were well, which Mr. Brooks assured me they were, and he agreed to eat supper with us, then bring me to the house and back home. I suggested that Armando get a good nap after dinner just in case someone needed me in the night.

I was surprised to find Lon Cao waiting for me in the front parlor of the Lawrence home. Mrs. Lawrence was resting in her usual chair and the baby in a cradle next to it.

"You know Mr. Lon," Mr. Brooks said, nervously.

"Yes, we've met." I looked at Mr. Brooks and Mrs. Lawrence. "How do you know Mr. Lon?"

Mr. Brooks face went deep red and he swallowed.

"His sister, Lon Yu, is my fiancée."

My eyes opened wide. "How on earth did that happen?"

"It's all very honorable," Mrs. Lawrence said quietly.

"Lon Cao and I are friends," Mr. Brooks said. "Have been for years. We knew each other as children. My sister and I were brought up in China. Our parents were missionaries. When Lon Cao wanted to leave China, he brought his sister here because he knew we were here. That's how I got to know Lon Yu. It broke my heart when Sing Lee kidnapped her."

"And yet you call her your fiancée," I said.

"We'll get as married as we can be," Mr. Brooks said fiercely. "I know it's not proper to marry a Chinawoman. But you don't know Lon Yu. She's the bravest, smartest, most wonderful girl."

Mr. Lon spoke up. "The problem is, we must get her far enough away before Sing Lee can put a bounty on her and get the American police to look for her."

"But I can't leave here," Mr. Brooks said, his eyes filling. "My sister and her family need me."

"Bobby, how many times do I have to tell you? We'll manage." Mrs. Lawrence smiled. She looked a little wan, but reasonably fit considering she'd given birth only three nights before.

"That's what happened the last time Lon Yu escaped," Mr. Lon said. "I helped her, but we had no protection from Sing Lee and the American police."

"I was supposed to be that protection," Mr. Brooks said, looking miserable.

"It is very honorable that you take care of your family," Mr. Lon said. "Lon Yu may be my sister, but she is only a girl. She understands that your family must come first."

Mr. Brooks knelt down next to his sister. "Delia, I promised Ma and Pa that I would take care of you, no matter what."

"You will best take care of me by being happy,"

Mrs. Lawrence said. "You can always send me money as you get it. Besides, the children are getting old enough to help out. We don't need you nearly as much as you think."

Mr. Brooks got up and looked at me. "I'm not afraid of having a Chinese wife. I just can't stay here with her. Too many people know me. If we go someplace new, like up north, folks will just think she's my servant or concubine. I can even take Lon Cao with me."

"I see," I said. "I presume I'm here because you need my help."

"We're pretty sure we can get Lon Yu out of her house during the day," Mr. Brooks said. "Lon Cao has a meeting with Sing Lee. I can get Lon Yu out of the window while they're having their meeting."

"The other girls are willing to help," said Lon Cao. "But we need a place to hide until we can get away during the night."

"I see. Are you hoping to hide her at my rancho?"

"You did offer help," Lon Cao said.

"I did, at that," I sighed. "Very well, then. When do you propose to do this?"

"Tomorrow afternoon." Mr. Brooks said.

I looked over at Mrs. Lawrence. There were some questions I wanted to ask her brother but I did not want to do so in front of her. Instead, I examined her and the baby, found both were well, and Mr. Brooks took me back home.

"How are you going to get up north?" I asked as we walked.

"I've got a couple horses," Mr. Brooks said. He gave me another pained look. "I know she says I shouldn't, but I am really worried about my sister and her family."

"Rest assured, Mr. Brooks, I will be there to help them."

"Mr. Lomax said the same thing. I mean, he doesn't know about Lon Yu, but I told him I wanted to go away to be married and he was all for it."

"That's good." We were walking onto Alameda

Street and I shuddered as I remembered the man who had accosted me. "Mr. Brooks, the man you helped rescue me from, he never actually said that he had killed the marshal. Only that he wanted me to stop looking for the true killer, because otherwise he could not stay here. Now, I took that to mean that he had killed the marshal. But it occurs to me now that it is possible there might be some other meaning and that you did have a very good opportunity to have killed the marshal yourself."

"No!" Mr. Brooks gasped and turned pale in the flickering light of the street lamps. "I swear, Mrs. Wilcox, I didn't harm him. I did not touch a hair on his head. I wanted to. He was riding me about Lon Yu and unnatural alliances. And him married to a Mexican."

"He knew about your affection for Lon Yu?"

Mr. Brooks shrugged. "He knew everything about everybody. He could be a real sharp one that way though he mostly didn't care. The only reason he was riding me was he wanted me to toughen up. I mean, I can draw as fast as anyone, and I can be tough when I need to be. I just don't like acting so tough, if you know what I mean." His face fell and he began blinking back tears. "I thought about giving him some extra laudanum. I really did, but I didn't do it. It wouldn't be right to. I hope that's not how he really died."

"He didn't, Mr. Brooks," I said softly. "I'm sorry to have upset you. I merely have to be sure. He didn't say anything about another bounty he hoped to collect did he?"

"No. Just rode me about Lon Yu and being weak."

I nodded and we went on along the street. I tried to think about anything except the next day and the marshal's killer and vandals and red paint, and while I did not succeed, I did get an idea.

So when Mr. Lomax and Deputy Smith came to the rancho early that next morning to collect my men, I told them my idea. But, alas, the vandal chose not to strike. I was not sure, but I hoped it was because Mr.

Lomax had been watching Reverend Bennett's home, while Sebastiano had watched Mr. Elmwood's.

Needless to say, I was quite annoyed, although I knew very well that the vandal had not struck on two consecutive nights. It was also quite probable that the vandal knew that the deputies were out looking for him. As to whether that would deter his activity or not, I had no idea. It was extremely frustrating.

I spent my morning hours sleeping, or rather, trying to. However, about mid-morning, I got another summons, this time to the Gaines home. Miss Gaines met me at the front door, the porch having been cleaned the day before. It still reeked of oil of turpentine.

"He's upstairs," she said, leading the way.

We stopped just outside the room's doorway and I looked in. Mr. Gaines was in bed, wheezing and coughing, his face even redder than usual with the fever.

"It started last night," Miss Gaines said softly. "He swore it was just the gripe. I tried to put a mustard plaster on him, but he wouldn't let me."

"That would have been good," I said. "And you've got cloths and water ready. Excellent. Why don't you fetch a spoon and we'll try some tonic? In the meantime, I'll try a different plaster."

Miss Gaines blushed a little but went to find the spoon. I moved quickly. Having stitched up all manner of wounds in all parts of the male body, I was inured to the sight of a man's bare chest. However, I knew Mr. Gaines' daughter was not and I wanted to spare her.

It also proved useful as I was able to prevent Mr. Gaines from either speaking or objecting much.

"I will apply this plaster whether you like it or not," I said, waving away his hands and pulling open his nightshirt. "It's up to whether you want to expose your daughter to your bare chest or not."

The poor man tried to growl at me, but only started coughing again.

I applied my plaster with plenty of oil of turpentine

and Mr. Gaines' breathing seemed to ease.

Miss Gaines returned almost before I was finished, but made no fuss as I pulled her father's nightgown back down over him. He coughed again, but it seemed a bit less ragged. I decided to leave before the cough eased enough for him to speak.

"Has he complained of any aches or pains?" I asked. She shook her head no. "Any diarrhea that you know of?"

"No. He's been fine that way."

"Has he been traveling at all?"

"I'm fine," he groaned suddenly from his bed.

"Have you taken any trips up north recently, Mr. Gaines?" I asked.

"No." He coughed again. "No visitors, either."

"Well, it's not likely cholera or typhoid," I said.

"Got chills," Mr. Gaines groaned again.

"It's not fever and ague, not this time of year," I said. "Besides, the way you're coughing more strongly suggests influenza, and we've had some of that in the pueblo of late. Now, take some tonic, and then try to get some rest. We'll be back with a little soup before long."

I dosed him, checked his forehead for the fever, then nodded at Miss Gaines.

We went downstairs.

"A good hearty chicken bouillon would be best for him," I said. "Do you have any?"

"It's already been started," Miss Gaines said with a smile. "Papa likes it for dinner and when he took sick last night, I thought it might be good if we needed to coax him to eat."

"You've got quite a good head on your shoulders, Miss Gaines," I said.

"Thank you, Mrs. Wilcox."

I looked at her, then decided I may as well ask. "That notice in the newspaper, what was behind that?"

"Oh, dear," she sighed.

"Pray forgive me. I shouldn't have asked."

"It's all right." She smiled weakly. "It was my fault of sorts." She took a deep breath. "Father can be very miserly. His family was wealthy, but then his father lost everything and died and left his wife and my aunts and uncles penniless. Father is terrified of it happening to me and my brothers. So he will not spend except what he must. However, last spring, he was courting a lady who had attracted him, and she objected to his miserly habits. So, Father told me, in front of her, that I could go out and buy whatever my heart desired. He is quite wealthy, so most of the stores in town were quite happy to extend me credit, and I'm afraid I did go a little wild. Father was furious, especially when some of the stores added items to the account that I did not buy. He spurned his lady friend and put that dreadful notice in the paper." She shrugged. "That's all."

"Do you know anyone who might want to champion you? Was there anyone who objected to the notice?"

"No one, really." She blushed prettily again. "Most of the time, Father only lets me out of the house to bring his lunch to his office, and I seldom receive callers. He only seems to trust Mr. Wilson. I think Father wants me to marry him, but I do not want to."

"I can well imagine why. He is a rather dreadful character."

The front door slammed and a young man bounded into the house. He had the same build and attitude of Mr. Gaines upstairs, though his face was somewhat paler.

"Lavina, who is this and what is she doing here?" The young man demanded.

"Timothy, this is Mrs. Wilcox. She's the doctor." Miss Gaines smiled at me. "Mrs. Wilcox, may I present my brother, Mr. Timothy Gaines."

"How do you do, Mr. Gaines?" I said, looking at him rather severely.

"Why'd you call her?" the young Mr. Gaines snapped. "You should have called Dr. Skillen. If he'd seen to the marshal, he might still be alive."

"That seems rather unlikely," I said, trying to once again to keep a hold of my temper. "After all, the marshal was murdered in his bed, and I don't see how Dr. Skillen could have prevented that."

The younger Mr. Gaines gaped for an instant. I turned to his sister as the sound of coughing erupted from upstairs.

"Miss Gaines, maybe you could have some of that broth brought up?" I asked, then turned and went upstairs.

I checked Mr. Gaines' forehead for the fever, then added a cold compress.

Mr. Timothy burst into the room. "Father!" he gasped. "Are you all right?"

"Well enough, now that Mrs. Wilcox is here," the older man grumbled. "I can breathe again."

Indeed, it did sound like his breathing was easier. His cough was still fairly rough, but not nearly as prolonged as it had been when I'd arrived. Miss Gaines appeared in the doorway carrying a tray with the bouillon in a small bowl.

"Here, Papa," she said, setting the tray down on the bureau. "I've got some chicken broth for you. Let me help you eat it."

I gathered my pots and tonic together. "He doesn't seem to be in much danger. But it can get worse in the evenings. I'll stop by before supper to make sure he's not too much worse off."

"Thank you so much, Mrs. Wilcox," Miss Gaines said, as she sat down next to her father on the bed. "Timothy, will you please see to getting her fee?"

"Father?"

Mr. Gaines coughed once more and waved at his son. "Get it."

"Yes, sir."

I followed the younger Mr. Gaines downstairs. He had me wait in the hallway while he went into another room. I received a whole dollar for my time. It could have been worse.

At the rancho, Lon Cao and Mr. Brooks had brought Lon Yu by and were planning to hide her in the barracks. She was very pretty and petite and wore that odd Chinese jacket and trousers, somehow making the strange man-like garb look delicate and womanly on her. Lon Cao had assumed Western dress and had cut off his queue. I looked at him, puzzled.

"I am not going back to China," he explained. "There is nothing for me there, and everything here."

"Mrs. Wilcox," Lon Yu said, smiling with relief. "I cannot thank you enough. Your kindness is overwhelming."

"It will be worth it to rescue you from the evils foisted on you by Sing Lee," I said simply. "It's too bad Mr. Sing turned down Mrs. Medina's offer."

"I would not want to go with her, either," Lon Yu gasped.

"She would never have forced you to work for her," I said. "It was part of the effort to help you escape. And now, Mr. Sing will not get a penny for you."

Lon Yu tittered quite charmingly, then followed her brother to the barracks house.

Olivia had arranged for a somewhat earlier supper than normal, as the men were going to be getting up early to go watch for the vandal. So I delayed my visit to the Gaines' for a bit, and it was just as well. Mr. Gaines' cough had worsened somewhat by the time I got there. So I administered another plaster, gave him some tonic and added a bit of laudanum to it, and he quickly went to sleep. I left more of the plaster and the tonic with Miss Gaines, instructing her to apply the plaster if he woke.

Mr. Brooks arrived shortly after ten o'clock to get Lon Yu. I was ready in my second best riding habit, which I'd been wearing all day. Mr. Brooks had two horses with him, fully packed for a journey.

"We should leave right away," he said. "But, Mrs. Wilcox, I remembered something. You asked if the marshal said anything about a new bounty that night, and he didn't. But I just remembered that earlier in the afternoon, as we were taking Lon Yu back to the jail, I heard the marshal laugh at someone and tell him he was next."

"Did you see who?"

"No, I didn't. I was looking out for Lon Yu, and right after that, Mr. Dye started yelling at the marshal."

"And then the bullets went flying." I sighed.

"I didn't want her to get hurt," Mr. Brooks said.

"Of course not. Well, your lady love is in the barracks, along with Mr. Lon."

In fact, Mr. Lon appeared a moment later and with him, his sister. Lon Yu ran to Mr. Brooks and the two embraced quite tenderly. It couldn't help but warm my heart to see it.

"Perhaps you should wait until closer to morning to leave," I said.

Mr. Lon shook his head. "Sing Lee is already searching."

Mr. Brooks looked up at the sky, which was clear. "We've got a good moon, too. Just enough to light our way. And there's an inn not far from the San Fernando mission. We'll go there first, then head to San Buenaventura and beyond. With luck, we'll be in San Francisco this time next week."

"Hopefully, that will be far enough," I said.

"It's either that or Sacramento," Mr. Brooks said with a grin. "Or maybe even the Nevada territory. I hear there's some good mining in those parts."

"Well, Armando and I will ride with you part of the way," I said. "It will make you harder to spot."

I called Armando, who saddled Daisy and one of the mules and we were off. We followed the river for a few miles, then Mr. Brooks waved us off.

"We can go from here," he said.

"Thank you for everything, Mrs. Wilcox," said Lon Yu from behind Mr. Brooks. Mr. Lon had the other horse. She reached out to me, then blew a kiss.

I must confess, I was feeling rather light-hearted

and gay as Armando and I rode back to the rancho. Armando thought it was all rather sick-making, but I teased him that he had his eye on one of the young girls in the pueblo. He shrugged, then frowned.

"I think I smell smoke," he said.

As did I, I realized, and I could distinctly hear the dogs barking furiously from inside the barn, where we'd locked them so they wouldn't follow us that night. We were actually already on the rancho at that point and a short run to the main yard revealed that there was, indeed, a fire. The roof of the adobe's front parlor was alight, and there was another small fire burning against the weathered wood of the winery's side wall. On the other side of the gate, I thought I saw someone running away.

"Fuego!" Armando screamed as he leaped off his mule. "Fuego!"

"Armando, get everyone out of the adobe!" I cried as I slid off Daisy and ran for the barn.

I found a shovel and ran to the winery. The dogs ran to the doors, barking with even more vigor. The fire at the base of the winery wall was small so I had some hope of putting it out. I could see that the fire in the adobe was advancing on my study and bedroom, but it had not yet reached the rooms where Juanita and the two Ortiz families slept.

"Fuego!" I screamed, adding my clamor to that of Armando as I frantically shoveled dirt onto the fire on the side of the winery. Suddenly, Hernan was at my side, still in his nightshirt, shoveling as fast as he could.

"The adobe," I gasped.

"They're all out," he gasped back. "Cuidado!"

He shoved me back as a flame licked toward us. Pascual joined us with another shovel. Several minutes later, the fire had been buried under dirt and Magdalena came by with a bucket of water and poured it over the small mound. Exhausted, Pascual stirred the ashes and I turned my attention back to the adobe, which was still burning.

The first thing I did was count the children. I nearly panicked when I was one short, but then realized that the missing person was Ramon, who often worked very late. I still ran up to Olivia.

"Everyone got out?" I asked her.

"Oh, yes." She coughed.

"Where's Ramon?"

"Still at work, gracias a Dios." She made the sign of the cross across her bosom and kissed her fingers.

"Are you sure?"

"I checked his bed, myself."

And as if it had been his intention to reassure us all along, Ramon came running up, followed by a whole troupe of neighbors bearing shovels and buckets. Fire was a terrifying thing in the pueblo. There was little enough water to spare, and the brush of the countryside surrounding us was often very dry and quick to light. Even the tiniest of sparks could ignite a massive conflagration. With Olivia and Juanita holding me, I watched as the flames engulfed my home.

CHAPTER FIFTEEN

It is impossible, even now, so many years later, to describe the stinking shell and mass of ashes that had been my home. Everything was gone. My medicines, my books, what few items I had left of my mother's possessions. My only memento of her was the small cameo locket that held a tiny lock of her hair. I seldom, if ever, took that locket off and so was wearing it that night. My best green bombazine dress was gone. All my journals and notes were gone.

My sole consolation was that no one had been seriously hurt and every one of my household had escaped alive. But we had nothing. I only had day clothes because I'd been wearing them. The Ortiz families had only their night clothes. Fortunately, Rodolfo and the Mendozas were able to give Enrique and Sebastiano some day clothes. Anita and Maria also handed over their extra dresses to Magdalena and Olivia, and their many cousins quickly provided for the children.

Of course we all retreated to the barracks house for what little remained of the night, but as the light of dawn spread over the rancho, and I emerged again to take stock, it looked even more hopeless. Worse yet, the gate to the rancho had been splattered with red paint. However, if someone had posted a list of sins, it was not there. There wasn't even an empty nail.

I pointed that out to Sebastiano.

"This wasn't the work of the vandal," I said. "Someone merely wants us to think that it was."

"I agree."

I started to cry. "Oh, Sebastiano, how can you ever forgive me? My search for the killer almost got you and your family killed!"

"But it didn't. Besides, if you don't find this person, he might try again and then where will we be?"

Sighing, he put his arm around my shoulders and gave me a quick squeeze.

There was so much to do and so much to think about. In a way, it was good that I had to focus on straightening out our lives rather than brood on how much we'd all lost. Still, I found myself bursting into tears at the oddest moments.

For example, sometime around mid-morning, a large package arrived with a note from Regina.

"I hope this is not presuming too much, nor that its source is too distasteful," the note read. "However, you have need, and we have plenty. If we offer it, it is only in thanks for the many gifts of your healing that you have brought us."

I was about to open it in the yard but then realized the men were present. So I went into the barracks. Once I saw what we had, I called Olivia, Magdalena, and Juanita immediately. Not to put too fine a point on it, there was a full supply of ladies' unmentionables, including corset covers, for all of us. There were also several dresses.

"I do not care where they came from," Juanita exclaimed. "I want to get out of these smoky old things so badly, they could have come from the Devil, himself!"

The package could not supply the entirety of our need, but it went a long way to help. There were many, many other gifts, too, but I am getting ahead of myself.

I had purchased fire insurance on the winery. So as soon as I could make myself presentable, I went into the pueblo proper to make a claim with Mr. Handley, my insurance agent. I was still wearing my riding habit, but with fresh unmentionables, I felt a great deal better and ready to do business.

I was, however, diverted from my purpose first by

a visit to my favorite dry goods store, where I placed an extensive order and received a letter, which I tucked into my pocket without looking at it. I also purchased a large leather bag to replace the one I'd lost. From there, I went to the pharmacy and purchased those supplies and instruments I could, which wasn't much, really. I'd only taken a few dollars from our winery safe, not realizing I'd need quite a bit more.

As I left the pharmacy, I noticed Sing Lee heading into the Clocktower Courthouse. I followed him, ignoring the stares I was getting. Indeed, it seemed as though those in the courthouse found it more odd that a woman would be there than a Chinaman. I found him in an office next to the courtroom, and he was swearing out a complaint against Sing Yu, or rather, Lon Yu.

"So how much did she steal this time?" asked the very bored clerk, who was a youngish man with thinning black hair and a front tooth missing.

"Two hundred dollars," Mr. Sing said. "And a gold watch."

"She most certainly did not steal a thing," I said.

The clerk looked up at me, then sighed at Mr. Sing.

"He says she did," the clerk said.

"I met with the young woman in question and she swore she took nothing," I replied.

I was, perhaps, stretching the truth. She had, in fact, said no such thing. However, I knew that Mr. Sing had lied about what she'd taken the last time she'd escaped and I knew that it was the practice to claim a theft in order to instate a bounty.

Mr. Sing glared at me, but I continued.

"In fact," I said. "This gentleman has a perfectly good offer for the young woman's contract. I witnessed the offer, myself. Is it not possible that he is trying to claim a bounty and get money for the contract at the same time?"

I was playing upon the unreasonable prejudices against the Chinese at the time, and that was, perhaps, not very kind of me. But I did not want Mr. Sing swearing out a bounty on Lon Yu and he had been very underhanded in his behavior toward her.

The clerk shrugged at Mr. Sing and turned away.

Mr. Sing glared at me, then left. He could not threaten me in front of the clerk, or any other American, but I did not doubt that he would have been very happy to cause me harm if he could. I thought of my burnt-out adobe and shuddered. Still, one could not let fear and evil persons rule. I left the courthouse and went to pay my call on Mr. Handley.

He had a full blond beard and hair, and spectacles on his nose. His office was nicely appointed with a large oak desk and several file cabinets and a view of the street behind him. He retrieved the file with my account promptly, then looked it over as I sat anxiously waiting.

"You say it was your house that burned, but the winery was intact?" he asked finally.

"Well, there was a smaller fire on the side of the winery," I said. "It's built of wood. I believe that the man who set everything on fire broke a window open on the adobe and tossed some sort of torch inside. That would account for it burning so quickly. There are no windows within easy reach on the winery building."

Mr. Handley winced. "Unfortunately, there is a problem."

"What do you mean?"

"Well, Mrs. Wilcox, it would appear that you have only insured your winery building against loss, but not your home."

"What?"

Mr. Handley shuffled some papers. "Well, you must understand, Mrs. Wilcox, we do not normally like to insure against fire, it being such a common occurrence, you know."

"I bought insurance on the understanding that it covered my whole property." I was close to tears at that point.

"Of course. That was the point. However, you must

understand that it is my job to sell the policies and to avoid paying claims."

"What? What is the point of insurance, then?"

Mr. Handley sighed. "Presumably to make a great deal of money for the stockholders." He sighed even more deeply. "However, I think we can make this right. Perhaps if we do not claim the full damages and pretend that it was the winery that sustained them. Yes, I can do that."

"I thank you, Mr. Handley. That is very kind of you." My brow furrowed. "It must be very difficult to be in the insurance business."

"It's not so bad if you can avoid submitting claims," Mr. Handley said. "There are those of my colleagues who will even cheat to avoid that, but I can't see how they keep getting people to buy their services when they do."

"You mean people like Mr. Wilson?" I asked, suddenly interested.

"I do not like to speak ill of others," Mr. Handley said. However, it was plain from the look on his face that he certainly thought ill of Councilman Wilson.

The which, in turn, started me thinking that I'd heard something about Marshal Warren having made a claim with Mr. Wilson that had not been paid. After I'd finished with Mr. Handley, I went over to Mrs. Warren's home and found that she had not disturbed any of the marshal's papers, what few there were of them.

"I only took his will," she said. "And found a few deeds for our properties. You're welcome to look at everything."

I went through every sheet of paper I could find, but nothing attracted my attention. There were a couple of letters from relatives, neither of which mentioned anything odd or suspicious, and the deeds to the various properties, as well as a couple of tax inventories.

Mrs. Warren held me back as I went to leave.

"Mrs. Wilcox, it is so very good of you to keep looking for Mr. Warren's killer when your own house has been destroyed."

I blinked back the tears. "Thank you, Mrs. Warren. But I'm afraid at this point, I'm searching for the killer as much for my own defense as I am to protect you. He's already threatened me once."

"But wasn't it the vandal that set the fire?" Mrs. Warren looked shocked. "That's what everyone is saying."

"No, it wasn't," I said. "But let us pretend that it was for the time being. I want the killer to think he is well-hidden."

I went on to the jail office. Marshal's Warren's replacement was due to arrive the following week, so Mr. Lomax was happy to help me search the marshal's papers. There were considerably more than at the house, but almost all of them pertained to his work as marshal, including various warrants, most of which were stuck between the pages of his ledgers, perhaps as a way to account for various bounties.

"But why are you so certain it wasn't the vandal who burned your home?" Mr. Lomax asked me as we paged through all the wanted posters and ledgers.

"For one thing, it happened so early in the evening," I said. "It wasn't even midnight yet. The vandal strikes in the early hours before dawn. And there was no paper proclaiming my sins, nor a nail to hang one on. We know the vandal usually hangs that first because there are no footprints in the paint. Finally, while there was a window broken at Mr. Carson's home, there wasn't at Mr. Gaines' or at the Warren house. So I must surmise that the one breakage was an accident. It would seem out of character for the vandal to do something so deadly as start a fire, especially if his goal is to alert people to the presence of sinners rather than send sinners to their doom."

"That makes sense," Mr. Lomax said. "But what's this?"

It was a warrant for the arrest of Pericles Wills, the brother of the unfortunate notary, Mr. Leander Wills.

"But he was killed a year ago, wasn't he?" I asked, looking again at the warrant. It was dated a little over a year before. "Look here. The complaint was filed by Mr. Robert Gaines, who claimed that his clerk, Pericles Wills, had stolen fifty dollars from him."

"And the marshal shot him, but as I understand it, Wills was drunk and drew first."

"That's what Mr. Brooks said he'd witnessed. Still, I could understand why our notary, Mr. Wills, would find it worth his while to ensure the marshal's death. And if someone caught him in the house, it would not be unreasonable that he was there to attempt to take whatever statement the marshal might give before dying."

"Only the marshal was doing well enough, and Mr. Wills saw an opportunity to finish him off." Mr. Lomax nodded. "The problem will be proving it."

I returned to the strongbox I'd been looking through. "Indeed. Oh, good Heavens, here's yet another who might be tempted to finish off the marshal. Mr. Wilson."

"What?"

"It's a letter to an insurance company complaining that Mr. Wilson has not paid the marshal's claim." I handed the document to Mr. Lomax. "It's dated October 29, and it looks as though it's not quite finished."

"That would make sense," Mr. Lomax said. "If the marshal started writing it, then something happened that interrupted him. That was the day he decided to go to San Buenaventura."

"Mr. Redona told me that he'd brought in the man Lon Yu had hired to help her on Saturday, and the marshal questioned him. He said they left right away."

"And the marshal didn't finish his letter." Mr. Lomax finished my thought.

"Which means that, at the time of his death,

Marshal Warren had an outstanding claim against Mr. Wilson." I racked my brain, trying to remember who else had said he'd had a claim against the councilman.

I looked through the strongbox again, and then at Mr. Lomax. He'd finished with the most recent ledger and hadn't found anything besides the warrant for Mr. Pericles Wills. The other ledger entries involved the whole range of petty crimes for which fines could be charged. Apparently, more serious matters didn't involve the same kind of bookkeeping as minor ones.

"I'd best speak to both Mr. Wilson and Mr. Wills," I said. "Would you care to join me?"

"I think I will," Mr. Lomax said, getting his hat.

However, we'd barely gotten out of the office when Mr. Lomax was summoned to quell a fight at yet another saloon.

"They're starting early today," he grumbled, running off.

I shuddered. For all I complained about how ineffective my various salves, unguents, and tonics were, I was loathe to be without them on a busy Saturday night. There was, however, little I could do about it just then. So I stiffened my resolve not to give in to tears yet again and went to visit Mr. Wilson, as his office was closest.

The younger Mr. Gaines was there ahead of me, quite loudly demanding that Mr. Wilson pay his claim. I couldn't quite hear Mr. Wilson's defense, but the councilman's voice sounded decidedly nervous. There were two clerks in the antechamber to Mr. Wilson's office and they kept looking across their desks at each other and shaking their heads.

"Can't get blood out of a stone," the one said, softly. He looked to be around thirty, with a neatly clipped beard.

"What do you mean?" I asked.

He shrugged. "I just hope you're not here with your own claim."

"I have my insurance elsewhere," I said.

"Good," the clerk said. "Because Mr. Wilson couldn't pay your claim even if it is covered. One of the companies he represents closed its doors last month and he's been scrambling to pay some of the claims out of his own pocket."

"Has to," said the other clerk, a young man with hardly any beard to speak of. "Won't be able to sell insurance policies if he doesn't. And if he doesn't sell insurance, we don't get paid."

"If he doesn't pay us this week, I'm going to find a new position," the older clerk said. "I can't pay my rent on promises."

"Me, neither," said the younger clerk.

I debated whether I needed to speak to Mr. Wilson, but then Mr. Gaines came out of the inner office and slammed the door behind him. He barely glanced at me as he stormed outside, and without a moment's thought, I hurried after him.

"Mr. Gaines!" I called as we came onto the Calle Principal.

He stopped and turned. "Oh. Mrs. Wilcox."

"I just wanted to inquire after your father," I said approaching him slowly.

"He's getting better," Mr. Gaines said, grudgingly. I surmised that he hadn't called another doctor, as he would have thrown that in my face the first moment he could.

"That's good to hear. You wouldn't happen to remember a clerk of your father's named Pericles Wills?"

Mr. Gaines rolled his eyes skyward. "The notary's brother. He was crooked as a country mile. It doesn't speak well of his brother."

"It might or it might not," I said. It seemed rather unjust of Mr. Gaines to assume that because the one brother was crooked that the other was, as well, even though I had my doubts about Mr. Leander Wills. "Apparently there was a warrant for Pericles Wills' arrest."

"He stole fifty dollars from us." Mr. Gaines growled. "You can't trust clerks these days. I have to check everything. They're always making mistakes."

"So the fifty dollars was the result of a mistake?"

"No!" Mr. Gaines' contempt washed over me. "He made the "mistake" on purpose to cover up the missing fifty dollars. Clerks are doing it every day. I'd fire the lot of them, but Father says we need clerks."

I could have suggested that they might have fewer problems with thieving clerks if they paid the clerks better, to begin with, but the suggestion would have fallen on deaf ears, so I didn't make it.

"Well, I'm glad to hear your father's health is improving," I said, instead. "Please commend me to your father and to your sister."

Mr. Gaines snorted and strode off, leaving me wondering how such a singularly ill-mannered person could have such a sweet and kind sister. Unfortunately, I had still to gain information from a still more ill-mannered man, Mr. Leander Wills. I caught him at the door to his office and made sure that he knew I would be waiting for him when he returned. He very reluctantly bade me enter and offered me a seat in front of his desk.

"So, are you here to hurl more accusations at me?" he demanded, shifting his bright blue silk vest as he sat down behind his desk.

"That has never been the point of my visits," I said firmly. "However, it is very interesting to me that you seem to believe it so. Could it be you do have a guilty conscience?"

He puffed himself up nervously. "Me? Well, I... No. I do not."

"You do have quite a few gambling debts."

He turned pale and blinked. "I have never taken a bribe. I swear I haven't!"

"I never said you had, Mr. Wills. Good Heavens. I didn't even come here to talk about those. I am here to ask you about your brother Pericles. I've been told the marshal killed him."

To my surprise, Mr. Wills broke down in sobs. "Oh, dear. Oh, dear. It was all my fault. Pericles had just been dismissed from his job for stealing some money and his boss had sworn out a warrant for his arrest. But it wasn't Pericles who stole the money. It was me. I was visiting my brother and he had some money on the desk before putting it in the company safe. I just took a few coins, but they were twenty dollar gold pieces. Pericles didn't see me do it. But I had to. I owed so much money. Then Pericles got drunk and drew on the marshal. It was terrible. Just terrible. If only that wretched marshal had listened. But he didn't. He simply shot my brother the second he got his gun out, and poor Pericles was too drunk to hit the broad side of a barn."

"By any chance were you out and about last night?" I asked.

"No," Mr. Wills said, still sobbing and far too wrapped up in his grief to get at what I was asking. "I was home asleep. I'm giving up gambling. It is the Devil's game. I'll not do it anymore."

"An excellent resolve," I said getting up. "Thank you for speaking to me."

I had no reason to believe that Mr. Wills would keep his resolve, but that didn't matter.

I returned to the rancho to see what I could do there to restore our lives. The burnt out shell of my adobe was still smoldering, with tiny wisps of smoke rising here and there through the ashes. There would be no way to recover anything, but the smoldering would soon be put out, as rain clouds were slowly pushing their way across the sky toward us. As I looked at the mess, the pain seared through me yet again. I wondered if I'd ever be able to look at the house ruins again.

Maria came and showed me how it had been arranged that we'd all fit in the barracks house so that I did not have to worry about anyone having a roof over their head come night time.

"Are you feeling well?" I couldn't help asking her.

"I am fine. The baby is moving," she said with a smile.

"But all the excitement," I said.

"It has not hurt me in the least. You'll see."

As it turned out, her confidence was misplaced, but that is for later. In the meantime, Olivia asked me to help set up the tables for dinner so that we could eat outside before the rain started. Still somewhat numb, I did so and found that there were a couple pots of stew and a host of loaves of bread that neighbors had brought by. We ate very well that afternoon.

Then Mrs. Elmwood arrived with a small crate containing unmentionables and nightclothes for the children and a dress for me.

"Some of the congregation wanted to help," said Mrs. Elmwood, a rather rotund woman with a fluttery aspect and green eyes that darted everywhere, looking at everything except the person to whom she was speaking.

"That is exceedingly kind of them," I said. "If I might, I'd like to have the names so that I can write my thanks."

Not having a front parlor, we were in the front common room of the barracks, which was fairly comfortable with a couple of sofas and three large chairs. Mrs. Elmwood had perched herself on the edge of a sofa.

"That's not necessary," she said with a nervous titter. She glanced up at the ceiling, then across the room at the wall. "Um. You don't think the reverend could have had anything to do with this or the vandalism, do you?"

"Of course not," I said, even though I wasn't sure. "It's possible he stirred something up in someone, but he can't entirely be responsible for that."

"The poor thing. Mrs. Hewitt was looking at him oddly the other day. He positively reeked of oil of turpentine, but the house is being painted and the boys keep leaving the paint buckets about and he is forever getting it on his clothes." She sighed deeply and looked at her hands. "I do wish they'd finish. The house is completely topsy-turvy and it's terribly unsettling."

"To be sure," I said, holding my tongue, as difficult as it was.

"Oh! Of course, you'd know. Oh, dear. I'm so sorry. So thoughtless of me."

"I understand," I said, even though I didn't. "Well, if you can't send me the names of our kind donors, would you please send my heartfelt thanks on?"

"Oh, gladly!" She bounced up and looked at something over my right shoulder. "You're very welcome, dear Mrs. Wilcox. You've done so much for our little congregation."

At that moment, someone called from the yard and as we emerged, I discovered it was a young woman asking me to help patch up her father. Our usual Saturday night exploits were, indeed, starting early, and I gathered what few things I had and went to help.

The very long afternoon stretched into a longer night. Sebastiano brought me some supper and the news that Maria had started her labor. It took a bit of quizzing him, but I was able to determine that I did have some time before birth was imminent, so I finished sewing up yet another knife wound, applied the poultice I'd been able to scrape together from Wang Fu's herbs and my own wine, and then mounted Daisy to go back to the rancho.

Maria's labor had not progressed well at all. She seemed cheerful, in spite of the more and more frequent pains, so I bit back my worry. The baby was not passing well, and it would only be a matter of time before the birth put both Maria and the infant in mortal danger. I gave Maria a bit of chloroform to ease the pain, but then heard the baby's heart rate stutter through my stethoscope.

I left the room we'd set up for the birthing for a moment to consider my options. Hernan was there outside the doorway.

"It's not going well, is it?" he asked, a worried frown on his face.

"No, I'm afraid it's not."

Hernan put his hand on my arm. "She will tell you to save the baby, not her. Please. Save her."

His dark eyes were filled with pain and worry. I took a deep breath and nodded. I ordered good, hot water from Juanita then pulled out the forceps that I had bought that afternoon, thanking our Loving Lord that I had made such a providential purchase. It was true that forceps were a pretty basic tool, as were the other instruments I had bought, but still, I was very glad I had them. I'd had to order some of the other items.

I didn't like using forceps unless I absolutely had to simply because they often caused tearing, which could lead to hemorrhaging. They could also break the fragile skull of the infant. And even if all that didn't happen, mothers often took sick afterward. We know now that it was probably infection from the tearing, but we didn't then.

Fortunately, I was able to deliver the little boy alive. He was quite a little moose, and it was no wonder he'd had difficulty passing through from the womb. Maria, however, began hemorrhaging, as I'd feared. I packed her womb with cloth after cloth and tried to force some water down her throat.

Dawn had broken about an hour before. The lamp glowed in the growing daylight. The baby, being held by one of his aunts in the other room, cried and Maria gave a little gasp. I held my breath. Then she began to breathe again and again. I checked the cloths. The bleeding had finally abated. Maria was going to live.

CHAPTER SIXTEEN

It was true that Maria wasn't entirely out of danger that morning, but there was little more I could do at that point. Juanita prevailed upon me to go to bed, promising to call me if there was the least change in Maria's condition.

Oddly enough, there weren't any nightclothes for me, but I was so tired, I barely noticed and slept quite soundly. Unfortunately, I also slept through church services, which annoyed me no end, but there was no help for it.

I checked Maria. She was very weak and had a small fever, but she was awake and had even nursed her new son, whom they'd name Elias, after his great-uncle who'd been killed. While I was very grateful that she had survived, as often happens when I either lose a patient or it becomes a near thing, I couldn't help wondering what I could have done differently to have achieved a better outcome. I have been told such ruminations can make one a better doctor. That day, however, my brooding provided no comfort or insights, but only served to make me even more depressed than I already was.

Juanita had found a red poplin work dress among those that had been donated and had already altered it to fit me better. The skirt was still a bit over-long, but she'd managed to take it in enough that I did not feel as though I were overwhelmed by it. She'd also found the letter I'd put in my pocket the day before and made sure I saw it. The rain had come the day before, as expected, and soaked the shell of the adobe, putting out the last of the embers, but releasing an acrid stench that seemed to permeate the entire rancho.

I don't know why I decided to sit out in the yard that morning. It was muddy and chilly. The rain had stopped for the moment, but it looked like it would start again. And looking at the shell that had been my home felt as though I were picking at a scab again and again. But sit outside I did, sipping coffee, sitting on a bench from the winery, and finally opening the letter I'd received the day before.

It was from my brother. Merriam had never written me before. That was the duty of his wife, Gertrude.

"My dearest sister," it began. I snorted. There was little love lost between the two of us, as he had made it plain that I was as great an embarrassment to him as I was to my father. As I have mentioned, we doctors were not well thought of back then, and no one of the social class into which I'd been born would have dreamed of becoming one. My being a woman only magnified the shame.

"As you know, our father's health remains in a precarious position." In truth, my father's health had always been "precarious," in that he constantly complained of some minor malady or other, but never seemed to sicken with it.

"In addition, Mr. Henry Wilcox passed away last week, and his passing has deeply affected our father." That was news. Mr. Wilcox was, of course, my Albert's father and a good friend of my father's, which was probably why he'd been able to arrange my marriage so quickly. The senior Mr. Wilcox had been grumpy and very full of his own worth to the world, or, in short, the elder version of my husband.

"Not surprisingly, Mr. Wilcox's passing has awakened in Father a new desire to see you safely back home where you belong. He has decided to forgive all and has instructed me to tender the offer. You will be well cared for and I have promised, as well, to see to your care even after Father goes to meet his reward. In addition, there are to be no limitations on your activities as long as they do not expose the family to shame or ridicule." Which did not mean automatically that I would be free to practice medicine. It meant I could as long as I could keep it a secret.

"Please come home and be the prop in our Father's old age that he needs. Affectionately, your brother, Merriam." Well, harrumph. I did not doubt he wanted me to come home and take care of our father. Our sisters, who'd had the good sense to marry and get away from the old coot, could point to the need to take care of their own families. I was the only one left who was unattached.

Had the letter arrived at any other time, I would have laughed at the thinly veiled attempt to get me to take on the noxious task of caring for our father. But as my eyes once again drifted over the ashes and burnt out walls, all I could think of was that I could go back to my beloved Boston. I could go to concerts and plays put on by people who knew how to play instruments and could act. I would not have to worry about a relentless sun turning my skin dark. I could walk down streets that were actually paved and enjoy bright springs, warm summers, and crisp falls. I could once again feel the exciting chill of snowflakes on my face and go ice skating. I could be where people didn't kill each other every night over gambling debts and silly arguments.

Now that the embers were out, I was able to go into what was left of the house. I found my study, and with a shovel I'd pulled from the barn, found the space where my desk had sat over a loose board in the floor. The board had burned through, and I was able to dig around the ashes to the strongbox underneath. It was singed, but intact and I was able to break open the lock. Inside were all my savings, several thousand dollars.

Most of the money that came from the winery business went into the safe in the winery. Every week, I distributed wages to everyone, took some more for the housekeeping, then took a small wage for myself. Some of it went to ingredients for medications or surgical tools. Some of it went to dresses and the like. But a goodly bit of it went into my strongbox, which had also held all of Albert's money while he'd been alive. He hadn't known that I'd been well aware of the box's contents even from the start, down to the penny. He'd also thought he was telling a great story when he told the aging couple that he bought the rancho from that he was giving them all we had. He'd barely given them a third of what he'd had. Between that and what I'd saved, myself, I could almost have lived out my days in comfort and security.

But now I had an offer from my brother for exactly that. True, I'd have to deal with my father and his many complaints. But I wouldn't have to spend all my time with him, and given the money I had, I could possibly have left him entirely. It was so tempting.

I hated Los Angeles. It was such a small backwater, filled with narrow-minded people and constant sickness and violence. Always, the violence. This is not to say that things were perfectly peaceful in Boston. But there, men almost never began shooting at each other in the middle of the streets. There, people were educated and even a woman could have a decent conversation or two with someone who would appreciate that she'd read a book.

I re-buried the box, then went over and sank onto the bench and began sobbing. I heard the ranch gate open and close but gave it no thought until I realized that Angelina was sitting next to me and holding me as I cried. A few minutes later, the gate opened, and a horse and buggy drove in, and then Regina was sitting on my other side, holding me, too.

I finally calmed down enough to tell them about my brother's letter. Regina blanched.

"You don't want to go, do you?" she asked, fearfully. She had good reason. Angelina and I were the only intimate friends she had and could have.

"I don't know," I said, wiping my eyes with a handkerchief I did not recognize. "I know Boston isn't perfect. People are just as venal and mean as they are here. But it is home to me and I miss it so."

"Of course, you do," said Angelina, patting my arm. "But this is your home, too. That is why you're so sad right now. And there are many people here who care about you and would not want to see you go."

"I can't imagine who," I sniffed. I shook my head. "That's not true, I know. I am wanted here, I suppose. It's just that I never wanted to come here. I was disgraced and forced to marry lest I be put out on the streets. That thought terrified me. It was the only thing I could think of worse than being forced to marry. And it's just so different here from Boston. So rough and violent and harsh and frightening."

Regina looked around, then blinked. "My darling, you know that I despair of you leaving. But." She reached over and patted Angelina's arm. "Thanks to you, I am no longer alone here. So, if you must go home, Maddie, do it. I give you my blessing, dearest, because there is nothing I want more than your happiness."

If ever I could have cursed Regina, I could have then. Such a beautiful sentiment, and of course, it released another drenching of tears. By then, the rain was starting again. Angelina and Regina got me into the barracks house before I got too wet. I thanked them and sent them on their way, then went to wash my face, which I did. I checked on Maria. She still had a small fever, but it was nothing that wouldn't be expected and it wasn't raging. If anything, she seemed a touch cooler than she had earlier. There was room for hope, especially since she was resting easily and not showing any other signs of contagion.

When I returned downstairs to the common room, I was surprised to see that I had more visitors. Many of them had brought donations. I suppose one should not cavil at anyone's generosity, no matter how tepid. But it was very hard not to notice that those of my patients and other friends from our Mexican community had brought armloads of shirts and dresses and bedding and pots and pans, some of them even new. Whereas, those offerings from the wealthier Americans in our community arrived piecemeal, a shirt here, a dress there, all clearly well-worn and some almost rags. Mrs. Carson sent over a set of journals, pens, ink, and blotting paper, all of it dusty as if the items had languished on a shelf in their store before being sent to me.

I write this not to complain about the offerings. We were hardly in a position to be choosy. Everything was very much needed and happily received. But the perceived stinginess of the offerings from the more well-to-do of the pueblo served only to ingrain in my memory the remarkable thing that happened next.

I think it was Enrique who answered the knock at the door. It had to have been a member of my household because the three who had knocked were immediately admitted. The room suddenly quieted.

There were two young men with dusky skin, carrying two large sacks each and attending an older Negress with skin as dark as ebony. Mrs. Biddie Mason had come to call. She was one of the wealthiest people in the pueblo and carried herself with the dignity of one who knew that she was. I forget the exact details, but she and her daughters had been brought here by their master in the 1850s. The master then tried to convince them that they were not free, or wanted to bring them back to Texas against their will, or some such chicanery, and the case had ended up in court where Mrs. Mason's testimony had been most eloquent. From there, she'd gotten a good job and started investing her money in real estate, of which she owned a great deal.

She was also known for her charity, which was why I was not entirely surprised to see her in the common room. But what she said next completely flummoxed me.

"Mrs. Wilcox, you have always treated my people

with dignity and kindness," she said, her voice quiet yet filling the room. "You have cleaned our wounds, delivered our babies, set our bones, and sat with us through fevers. Many times when no one else would. And now this be your hour of need. So, we bring you our charity."

I blinked back tears. "I don't deserve it. I've done nothing but what any decent God-fearing woman would do."

Mrs. Mason chuckled a little bitterly. "There not be a lot of God-fearing people then. But you be one of them. Thank you."

The young men left the huge sacks, then took Mrs. Mason's arms.

"Please. Stay," I asked. "We have some food and we can talk."

But Mrs. Mason and the young men had already left. When the sacks were opened, they were filled with heavy wool blankets. Mrs. Mason could have paid for all of them, but I later found out that almost all of the colored people in the pueblo had contributed. Truly, those who had the least had given the most.

I went back upstairs again shortly after to attempt to regain something of my composure. I was not alone in my distress. While the men had all been stoic in the face of what had happened, Magdalena assured me both Sebastiano and Enrique had shed tears. Hernan could not be induced to leave Maria's side, nor could Rodolfo's wife, Anita. The children were fretful but trying very hard to be cheerful for their parents' sakes. As for Magdalena, Juanita, and Olivia, who had lost just as much as I had, we were all prone to crying and all manner of unseemly displays of emotion. As I placed one of the blankets that Mrs. Mason had brought on my bed, I sank down once again, only to hear Juanita crying on the bed next to mine. I flew to her side.

"Juanita, dearest, it will be all right," I told her, rubbing her back. "We will rebuild."

"I heard what you were saying to Mrs. Medina

and Mrs. Sutton about that horrible letter from your brother. That you want to leave us."

"Oh, dear." I sank back, feeling horribly ashamed. "I don't know what I want to do. It's all so confusing."

"It's not for me!" Juanita bolted upright. "You belong here. This is your home. We are your family. You embarrassed those people in Boston by being what you are and the first thing they did was throw you out. We found out and we loved you all the more."

I tried to find the words to admonish Juanita, as she had added a few words to her outburst that were anything but polite.

"Do you think they will let you be the doctor that you are?" she continued. "Do you think they will let you be a winemaker?"

"Juanita, I only make wine for the money.'

The next word out of her mouth was unbelievably foul, but, alas, apt. "You do it because you love it, too. I know. Even with Sebastiano and Enrique as your partners, you are standing over their shoulders, making sure everything is right. You take as much care with your wine as you do your patients. And when everything was on fire, what was the first thing you tried to save? The winery."

"It was a much smaller fire."

"But you trusted Armando to get us out of the adobe. You took care of the winery." Juanita paused. "It was the right thing to do. We were already out of the adobe, and I know you would have sacrificed the winery for us."

"Of course, I would have." I blinked my eyes, trying to remember those terrible events and realized that I had seen everyone outside the adobe before I ran to the barn to get the shovel.

"And now you want to leave us. Fine thanks that is for all we've done for you." Juanita folded her arms across her chest and huffed loudly.

"But I don't know," I said, finally. I started sniffling again and found the handkerchief that I did not recognize. "Juanita, it's as I told Regina and Angelina, I never wanted to come here and I do miss Boston. And I do not always feel as though I belong here. I don't know what to think right now."

Juanita sniffed and relented a little. "I guess I can understand that."

"Thank you, Juanita."

There really wasn't anything more I could say.

Later, all the men of my household woke up at three in the morning. Mr. Lomax and Deputy Smith arrived shortly after. They were going to attempt to watch the pueblo and possibly catch the vandal. I was so proud of Sebastiano and Enrique and the others, especially Hernan, who had left his beloved wife's bedside, and I told them so. I caught one brief glare from Enrique, which I supposed I had earned. They went off.

Forced to stay behind, and feeling rather nettled that I was, I made another decision. The men had already been talking about tearing down what remained of the adobe's walls. I did not want them exploring the foundations.

I found a shovel and walked around the yard, and then into my vineyards. I walked back to my yard. I slipped into the winery and lit a lantern. Far back against the back wall, I dug another hole. Then I went back to the remains of the adobe and dug up my strongbox. It was no small task to lift the box up out of the hole and then drag it into the winery, but I managed and buried it well against the back wall. Then I went and swept away the tracks that I had made.

It was not the best of solutions. I would have to open the strongbox every so often to add money and occasionally take some. But it would suit until we could get a new adobe built.

CHAPTER SEVENTEEN

Mr. Lomax stood next to me in Mrs. Glassell's front parlor. I could see that he was desperately trying to keep a straight face. The situation was absolutely not in the least bit funny. That only made the desire to laugh worse.

The watchers had spent yet another fruitless night watching, until, near dawn, they'd heard shots being fired on the Calle Segundo. That they'd missed the target of those shots was not their fault. The miscreant had managed to get his notice posted and his paint spilled, but had, not surprisingly, fled the second the gunfire erupted.

He had left several buckets behind. Alas, they were ordinary wooden buckets with no marks of any kind. Moreover, the buckets were available at every dry goods and hardware store in the pueblo, and they were often purchased a gross at a time for various industrial uses, so it seemed unlikely we'd be able to trace the vandal that way.

Mrs. Glassell, for her part, was not the least repentant. Her husband happened to be away at the Anaheim colony that night. One would have thought that to leave his wife alone in the house with a violent vandal on the loose might not have been safe for the wife. One would not have known Mrs. Glassell.

Her remarkably huge pistol still sat on the end table next to her chair. She had changed to day wear, in this case a nice blue bombazine dress. However attuned and obedient to the niceties of society Mrs.

Glassell was, she was not to be easily cowed by the violence that haunted our streets. The woman knew how to shoot.

"I can't believe I missed him," she complained, not for the first or even second time.

"It was dark," I said, trying to sound soothing. "And you were called out of bed unexpectedly."

"Bosh!" Mrs. Glassell snorted. "That's exactly when I need most to be on my guard. Did you find the list of sins?"

"Yes," I said, handing her the large sheet of brown paper.

"Greed and pride," she muttered. "Well, I suppose if one is going to be successful in business, one could call it greed. But pride? I simply do not understand that one. Mr. Glassell is the soul of modesty."

I could have made an argument against that, as Mr. Glassell was rather prone to holding himself above others. I was not, however, going to say so to his wife. There was that rather large pistol to take into account.

"So why were you not watching our house?" she suddenly demanded of Mr. Lomax.

"We did not consider your husband a sinner," he said.

I had to give him credit for thinking of the kindest response, and one that, now that I think about it, may even have been true.

"Oh." She shifted herself. "Well, that's some consolation, I suppose." She turned her glare on me. "Well, Mrs. Wilcox?"

"I do not understand, Mrs. Glassell."

"Why haven't you found this fellow? Good heavens. You were certainly quick enough last time."

I swallowed. "The vandal, while frightening, has not killed anybody. The man who murdered the marshal and who has tried to murder me twice is considerably more dangerous."

"And how do you know they are not one and the same?" Mrs. Glassell pulled herself upright. "After all, it seems unlikely we should have two such crimes occurring in the pueblo independently of each other."

I had to give her credit for that thought, as well.

"It does seem unlikely, indeed, and I did at first think they were the same person," I said. "However, I had an encounter that has led me to believe that we are dealing with two separate criminals. As the vandal has only wreaked minimal havoc and possibly some embarrassment, whereas the killer has not only taken a life but almost taken mine twice over, I thought the latter seemed more urgent."

"Yes, I suppose it would be," said Mrs. Glassell, conceding my point, but doing so most reluctantly.

"It's probably for the best that you scared the vandal away," said Mr. Lomax, still trying not to laugh. "He might think twice before trying to strike again."

"And Mr. Glassell will be spared having to make excuses or even pay a bribe or two," I pointed out. "That will make him happy."

Mrs. Glassell simpered. "Yes. It will. He gets in such a lather when I shoot someone. But it's always in self-defense."

"Naturally, Mrs. Glassell." I stood up quickly before Mr. Lomax could lose his reserve. "And to be clear, you did not see anything that might help us identify the vandal?"

"If I had, he'd have been wounded, at the very least!' Mrs. Glassell snapped. "I have very good aim, you know."

"Yes, I do," I said. "Thank you very kindly for speaking with us. Mr. Lomax, I think it's time we were off."

"Yes, ma'am," Mr. Lomax managed to get out.

We were, of course, forced to go through the back of the house. I thought Mr. Lomax would not make it without laughing, but he managed admirably. That being said, once we were on the street and out of Mrs. Glassell's earshot, he caved in. I did not. Armando, who was once again shadowing me, had waited outside the house and joined us, looking quizzically at Mr. Lomax.

"Pray forgive me, Mrs. Wilcox," Mr. Lomax gasped once he was able to. "You did not tell me what a pistol she is."

"Or that she has," I said, oddly missing his pun. "Good heavens, that thing is a monster. Worse yet, she is not in the least afraid to use it."

"I'll have to tell the men to keep an eye out for it and her." Mr. Lomax couldn't help chuckling again. "You can't help but admire a woman with that kind of spunk."

"Perhaps, but her actions may have only served to thwart us. She may have driven the vandal back into hiding and made it nigh unto impossible to find him."

"If he never strikes again, is that such a bad thing?"

I sighed. "Probably not, except that we'll be forever wondering if we'll be attacked again. That would be dreadful."

Mr. Lomas sobered. "Yes. I'm afraid it would be." He began chuckling again. "But no one else has her gun."

Perhaps it was my mood that day, which was hardly salubrious, or perhaps Mr. Lomax's humor was misplaced. Nonetheless, I took my leave of Mr. Lomax rather promptly. While Armando and I were heading back toward the rancho, we went past the Plaza church and I was hailed by Father Jimenez.

"Mrs. Wilcox! I'm so glad to see you," he exclaimed. "And you, Armando."

The boy grinned, nodded, but held his tongue

"As I, you," I said to Father Jimenez. "I need to offer so many thanks to your parishioners for the many, many kindnesses we have received."

"Only their gratitude for the many kindnesses you have bestowed on them," Father Jimenez said. "But I remember now something about Reverend Bennett. I told you I had seen him before."

"That's right, you did."

He nodded. "I remembered where. It was in San Buenaventura. I was there last year to visit some of my brother priests." He frowned. "I do not remember how it was that I saw him, but I am confident that it was in San Buenaventura."

I smiled although I did not feel it. "That is something, at least. Thank you, Father, for telling me."

"I hope it helps."

I shrugged. "I do, too."

We said our goodbyes and Armando and I started back toward the rancho, then I paused. If we were to rebuild, I needed to be sure my accounts were in order with a variety of merchants in the pueblo. So we retraced our steps back to the Calle Principal and visited the hardware store.

Mr. Ivins, the owner, was particularly glad to see me. He was relatively tall and very well-rounded with a reddish beard and hair.

"I have been expecting you, Mrs. Wilcox," he said, nodding at Armando.

"To be sure," I said. "As you have guessed, I shall shortly be in need of your merchandise. I want to be sure my account with you is in order."

"Very much so, Mrs. Wilcox. There are few in this town I can say that about, but for you, there will be no problem."

"Thank you," I said. I saw the buckets stacked nearby and suddenly thought of something. "You sell a fair amount of paint, do you not?"

"Yes. All the colors of the rainbow, although whitewash is the easiest to get."

"What about red?"

Mr. Ivins frowned. "Most of that goes to the Hewitt factory, but I've had a barrel go missing the other day. I would not want you to think the worse of me. It was stolen. I filed a claim with Mr. Wilson, but he doesn't seem to be doing much about it."

"I'm not entirely surprised," I said. "And I believe you about your paint being stolen. You would have denied it otherwise. Well, thank you for your time, Mr. Ivins. I will be contacting you soon, I'm sure."

I left thinking about other things than replacing my adobe. I was not far from the buggy manufactory, so I decided to visit Mrs. Hewitt once again.

I was somewhat surprised that she agreed to see me, and left Armando in the company of the factory foreman. I was even more surprised, upon arriving in her office, to find Mrs. Hewitt near tears.

"Oh, Mrs. Wilcox! How can you forgive me?" she sobbed.

"I have no idea until I know what I am supposed to be forgiving your for," I said. I suspect, now in retrospect, that was a bit harsh, but my nerves were stretched quite a bit at that point.

"I should have been more forthcoming with you when you came to ask about the paint," Mrs. Hewitt said, dabbing her eyes. "Perhaps if I had, you would not have suffered so great a loss. It's all my fault."

I did my best not to roll my eyes heavenward. "That may be true. But it's also probable that the person who set the fire at my home was not the same person who has been vandalizing houses in the pueblo. But if you are more forthcoming now, perhaps it will make it easier to separate the two and find out who they are."

"That's the problem," Mrs. Hewitt sniffed. "I do not know who it could be, but it is true that there is a good amount of red paint missing from the manufactory. We usually keep the barrels in the yard, so anyone could have taken it. No one has ever stolen paint from us before, so it didn't make sense to worry about it. But then supplies began to run low right around the beginning of this month. When Mr. Lomax, and then you, began asking about it, I became afraid. As you know, I can't afford the least scandal connected to the manufactory. The worst of it is, I've been waiting for the vandal to attack us. I cannot believe that Mr. Hewitt's sins are that great a secret."

I thought for a moment. "That is true. Although, I have never heard anyone speak of his drunkenness."

"That's a blessing," she said, sighing. "Oh, Mrs. Wilcox, I am so sorry."

"Mrs. Hewitt, as I said, I have no reason to believe that the vandal attacked my house. It was more probably in connection to the marshal's death. But it does help to know where the paint is coming from. Perhaps if you were to secure it, it would be harder for the vandal to use it for his nefarious purposes."

"I already have. Although I fear the vandal has already secured sufficient for a few more attacks."

"Then we shall have to hope we can find him quickly." I tried not to let her see my sigh.

I left shortly thereafter, collected Armando, and once on the street, felt somewhat at loose ends. There was a saloon nearby, not one I usually sold wine to, but it did give me an idea. Mr. Uribe's saloon did buy my wine and it would make sense for me to visit and reassure him that I could complete any orders.

I went to the back of the saloon with Armando in tow. Mr. Uribe was not in, but Mr. Sedonez was. His full hair was white, even though he was not all that old, and he wore a full, white mustache.

"I'm glad to see you, Mrs. Wilcox," he said, seating me in the large back room where the barrels and bottles of whiskey were stored. Armando was, once again, waiting just outside. "Mr. Uribe asked me to order another barrel of angelica last Friday and I didn't get a chance to before now."

"I'm glad of it, Mr. Sedonez," I said. "Your saloon seems quite popular. I've heard several people tell me that they were here the night the marshal died."

Mr. Sedonez chuckled. "We had several celebrations going on. Poor Emanuel Mendoza, he didn't leave until close to dawn. And Mr. Dye was in no better shape, although Mr. Bonner was kind enough to get him back to his room."

"That's very interesting." I thought of another

question. "Have you heard any clerks complaining about their bosses?"

That made Mr. Sedonez laugh out loud. "They all complain about their bosses. It doesn't matter who."

I frowned, trying to remember what all I knew about the paint victims. "Well, somebody has taken umbrage over the treatment received by various clerks in the pueblo, specifically Mr. Carson's and Mr. Gaines'."

"That does not surprise me." Mr. Sedonez shrugged. "Mr. Carson is frequently in an ill-temper, thanks to his stomach. So he will throw things and sometimes even hit his clerks. One of them lost a tooth last month. And everyone knows what a miser Mr. Gaines is."

"I did not until recently," I said. "Can you think of anyone else who has been complaining about his boss with a certain degree of legitimacy?"

Mr. Sedonez thought. "I can't say. I don't really listen to too many fellows. I'm usually too busy. But if I hear anything, I will certainly let you know."

I thanked him and rose to leave. But before I could, there was a disturbance from the front of the saloon. Mr. Sedonez asked me to wait and went out front. A minute later, he dragged Mr. Bonner into the back and tossed him onto the floor near a barrel of beer.

"You will wait there until I can pay Mrs. Wilcox for her wine," Mr. Sedonez said, going to the strong box while keeping one eye on Mr. Bonner. "You see, we pay for our wines first, then we sell them."

"Oh, dear," I said, eyeing Mr. Bonner. "You haven't paid your tab?"

"Walked out on me twice last week," Mr. Sedonez said. "I'm not letting it happen again."

"And why are you drinking at a saloon in the middle of the day?" I asked Mr. Bonner.

"Please don't tell my boss. I only take a nip or two, chat with my friends," Mr. Bonner whined.

"And yet, you seem so religious," I said. "You go to the revival meetings."

"Only to keep my job," he grumbled. "Mr. Stonefield, he's the churchgoing type. You can't work for him if you aren't."

"I expect he would frown on your habit of drinking during the day."

"Please don't tell him!" Bonner wailed. "I got enough troubles around here. Everyone thinks I'm the fellow painting up the houses as it is."

"Why would they think that, Mr. Bonner?" I looked at him and folded my arms.

"Because I'm a Yankee," Mr. Bonner said. "From Pennslyvania. I even fought in the war for the Union, though I don't say that too often around here. But some folks know. And now they think I'm painting things up and I'm not."

Mr. Sedonez handed me my money and I put in in my leather bag.

"Well, I'm not going to say you are without better proof," I said. "I've had enough people suggest the same about me. And it seems to me, you'd be a better target than not." I looked at him again. "It also seems to me that the last time we spoke, you said that you had a significant grievance against the marshal. Where were you the night the marshal died?"

Bonner looked frightened. "I was here, then I took Joe Dye home to his room. I have a room at the same house. Mrs. Jameson's place."

"And you were not concerned that Mr. Dye was not in jail as he should have been?"

Mr. Bonner shrugged. "He said they hadn't made him stay in jail. I took it to mean that they weren't holding him."

"Interesting," I said. "Were you out on the streets early that next morning?"

"Only to go to work, ma'am. I swear. I have to leave before dawn to get to the ranch."

"Did you see anybody on the streets?"

"No, ma'am." Bonner seemed somewhat calmer.

I nodded, then thanked Mr. Sedonez again and

left the saloon. Fetching Armando from where he was waiting, I decided that it was time to go back to the rancho. Again, I was waylaid in my purpose, this time by Mrs. Judson, herself.

"Oh, Mrs. Wilcox, I am so glad to have met you," she said.

"I am glad to see you, as well," I said, wondering why she was in that part of the pueblo.

While not the roughest of our neighborhoods, it was not one frequented by the ladies of society.

"I've just come from the Monteros," she told me, as if in answer to my musings. "You are quite right that they do make the best gloves."

The Monteros were tanners and their tannery was on the edge of the pueblo, as it was a very smelly enterprise. And they did make gloves that rivaled anything I'd been able to buy back home. More to the point, there was no reason to doubt Mrs. Judson's word about why she was there. The route between her home and the tannery ran right along where we were.

"I was just going to send you a message," Mrs. Judson said, taking my arm as we walked. "This is somewhat awkward, but I fear I have been remiss. Please understand that our motives were of the best."

"I am confident they were," I replied, although I seriously doubted that. "But in regards to what?"

"We were afraid you would take it amiss if we asked you to join the committee for the monument to General Lee. You being a Yankee and all. We did not wish to offend you. But now, we're afraid we may have been mistaken."

"How do you mean?" I asked.

"Well, it has gotten abroad that you might be leaving us," Mrs. Judson said. "What with that terrible fire and all. We… Well, I and several of the others, we do not want you to think that you are not welcome here in Los Angeles, that we would not want you to stay."

I stopped walking and Armando almost bumped into us. It was, perhaps, the most awkward compliment

I had ever been paid, but it was also strangely touching.

"So kind of you to say so, Mrs. Judson," I said finally. "What you heard about was a letter from my brother asking me to come home and take care of our father. And it is true that I have considered doing so, but only because he is my father, and I do owe him some respect and care. That being said, I have no reason to believe that he is in any great need of my help, and, as such, seriously doubt I will be leaving the pueblo any too soon."

Mrs. Judson brightened considerably. "Oh, that is wonderful, indeed." She patted my hand as we began walking again. "To tell you the truth, I would be quite bereft if you left us. I shall have to make a point of having you to tea more often."

"That would be very congenial, Mrs. Judson," I replied. "I will endeavor to make myself available and to return the invitation."

"Now, the ladies will be joining me very soon for our committee meeting. You simply must join us. Will you?"

Such a meeting was not to my taste, but Mrs. Judson's kindness was endearing and I agreed to go. I soon found myself packed into her parlor with Mrs. Carson, Mrs. Glassell, Mrs. Downey and a couple other women whose names I've forgotten and do not care to remember. We were making paper nosegays to sell to raise money for the monument. I, personally, thought it was a bit of a wasted effort as it was going to take considerably more money to pay for the fine statue and pedestal that was being planned. But it seemed relatively harmless.

Mrs. Glassell was chattering on about her fine, new buggy when Mrs. Hewitt joined us. One of the unnamed ladies asked Mrs. Hewitt whether Mr. Wilson was going to pay her claim.

Mrs. Hewitt looked as though she were about to burst into tears again, but she managed to compose herself.

"As a matter of fact, no, he hasn't," Mrs. Hewitt said. "In fact, I doubt he will."

"He must have cheated everyone in the pueblo," Mrs. Carson said.

Or something of the sort. I was barely listening. Someone else mentioned, "that dreadful Yankee singing that horrible song."

I must concede that the Battle Hymn has never been one of my favorites, and I was thinking that when it suddenly occurred to me that the hymn, in many places, was only that. It was a song about the Lord as we see Him in Revelations, meting out his justice to the Glory of the Eternal Father.

"His truth is marching on," I muttered.

"What's that?" asked Mrs. Glassell.

"The vandal," I said. "He's not a Yankee."

"Then why would he be singing that dreadful song?" Mrs. Carson snorted.

"Because, if I'm right, it's his favorite hymn," I said. I looked at Mrs. Hewitt. "I want everyone here to know that you are completely innocent in this matter. You would have no way of knowing what you are harboring. In addition, it is entirely possible that I am wrong." I glared at the other women. "I do not want a hint of scandal to fall upon our dear Mrs. Hewitt. Is that clear?"

The other ladies agreed noisily as Mrs. Hewitt turned white.

"Do you promise, not one hint?"

They all agreed immediately, to no one's surprise.

"Mrs. Hewitt, do you have occasion to do business with Mr. Robert Gaines?" I asked. I needed desperately to know but did not like having to ask her in front of the others.

"Of course. He's our land agent," she said in a tiny, terribly frightened voice.

"What about Mr. Carson?"

"We supply all the stationery for the manufactory," Mrs. Carson said proudly.

"And, Mrs. Glassell, you just got a new buggy from the manufactory, did you not?" I asked.

"A very fine one, indeed," Mrs. Glassell said, a little pompously. "Mrs. Hewitt has every right to be very proud of her husband's business."

"That's everybody except Marshal Warren," I said, thinking furiously. I bounced to my feet. "My apologies, Mrs. Judson, but I may have found the vandal. Mrs. Hewitt, you may wish to join me." I turned again to the other women. "Not one hint of scandal. You promised and your good word can help Mrs. Hewitt at a time when she and her husband are completely innocent."

I dashed from the house without waiting for the maid to show me out. Mrs. Hewitt and Armando scrambled after me.

"Do you mean that I am harboring the vandal?" Mrs. Hewitt gasped as she trotted along after me.

"Not with any intention of doing so," I said. "I promise you, Mrs. Hewitt, you and your husband are blameless. However, I fear the vandal may, indeed, be one of your employees."

"Oh, no!"

I stopped suddenly and she nearly ran into me. "Mrs. Hewitt, would you rather I left things be?" I felt horribly guilty because the consequences of having the vandal as an employee could very well reflect badly on the manufactory. "I could, you know. I may even be able to frighten the fellow enough that he won't attack anymore."

Mrs. Hewitt trembled, then stood up straight. "No. If the vandal is one of my employees, then we will rid ourselves of this scourge and we will bear the brunt of the consequences. I will not allow this to continue and I will not shirk my duty."

We went straight to her office, although I did send Armando after Mr. Lomax. Mrs. Hewitt stopped long enough to speak to the foreman, and very shortly, Mr. Frank Hill was standing in the office with Mrs. Hewitt, Mr. Lomax, Armando and myself.

"Mr. Hill, I'm sure you're aware that there is a full barrel of red paint missing from the manufactory yard," Mrs. Hewitt said.

Mr. Hill swallowed but said nothing.

"Mr. Hill," I said firmly. "We have reason to believe that you stole it."

"I didn't steal it, Mrs. Wilcox," Mr. Hill said quickly. "That would be wrong. I left some money behind for it. You can ask the foreman if there's some extra in the wages safe."

"But you did take it to expose to the pueblo people whose sins seemed to be overwhelming and yet overlooked," I said.

"It was kind of a joke." Mr. Hill said. "Folks were saying what a wonderful fellow the marshal was and I knew better. I thought folks ought to know about it. And then there was that awful Mr. Wilson paying his attentions to Mrs. Hewitt, and her a married lady."

"You needn't recite the whole litany," I said.

"What about Mrs. Wilcox?" Mr. Lomax said, severely.

Mr. Hill trembled. "I didn't set fire to her adobe. I didn't even put the paint there. I swear."

"We already know that, Mr. Hill," I said.

"Besides everyone knows your sins," he said to me.

"I suppose that's a comfort," I said drily. "Who else knew what you were doing?"

"No one, ma'am. I did it all, myself." Mr. Hill said.

"So Reverend Bennett did not encourage you?"

Mr. Hill snorted and laughed. "Reverend Bennett is no man of God. He talks a good piece, but he don't know his scriptures that well. And truth be told, I've seen him on Calle de los Negros, sating his flesh."

"He told me he was trying to win over those addicted to opium," I said.

"He may be, but I saw him kissing one of those hussies as he left one day." Mr. Hill sighed. "I guess that's why I thought folks should know about the marshal."

"And yet, you continued to play piano for the reverend," I said.

Mr. Hill shrugged. "I liked the revival meetings. We need more of that around here."

"To be sure," Mrs. Hewitt sighed.

Mr. Lomax stepped forward. "Mr. Hill, I'm going to have to place you under arrest."

He got Mr. Hill bound and the two left, with Mrs. Hewitt, Armando and I watching after them.

Armando laughed. "That was really something, Mrs. Wilcox."

"Thank you, Armando," I said softly. I looked at Mrs. Hewitt. "That was incredibly brave of you, Mrs. Hewitt. I will do everything in my power to prevent others from thinking ill of you."

She shrugged. "It doesn't matter. The reverend laid hands upon Mr. Hewitt the other night. Mr. Hewitt swore he would never drink again. He was completely sauced by Saturday night." She looked at me. "It's going to come out at some point or another. I may as well steel myself to it."

I left the manufactory feeling rather downcast, even though we had stopped one bit of trouble in the pueblo. As it turned out, Mrs. Hewitt was able to conceal her husband's dissolute habits over the next several years. Although once Mr. Hewitt finally died, no one in the pueblo was particularly surprised to see work at the manufactory continue as always.

CHAPTER EIGHTEEN

Armando, for his part, refused to leave me until I was safely inside the gates of the rancho. Only then did he agree to send invitations to Regina, Angelina, and Mr. Lomax for that evening after supper. I did think to ask the others if they minded, but they all agreed that we needed to find the marshal's killer as soon as possible.

As soon as we'd eaten supper, Anita shooed the children upstairs while Olivia brewed tea and Magdalena set out pan dulces. Hernan was still sitting by Maria's bedside. However, when I checked her, her fever had broken and her appetite was returning with a vengeance. There was hardly enough soup in the house to sate her. I did insist that she stay in bed, but she was happy to fondle her little Elias, who was also faring well and lustily. Indeed, it was probably his ferocious appetite that was driving Maria's. Hernan's cousins, Emilio and Pascual, had decided to stay with their grandmother in the pueblo, to make a little more room in the barracks house.

Sebastiano joined my little party, while Enrique decided to help Anita listen to the younger ones' lessons.

"Very well, then," said Angelina once we were all settled and she had placed her wooden lap desk in her lap. She pulled out her list and opened her ink pot. "I have some most interesting news. But first, there are several people we can scratch off the list of possible killers. Constable Brooks, for one."

"Yes, he was there when the killer attacked me," I

said. "And probably Deputy Redona, too. His arm was in no condition to have smothered the marshal, who did, now that I think about it, definitely fight back."

"Mr. Villega remains a possible killer," said Sebastiano. "He nearly lost his job because of Maddie and so it would make sense for him to threaten her because he wanted to stay here."

"To be sure," I said. "But he talked as though he expected the marshal to die of his wounds that night. That would seem to indicate that he did not kill the marshal."

"What about Mr. Bonner?" Mr. Lomax asked.

"I spoke with him this afternoon," I said and recounted our conversation. "He was not acting guilty or afraid I suspected him, however, he was abroad at the time we think the marshal might have been killed. Mr. Sedonez also vouched for Deputy Dye and Mr. Mendoza, and neither, apparently, were in any shape to commit the murder."

"Very well," said Angelina. "That leaves Mr. Wills and Mr. Wilson. And I have news about Mr. Wilson that is very suggestive. He's closed his office and is selling his house. He said he wants to move to San Buenaventura where he has some land. Or that's the report, anyway."

"And I can add further to that," Regina said, with a smug smile. "I shouldn't say this, but Mr. Wilson stayed over at my house Friday night. It was almost as though he wanted to be seen there, and left very ostentatiously the next morning. If he had paid someone to set the fire here, it would serve him well to be seen elsewhere."

"That's true," said Mr. Lomax.

"But where would he have gotten the money to pay someone?" I asked. "As I understand it, one of the companies he represents recently closed its doors and he has no money to pay claims."

"And why would he blame Maddie for making it impossible to stay in Los Angeles?" Sebastiano asked.

Regina chuckled. "She makes an easy target, of

course. And she is rumored to have been very harsh with him. But why would Mr. Wilson go to such an extreme? After all, insurance fraud is not likely to get you hanged."

"Not by the law, at any rate," said Mr. Lomax.

"There is also Mr. Wills," I pointed out. "He cannot vouch for his movements at any of the critical times, and he not only had revenge as a reason for killing the marshal but feels acutely guilty about his brother's killing, as it was his theft and not his brother's that incited his brother's drunken attack on the marshal. Finally, there are Mr. Brooks and Mr. Redona's reports of the marshal's actions that day, namely that the marshal had his eye on collecting a second significant bounty on someone no one would expect."

"Both Mr. Wills and Mr. Wilson fit that description," Angelina said.

"And Mr. Wilson is even now heading to the very place where the marshal found out about the bounty," Regina added.

Mr. Lomax sighed deeply. "I guess I'm going to be riding out to San Buenaventura tomorrow."

"I'll go with you," Sebastiano said quickly, glaring at me to ensure that I did not volunteer to go, also.

There was little more to settle. Angelina and Regina left soon after and Mr. Lomax followed. The next morning, he arrived with the sun. Sebastiano had saddled one of the mules and the two made their way north along the river.

As I watched them leave, I remembered what Father Jimenez had said about Reverend Bennett, namely that the priest had seen the reverend somehow in San Buenaventura. With all that seemed to be converging on that city, I thought I might as well ask the reverend about it. Perhaps he'd been there before coming to Los Angeles and might know what the marshal had seen.

It was fate, possibly, but I had no sooner arrived on the Plaza with the intent of going to the western part of the pueblo to find the reverend's rooming house when I saw the man, himself, going into the restaurant at the Pico House. Most of the hotel restaurants in the city served breakfast to the public, as there were so many single men in the pueblo who required one.

I hitched Daisy to the post in front of the hotel, and Armand hitched the other mule. He went in with me to talk to his other cousin Lupe, who was working that morning in the restaurant.

The reverend was sitting alone with a newspaper and a cup of coffee. I made my way over to the table.

"Pray excuse me, Reverend," I said.

He quickly stood. "Mrs. Wilcox. Good to see you. Please join me."

"Thank you, Reverend," I said, sliding into the chair he offered. "But please do not order for me. I only wish a word or two, then I have business to transact with the restaurant manager."

"Very well, then." The reverend seated himself. "How may I help you this morning?"

I decided to start with something a little more innocuous than the marshal's death. "You may have heard that Mr. Hill was arrested yesterday."

"Yes, I'd heard he'd confessed to being that terrible vandal."

I looked at my hands. "He made a rather awkward accusation of you. He'd apparently seen you kissing a prostitute down on the Calle de los Negros."

The reverend shifted uncomfortably. "And, eh, what do you intend to do about it?"

"Not much," I said with a smile. "Believe me, I understand how one can be tempted."

He sighed. "And my sinful life is not all that far in my past." He looked at me. "I am quite serious, Mrs. Wilcox, when I tell you that I was once the worst of criminals. Any day, I expect the ill fruits of my sinful ways to bear down upon me. It was a miracle that I found the Lord and heard my true calling."

"That would also explain why Mr. Hill did not

think you knew your scriptures all that well."

"Oh, I know them." Reverend Bennett smiled ruefully. "Or I did. I was beaten when I didn't. You see, I was an abandoned child back in Brattleboro, Vermont. Reverend Aloysius Bennett took me in, gave me my name. He was, however, not a kind man, and I, sadly, rebelled against him. I left as a young man and entered into a life of crime and all manner of ill deeds. Then one day I was given a Bible and I meant to throw it away, but instead I began to read it again and saw a different Jesus than my foster parent had taught me. A Jesus who loved and forgave. I confessed my sins and became the man I am today."

"That's quite a moving story," I said.

"Thank you. It has been quite well received here and I truly appreciate it." His eyes shone with tears and I looked away.

"Well, I was going to ask you if you'd been to San Buenaventura in your travels," I said.

"I passed through last spring, but haven't been back."

I frowned. "Well, I'll just have to wait for Mr. Lomax and Mr. Ortiz to get back then. The marshal apparently saw something there and they just left this morning to find out what it was."

The reverend swallowed. "They did?."

I got up and he scrambled to his feet.

"Thank you for your time, Reverend," I said.

"You're very welcome, Mrs. Wilcox," he said, nervously looking through the window.

I went to the foyer of the hotel but looked back at the reverend, who was hastily gathering his things together. He'd seemed quite calm and relaxed before.

There was something very odd, indeed, about the reverend. Armando and I went to the telegraph office and I sent a telegram to the sheriff in Buenaventura, inquiring after particulars. At the very least, I would know if the reverend had been lying about his background, if not to what extent. I was not surprised to see the reverend rush into the livery stable nearby.

Armando and I were passing the dry goods store when the shopkeeper hailed me and handed me a letter. It was from Mr. Brooks. Behind us, the reverend tore down the street on a black gelding, running the poor horse for all it was worth toward the north end of the pueblo and the river.

I looked at the letter and noted that it had come from a hotel in San Buenaventura. I opened the envelope to find Mr. Brooks note - he and the Lons had safely arrived and were leaving almost immediately. He would write again when they were settled. However, he'd stopped at the sheriff's office and found the enclosed.

I looked at the sheet of paper that had been folded and included with the letter. It was a wanted poster for a horse thief and murderer. The bounty was one thousand dollars and while I did not recognize the name, I knew the face.

My heart pounding, I stuffed the letter and poster in my leather bag.

"Armando," I almost screamed. "We've got to hurry! I just sent Marshal Warren's killer after Mr. Lomax and your uncle!"

There was no time to seek reinforcements. Armando had a pistol on him and I had nothing but my anger, but that would have to do.

We ran our mounts as fast as we dared and as long as we dared. The road to San Buenaventura was well marked and we passed farms and vineyards, expanses of brush where cattle grazed. The road was flat a good ways, then began to climb into dry, brown hills crowned by huge light brown boulders. We were trotting Daisy and the mule when I heard gunshots. I was about to kick Daisy into a run, but Armando had drawn a pistol and waved at me to stop.

He was right. Someone was yelling just beyond the bend. Armando and I slid off our mounts and tethered them to some scrub. We couldn't quite make out what the man was yelling, but it was along the lines that he was not going to let his targets go and ruin his home for him. Armando and I scrambled over the rocks, no easy feat for me, as I was wearing my second best, actually at that moment my only, riding habit. But I'd climbed all manner of rocks and trees in skirts in my youth. I wasn't about to let my hoops stop me.

As we crested the boulders, we could see the slope of the hills rolling downwards. The road going down crossed back and forth along the slope's side. I gasped silently when I saw the chestnut mare Mr. Lomax had been riding trotting loose with our mule behind. Neither Mr. Lomax nor Sebastiano were in the saddles.

"I know you're out here," Reverend Bennett screamed. He came out from behind an oak tree, and I noted that his horse was missing. In his hands was a large revolver.

Armando pointed at another tree some ways down the slope from the reverend. I saw boots scrambling backward into the cover of a scrub bush. It was only a matter of time before Reverend Bennett found either Mr. Lomax or Sebastiano or both.

I looked at Armando and pointed at the gun. He shook his head.

"We're too far away," he whispered. "If I miss, it will just give us away and that won't help the others."

I had to believe that Mr. Lomax or Sebastiano were either wounded or worse, as they were both armed and under good cover. I didn't think it would have been that hard to return the reverend's fire if they had been able-bodied.

Reverend Bennett suddenly bent to the ground and picked up not one, but two pistols and stuck them in his belt. "Looks like you fellows lost something!"

That explained why no one had been shooting at the reverend. The only problem we had was that if Armando or I tried to crest the rocks and head down the slope, we'd be in full view of the reverend and I did not doubt he'd be happy to shoot us.

The sun beat down on us and a dry wind blew from the northeast. Something triggered a small rock slide and the reverend jumped, then let off a couple shots into the brush somewhere between where Mr. Lomax and Sebastiano were hiding and where Armando and I were lodged. The reverend, gasping for air, whirled around, looking, searching for his prey. I motioned Armando to slide down next to me behind the rocks.

"We've got to distract him," I said. "Do you think he's carrying any extra bullets?"

"Can't be that many if he is," said Armando. "He's not wearing a gun belt. But he does have those two extra revolvers."

I thought. "How many shots have we heard? Two just now and maybe two as we rode up?"

Armando nodded.

"All right. That leaves two in his gun, plus another twelve from the two others. Best assume he has more shots than we think, right?"

"Of course."

"What we need to do is distract him and get him to empty his guns, then, if we can, get him to come towards us. But don't shoot until you're sure you can bring him down."

Armando pointed to some rocks close by. "I'll go that way."

"Do it slowly and carefully," I said. "The way your uncle and Mr. Lomax would be moving."

Armando slipped away, but in doing so, accidentally let loose some rocks, which clattered noisily down our side of the hill. Reverend Bennett fired again and I heard the ping of the bullet striking a rock just above my head. I carefully eased myself to where I could peer over the rocks and saw the reverend climbing back up the slope. A rock clattered to the ground just behind him and he whirled, his revolver still at the ready. He started down the slope again, but as soon as the road passed behind the huge oak tree and my sight of him was obscured, I threw a handful of rocks down the slope immediately beneath me. A second later, the reverend was scrambling back upwards, foregoing the road that looped back and forth and tackling the slope in a straight line.

Armando threw some more rocks to the reverend's right. His head danced in that direction, and it seemed he was starting to panic. I threw some rocks to my other side and he let off three more shots. So he'd either reloaded before we got there or we'd miscounted. Neither was a help to us. Armando let another rock fly and this one bounced off the reverend's left shoulder. The six-gun was in his right hand, so the hit did little more than make him angry. He tackled the slope again, taking a middle course between where I and Armando were hiding. I threw a rock that landed behind him. He whirled, slid a little and lost his balance, dropping the pistol in his hand to catch himself and one of the other two pistols from his belt. The two guns slid all the way down the steep slope to the road below. I wasn't sure, but I thought I might have seen movement next to the road. It was the last thing I wanted the reverend to see, so I threw some more rocks at a spot near where Armando was hiding. It was, perhaps, foolish, but I knew that with the two pistols gone, he only had the one and no more than six shots, unless he was able to reload. I hoped that by that time he'd be close enough for Armando to get off a good shot.

The reverend must have seen me, for all of a sudden, I saw him grin beneath his beard and aim that one revolver my way. I ducked behind the rocks. I could not see where Armando was. I knew that if the reverend crested those rocks, he'd have a tremendous advantage over me, in being above me, as well as being considerably larger. I frantically looked around for any small advantage I could take. There was plenty of sand and dirt. I grabbed up two handfuls and pulled a good-sized rock into my lap.

I could hear the reverend scrambling up over the rocks, his breathing heavy. I was waiting for him and the second I saw his face, I threw the sand and dirt into his eyes. He howled but kept coming. I heard someone else running towards me and then the report of a gun.

The reverend crumpled and fell backward down his side of the slope. I scrambled up to look and saw his body rolling and stirring up great clouds of dust, until he landed on the road and lay on his back. Suddenly, Mr. Lomax appeared from below him and trained a small rifle on the reverend.

As it turned out, the reverend was in no shape to fight back. Indeed, as I found when I'd made my way down the slope after him, he was just barely alive.

"I tried to be good," he whispered to me. "I wanted to be good. It was the first place I ever belonged."

"Our Lord is a forgiving God," I said.

He gasped. "I did not want to kill the marshal. But he was coming for me. I did not want to give up my first real home."

"I understand," I replied.

I don't know that I did, entirely, but it was not my place to make that judgment.

I debated how best I could make Reverend Bennett as comfortable as I could as he lay waiting to meet Our Maker. The only thing I could think of was to recite the parable of the workers in the field, hired on later and later in the day, only to be paid the same wages as though who had been working all day. I had always thought it rather unjust, but I could see how it might be a comfort to a man who had only just added to the long list of his sins and now faced Eternity.

The reverend was still alive when Sebastiano limped up, holding his right arm. Both he and Mr. Lomax were exceedingly dusty. Armando, who had fired the near fatal shot, came scrambling down the slope in a rush of dust and small rocks.

Mr. Lomax later explained that once we'd distracted the reverend, he'd been able to coax the horse and mule to him and retrieve the rifle. He and Sebastiano had both lost their guns and their mounts when the reverend had shot at them from the road above. Their mounts had shied and reared and both men had been thrown. Sebastiano's arm had been grazed, as had Mr. Lomax's heel.

"I didn't kill my foster father," the reverend gasped. "They all thought I did. I killed others, but I did not kill Aloysius Bennett."

I did not understand the meaning of his words, but I squeezed his hand.

As soon as the reverend had breathed his last, I tended to the others' wounds. Both men were bruised, but, thankfully, had not broken any bones. I cleaned Sebastiano's arm as well I could with their store of water, then cleaned Mr. Lomax's heel. The boot had taken the worst of the shot and I worried that Mr. Lomax would be hard-pressed to replace it.

Armando's wound was harder to take care of. He tried to act tough and as if it didn't matter. But he'd killed a man and that is no easy thing to deal with, especially when one is of such tender years as he was, not entirely a youth, but not quite a man yet, either.

"I say we leave him," Sebastiano grumbled as he nodded at the corpse.

I drew my bonnet up. "No. We'll take him home to be buried."

"But he tried to kill us, and you. He killed the marshal." Sebastiano was getting quite angry.

"True," I said. "But it is up to us to show him Christian mercy and charity, nonetheless. He told me something of his life earlier today. Perhaps if someone had shown him some charity, he would not have turned as bad as he did. And I do believe he was, in his own way, trying to be good."

Sebastiano suddenly burst into laughter and I looked at him through my tears.

"Que tu eres loca!" he laughed. "But you are right."

"Armando, please fetch Daisy and the mule," I said. Keeping him busy would be the best thing for him.

I must give the boy credit. He managed quite well

in the days following. There were a few nightmares, but he got plenty of attention and the story of how he had rescued me grew considerably.

It was well after dark by the time we'd returned to the pueblo and brought the reverend to Angelina.

The next day, I went to Mrs. Warren and told her what had happened.

"I don't care to lie," I explained to her. "But I don't necessarily have to say everything about how your husband died."

She nodded. "The city council has asked me to let everyone think Deputy Dye killed Mr. Warren. It would be better for the pueblo. I would prefer it, if you don't mind."

"Not much, really. We don't have to explain how the reverend died, either. Most people seem to believe it was bandits on the road."

"We have enough of that, too," Mrs. Warren said sadly.

Joseph Dye was tried for the murder of Marshal William Warren in February. As everyone expected, he was acquitted, even though Mrs. Warren read an impassioned speech about what a terrible thing he'd done. It had been written for her by the city council, but as she pointed out to me later, the reverend would never have been able to kill the marshal had the deputy not wounded him first, so in a way, Deputy Dye had killed the marshal. I did not like it, but it was out of my hands.

In any case, Marshal Baker almost immediately fired Dye, and the man spent the rest of his days going back and forth between Los Angeles and San Buenaventura. He eventually, over ten years later, was shot and killed by his nephew, but not before others had met their ends at his hands.

Mr. Hill served two months for the vandalism he'd perpetrated, then left the pueblo. The last we'd heard, he'd taken up with a traveling preacher.

Some weeks after the events I've described, I got

a letter from Brattleboro, Vermont. The writer, a Mrs. Waldorf, inquired after Mr. Jeptha Bennett. I was surprised that the reverend had been using his own name. Mrs. Waldorf wrote that she was Mr. Bennett's foster sister and Reverend Aloysius Bennett's daughter. Her father had died under suspicious circumstances, and everyone believed that it had been young Jeptha who had committed the crime. Mrs. Waldorf had never believed so and had tried to stand by Jeptha. But the young man had run away, and there were rumors he'd become an outlaw.

As I'd later found out from the sheriff in San Buenaventura, Mr. Bennett was better known to lawmen north of Los Angeles as Tom Wildman, although they'd heard he'd taken on the disguise of a traveling preacher, and he'd committed all manner of crimes, from robbing stages, to stealing cattle, and at least five murders, and those were the crimes they knew about. There was good reason to believe that Tom Wildman had made his way across the continent engaging in any number of ill deeds.

I could not help but feel terribly sad for Reverend Jeptha Bennett. He was, most certainly, an outlaw, but I do believe that in the end, he had been converted to the True Path and was trying to be good. In fact, I was certain it was that desire that had saved my life when he accosted me in the streets. The poor man had never known what it was like to feel wanted and that he belonged, and the first time he did, his past caught up with him.

As for me, well, I stayed in Los Angeles. I wrote my brother back, explaining that I felt ill at ease accepting an invitation from our father at my brother's behest. If Father wanted me back that badly, I'd rather see the request in his hand, as I had no interest in going where I was not wanted. I eventually got a letter from my sister Carrie that said Father had softened toward me, but I had chosen the wiser course by staying where I was, as Merriam had, indeed, been looking for someone to take care of Father who, for all his complaints, would probably outlive us all.

The letter came with an exceedingly large crate, which, when I finally got it open, contained my mother's desk. Carrie explained in her letter that since I had lost everything in the fire (I had written to her about it, as well as about Merriam's letter), perhaps I would like this memento of our happy childhood at our mother's knee. That did bring on a most unseemly display of tears. Fortunately, the adobe had been rebuilt, a phoenix rising from the ashes, and there was a brand new study that required just such a desk. Sebastiano and Hernan wrestled the old roll-top desk into at least three different places until I was satisfied. Then I stepped back and rolled up the top.

It definitely belonged right in that spot.

HISTORICAL NOTES

Death of the City Marshal is based on the actual killing of Marshal William Warren by his deputy Joseph Dye. The description of the fatal gunfight is based on Scott Zesch's compilation of the testimony and newspaper accounts of the event in his book The Chinatown War, which I also read along with the newspapers.

So, I was massaging the actual history by positing that Marshal Warren was smothered by someone else. Bobby Brooks was modeled on Robert Hester, who did have his hand injured in the affray. But Mr. Hester remained in Los Angeles, as did Sing Yu, the unfortunate prostitute that was the model for Lon Yu (Lon Yu was the name that appeared in the local newspaper accounts of the time). Lon Yu's relationship with Mr. Brooks is entirely fictional.

Joseph Dye's end was accurately portrayed by Maddie, as was the violence of the pueblo. A contemporary historian once claimed there was a murder a day in the pueblo. Given that this chronicler was more than a little generous with his facts, that number is probably very much exaggerated. Nonetheless, even 13 murders a year (as posited by Mr. Zesch) in a city of 7,000 people is a heck of a lot (currently L.A. sees roughly 7 homicides per 100,000 people per year).

COMING SOON

Please enjoy this excerpt from the next Old Los Angeles mystery, Death of the Chinese Fieldhands

When the darkness of evil holds sway, how does one keep it from overtaking one's heart? Before the terrible events of the autumn of 1871, I had several ready answers, none of which preserved me against the horrors that took place. The sheer hatred that propelled the events I am about to relate in these pages of my memoirs, I do not understand, even when it infects me with the black cloud of its fury.

It still troubles me at times, mostly late at night, after I am confronted by it during my daylight hours. Or after I lose a patient that I would not have lost but for the ignorance or prejudices of others. All I know is that my own anger is not the answer, no matter how much I would prefer to unleash it. I had to learn that the hard way.

It had been a long day that Tuesday, October 24, and it was a blessing for my three Chinese field hands that it was. The day started with bringing in the last of the grapes for the Angelica. My vineyards and winery were my principal support in those days. We had already harvested the cabernet and merlot two weeks before and the wine would soon be ready to move from the vats in which the grapes had fermented into the casks where it would age. The grapes for the Angelica were always harvested last, as they did not ripen readily. Indeed, even when some of the grapes had already turned to raisins, there were still several green grapes among the clusters.

As the sun slowly sank into the horizon, Wei Li and Wei Chin were still walking through the vats with several of the Ortiz children, crushing the grapes in preparation for fermentation. Wang Fu was busy cleaning the harvesting baskets, along with my partners in the venture, Sebastiano and Enrique Ortiz. I was wearing my red poplin work dress and moving the cleaned baskets to the back part of the winery barn.

We heard the first of the gunfire around five-thirty.

"Sounds like the big fight has started," Hernan said, playfully nudging Wei Li.

Hernan Mendoza was one of the other field hands on Rancho de las Flores. He'd just brought in the last baskets of grapes. Wei Li grunted and kept walking the vat.

Wang Fu had told us earlier that there were rumors that there would be a fight that day between two rival companies on the Calle de los Negros, where the Chinese principally lived. The companies were home organizations that, by themselves, helped the Chinese who came to our fair shores navigate a society that, to them, was utterly strange and even barbaric. But as so often happens, there was a criminal element known as Tongs that became attached to some of the companies. It was rumored that one of the companies had hired Tong assassins from San Francisco to fight against the leader of a rival company.

Even so, we were not terribly concerned at first. After all, Los Angeles was a very rough place in those days and the sound of gunfire was almost pervasive. But then, not only did the reports continue, they grew as if more and more guns were being fired.

"You would think there was a war on," Sebastiano said, shaking his head.

"It may be," said Wang Fu quietly. He looked up at the Wei brothers.

I wiped my hands on my apron. "That most

certainly means there are injuries. I'd best get my bag and head over there."

Enrique and Sebastiano groaned quietly but did not bother to deter me. It would have done no good and they knew it.

"I go with you," said Wang Fu. His accent was getting much better, but it was still very heavy.

He had been trained as a physician in his native China and was becoming quite a big help to me.

Armando, Enrique's son who was sixteen at the time, burst into the yard. Dark had settled by that point, and Armando was returning from his job at the Pico House hotel, around the corner from the Calle de los Negros.

"Wang Fu! Wei Li! Wei Chin!" Armando looked around, frantically. "Are they here?"

"We are in the grapes," Wei Chin said, nervously laughing.

Armando gasped. "You can't go home. There's a mob. I saw them take Ah Wing, one of the kitchen boys. They're calling for a lynching!"

"But what did this Mr. Ah do?" I asked.

"He didn't do anything!" Armando gulped, his face ashen in the light of the lamps scattered about the yard. "Leastways, I don't think so. But he was trying to run away and some men caught him and Marshal Baker found a gun on him. They were screaming to lynch him and all of the Chinese, too. I was hoping our fellows would still be here, so I ran as fast as I could."

"Maddie," said Sebastiano. "Maybe we'd better wait to take care of people until things settle down."

I frowned, then shook my head. "That might be too late for the worst injured. But let us not throw all caution to the wind. Wang Fu, why don't you stay here? We can have the casualties brought here and you can tend to them. Enrique, you can keep guard. Sebastiano, shall we?"

"Let me get my guns," Sebastiano said. "Armando, get yours and the rifle."

Both the Wei brothers and Mr. Wang looked at me and Mr. Wang spoke first.

"There is the Lee wash house and laundry," he said. "That is where we live. Please find Lee Won and Lee Ma. They are good people. If as bad as Mr. Armando say, they will be safe with you."

By the time we made it to the Calle de los Negros, it was worse than what Armando had said. How do I describe that most terrible of nights? Mere words cannot convey the acrid stench of human blood and fear, the screams, the harsh laughter of the mob.

Sebastiano insisted that we skirt the group crowded around the Coronel adobe, which we later learned was at the center of the riot. The other buildings on the Calle de los Negros were dark, although one would catch the occasional glimpse of a flickering torch inside a window. Raucous shouts confirmed that there was looting going on.

Near the end of the calle closest to the Plaza, we found the Lee wash house. It, too, was dark. Sebastiano called out and slowly slid into the door. He came out a few minutes later, shaking his head.

"Oh, good. They escaped," I said.

Armando shook his head and pointed toward a wagon that had been turned over. Muffled sounds of hushing came from within, then silence. I nodded at Sebastiano and Armando, and we approached the wagon slowly, certain that whoever was underneath the overturned box was terrified beyond all reckoning. I knelt next to the box.

"I'm here to help you escape," I said slowly and softly. "We will not harm you. We will bring you to safety."

There was dead silence within. I nodded at Armando and Sebastiano and they slowly raised the wagon box. Huddled inside were two women and three men. They drew back in terror as they saw me.

"Lee Won? Lee Ma?" I asked. "Wang Fu, Wei Li and Wei Chin sent us to find you."

The oldest of the three men looked at me warily. "Wang Fu?"

There was more shouting and the bouncing light of torches slowly made their way toward us.

"Yes, Wang Fu," I said. "Hurry. We must get you to safety."

One of the women chattered at the old man, and he nodded.

"I Lee Won," he said. "We go."

We hurried along the adobe on the eastern side of the Plaza, hoping to get to Wine Street, and then from there, to Alameda Street and back to the rancho. But a crowd burst into the Plaza from Bath Street, so we slunk up Republic, in front of the Pico House and went cautiously along the Calle Principal toward the jail. It was a very long way around to the ranch, but we hoped we'd be able to take Calle Primero down to Alameda and from there get back to the rancho, having gone around the worst of the riot.

We had gotten to just beyond the new Merced Theater when we saw a mob coming from behind us. We ducked onto Arcadia Street to hide, little realizing what a terrible mistake we'd made. We pressed ourselves into the doorway of a darkened adobe, but we could still see the corral at Aliso and Los Angeles streets. Three bodies dangled from the gate's crosspiece, black against the flicking orange light of the torches. Men were binding a fourth struggling man, slipping the noose over his neck, while what looked like a boy was dancing on the top of the gate.

I couldn't help it. I burst from our hiding place, screaming at the men, but they did not hear me. Two other men tried to make themselves heard as they confronted the crowd, but they were pushed back or ignored.

I started to rush forward, but Sebastiano held me back.

"We cannot help them," he growled softly. "Not now. We must save Wang Fu's friends."

I looked back. The two men continued their fight to be heard over the mob and I had to give Sebastiano the truth of his reasoning. Loathe as I was to admit it, there was nothing I could do there, although it still grieves me to this day that I didn't try harder to stop the mob. We slipped our small group back up to the Calle Principal and were debating which way to go when a group of about eight men suddenly bore down on us, guns drawn.

"You'll give us those heathens," the leader called out. I could barely make out his face in the dark and the flickering torchlight, but he was dark-haired with a badly kept beard.

"I most certainly will not!" I said, positioning myself in front of our little band of refugees.

"Either hand them over or we'll shoot you like dogs," the leader crowed.

The men behind him laughed. Terrified, not only for myself, but for the people I guarded and my dearest of friends, I pressed my lips together.

"Shoot her, McKinley," growled one of the men behind the leader, I couldn't see who. "It's that lady doctor. She'll finally get what she's got coming to her."

It was not a sentiment with which I was unfamiliar, but it had never been used as an excuse to kill me before. The leader raised his gun. Armando and Sebastiano both cocked theirs.

"Hey, look over there!" a third man cried. "Let's go get after some of that!"

The men dashed off, although one lingered a moment. The torchlight glinted off the gold anchor watch fob that dangled from his vest pocket.

I swallowed and looked at Sebastiano. He nodded.

From there, we kept to the dark corners and eventually made it back to the rancho, thoroughly shaken but unharmed in body.

There was a great deal of chatter among our field hands and our guests in that so very odd language of theirs. In addition to Mr. and Mrs. Lee, an older couple with graying hair, there was Lu Ang, a spindly fellow who could not stop shaking, and An Wu and An Mei, a young couple. An Mei was Mr. and Mrs. Lee's daughter and had only recently married Mr. An.

Wang Fu was very relieved to see the Lee family, but the Wei brothers seemed more concerned about something else. I asked Mr. Wang what that might be, but he shrugged as if he didn't want to tell me.

Among my household, Enrique's wife, Magdalena, seemed very perturbed to find that the "Chinos" were going to be spending the night in the large barracks house where most of my hands and their families lived. Sebastiano and Enrique each had an adobe to house their respective families. The barracks housed both Rodolfo and Anita Sanchez, and Hernan and Maria Mendoza and their growing family, along with Hernan's cousins Emilio and Pascual Mendoza. I was not happy with Magdalena's attitude but was saved from remonstrating with her by Armando. We had often teased Magdalena that her darling son could tease her into doing anything he wanted. But that night I was profoundly glad of it. It must have been the resilience of youth, for Armando was able to translate to his mother the horrors we had witnessed in such a way that her prejudices were abandoned in favor of the Christian charity that I normally associated with her.

It was a sleepless night, nonetheless, and the dawn the next morning fell upon quite the grisly spectacle. Eighteen men in all had been lynched in three different locations. Many of the men had been mutilated as well. The bodies were cut down and the inquests began. The funeral for the victims was held that same day. I attended with Mr. Wang and his fellows. Mr. An was horrified to find that one of his cousins was among the dead.

Among the good citizens of Los Angeles, most denied any involvement, some legitimately, others less so. As the days went on, those of the more settled class blamed the ruffians and transients in the pueblo. The newspapers published hypocritical essays on the rule of law. Lu Ang was gone to Wilmington by the end of the day after the funeral, presumably to catch the next steamship to San Francisco. Whether he stayed in California or returned to China, we never found out. The Lee family, however, elected to stay, as did their son-in-law and daughter. With a sudden dearth of laundries (which at the time were mostly run by the Chinese), they actually did rather well, although it was not easy for them.

Wang Fu chose to stay, for which I was heartily glad. The Wei brothers, however, informed me that while they would wait until spring, they would be leaving to go back to China. Wei Chin, whose English was significantly better than his brother's hastened to reassure me that this had been planned before the riot.

"We come here to make money to take back to China," he explained. "So our family live easy. We have money now. We go. We wait 'til spring because no storm on ocean." He smiled impishly. "And we like you, Miz Wilcox. We help you prune vines, then we go."

There was naught I could do but give him my blessing.

A week passed and there was significant talk of witnesses and indictments. Still numbed by the shock of it all, we clung to the rhythms and tasks of everyday life. The wine fermented. We added the brandy we'd made the year before to it and we put it in casks. We racked the cabernet and merlot wines together and made a lovely claret, as I recall. I read and re-read all of my medical journals and went on a crusade to teach housewives the importance of sanitation in the home. We tried to pretend that everything was normal. So, I didn't think anything of asking Wei Li to take our goats and pasture them in the far end of the vineyard that day, the first week of November. None of us did.

Until Wei Li didn't come back.

OTHER BOOKS BY THIS AUTHOR

I'm so glad you liked this book! Please check out my other novels, available in print or ebook at your favorite retailer:

Freddie and Kathy Series
Fascinating Rhythm
Bring Into Bondage
The Last Witnesses
Blood Red

Operation Quickline Series
That Old Cloak and Dagger Routine
Stopleak
Deceptive Appearances
Fugue in a Minor Key

Old Los Angeles
Death of the Zanjero
Death of the City Marshal

Mrs. Sperling
A Nose for a Niedeman

Brenda Finnegan
Tyger, Tyger

Romantic Fiction
White House Rhapsody, Book One

Fantasy and Science Fiction
A Ring for a Second Chance
But World Enough and Time

And I would be honored if you left a review for this and any of my books on GoodReads or any other retail site. It really helps.

CONNECT WITH THE AUTHOR

Thank you for sticking it out this long! Please join my newsletter. It's the best way to stay up-to-date on my upcoming projects, blog posts and even games and giveaways.

Sign up here: http://eepurl.com/zH0Ab

Or connect with me on your favorite social media platforms:

Visit my website: http://annelouisebannon.com
Friend me on Facebook: http://facebook.com/RobinGoodfellowEnt
Follow me on Twitter: http://twitter.com/ALBannon
Favorite my Smashwords author page: https://www.smashwords.com/profile/view/MsBriscow
Connect on LinkedIn: http://www.linkedin.com/in/annelouisebannon
Follow me on Pinterest: http://pinterest.com/msbriscow

ABOUT THE AUTHOR

Anne Louise Bannon is an author and journalist who wrote her first novel at age 15. Her journalistic work has appeared in Ladies' Home Journal, the Los Angeles Times, Wines and Vines, and in newspapers across the country. She was a TV critic for over 10 years, founded the YourFamilyViewer blog, and created the OddBallGrape.com wine education blog with her husband, Michael Holland. She is the co-author of Howdunit: Book of Poisons, with Serita Stevens, as well as author of the Freddie and Kathy mystery series, set in the 1920s, the Old Los Angeles series, set in 1870, and the Operation Quickline series and Tyger, Tyger. She and her husband live in Southern California with an assortment of critters.

CPSIA information can be obtained
at www.ICGtesting.com
Printed in the USA
LVHW111626250419
615549LV00001B/26/P